GASLIT

RR HAYWOOD

1899 INC

Copyright © 2024 by RR Haywood

All rights reserved.

No part of this book may be reproduced in any form or by any electronic or mechanical means, including information storage and retrieval systems, without written permission from the author, except for the use of brief quotations in a book review.

FOREWORD

Dear Reader,

I released a novel in 2014 called Huntington House. It was an early novel for me, and I was never really happy with how it turned out.

Eventually, I scrapped that story and re-wrote the whole book with a new plot and characters and a new ending too.

Mike Humber still goes to Huntington House, and there are a couple of similar scenes, so if you have read the 2014 version you might feel a sense of familiarity - but otherwise this is very different.

But still very dark...

I hope you enjoy it.
Please do leave a review.

Much love,
RR Haywood 😊

GASLIT
A Twisted Tale Of Manipulation & Murder

1

Day One

I arrive at the single line station in Huntington village a few hours after leaving London.

The house is a few miles away, but I'm flat broke and can't afford a taxi. I pull my rucksack on my back and set off walking.

At least the weather is nice. Mid-October and cold and clear, with that lovely, crisp feeling in the air.

I find the entrance to the driveway along a country road next to a big, ornate nameboard.

Huntington House

I can only just make out the top of the roof from the road, which tells me the driveway is long. That's all I need after walking for an hour already.

I set off, and the house slowly comes into view. A big,

old stately home with grey walls and ivy growing up the front. Three levels high with dark, imposing windows. I guess in summer it would look pretty. Now it just looks bleak. But then I'm not in a position to be picky about where I work.

The brand-new Range Rover parked up outside the house, with a fat man sitting inside it, tells me two things.

First, that he's minted as a car like that costs well over one hundred grand. Second, it tells me the man is an entitled prick by the fact that he sits in his car, watching me walk the mile long driveway instead of coming to pick me up.

'You must be Michael Humber?' the man says and only gets out when I eventually reach the gravel parking area in front of the house. Ginger hair, ruddy cheeks. Startling blue eyes. He extends a pudgy hand towards me. His stomach straining against the flannel shirt and tweed jacket. 'Lord Charles Huntington.'

Nice of him to tell me he's a lord.

'Yes, it's just Mike. Nice to meet you, sir.' I shake his sweaty, limp hand.

People say you can tell a man by the measure of his handshake, but anyone can fake a firm grip or try, and bely a weakness of character by giving a floppy shake.

'Well, you're early, so that's a good sign. Have you travelled far?'

'From London. I got the train into Huntington village and walked in from there. Lovely day, and I knew I was early, so...' I don't want to tell him I'm broke.

'Walked all that way, eh? You should have said. We could have picked you up.'

He literally just watched me walking along the driveway.

'No, it's fine. It's a lovely day, and I love walking.' I hate walking.

'That's wonderful! Right, well, obviously, we did our due diligence on your background.'

'I did disclose it in the email,' I say quickly.

'Yes! Yes, you did. Very honest of you. But let me say this. I think it was awful what they did to you, sacking you like that.' He shakes his head, looking all serious. 'Their loss is our gain, though,' he adds.

I'm not sure how to answer that. Does that mean I have the job already?

'Well, this is the house. It's been in our family for generations,' he says with an arm outstretched to present the house. 'Did you get the gist of what we need?'

'There's a legal issue, and you need someone living here. Is that right?'

'Pretty much the crux of it. I won't bore you with the full details, but there is a rather heated legal, er...shall we say, entanglement? My father, Lord Huntington, the title is hereditary, you see. But yes. He died, and we were all terribly sad as you would be, but there now appears to be an issue over some claims to inheritance, and well, it's all very personal, but until we get that sorted, we can't live in it. Which is stupid, but there it is. We can't even go inside unless we get all sides to agree, and the court has to ratify it. Bloody mess. And it was dragging on, and we had all sorts of issues with people saying they'd get inside and claim rights, but finally, we got the lawyers to get everyone to sign a contract, promising they won't try and get in until the court hearing. And the only way we could do that was by employing someone to stay here and keep us all out!'

There's nothing like a death and a contested will to bring out the best in people.

'Understood, so you want someone here to stop anyone entering or trying to move in and claim squatter's rights or possession by their virtue of residency?'

'Yes! That's it, old chap. Well done, you!'

Patronising shit.

'Thank you, very kind.'

If I had a cap, I would be doffing it. He stares at me with a big smile. It seems he wants something, but I don't know what.

'Well, do you want the job then or what?' he asks.

'Er, well, yes, of course, but...' This is the quickest interview I've done. He didn't ask me for references or where I see myself in five years, or if I would say I'm a team player or not. He didn't even tell me they're a mad bunch here and it's amazing they get any work done with all the japery.

'Great, well, here's some petty cash in case you need anything, and we'll get the salary paid into your account. You'll find a list of emergency numbers on the telephone table in the main entrance.'

'My account?'

'Yes, you do have a bank account, don't you?'

'Yes, of course.'

'We'll get the money paid into that. Do you have the details?' He takes out a pen and notepad to jot down my account number and sort code.

'Let me get the keys.' He hands me a jailhouse bunch of keys on a large metal loop.

'That's a lot of keys.'

'It's a big house. I would go in and show you round, but sadly, the courts prevent me from crossing the threshold. It's also Grade I listed, so do be careful, and are you familiar with gaslights?'

'Gaslights?'

'Yes. Gaslights. It's gaslit, you see. One of the only stately homes in the country that still uses them. I say uses them. The house is fully fitted with modern lights, but there's still a few gaslights on the walls. We're not allowed to remove them. They still work too. That's why I'm saying all this. You might hear a hiss coming from them. Very faint. But that's alright. It's a tiny feed of gas, keeping the pilot light on inside the mechanism. No need to call the gas board out, eh?'

'Okay. So I don't do anything with them?'

'No need to touch them. Anyway. I always think the best to get familiar is to look for oneself. Would give you a tour, but not allowed in my house. Right! Splendid! Well, I hate to rush off, but well, I...have to rush off.' He shakes my hand again; then he's off in his nice car, leaving me standing there, holding the jailhouse keys, and looking about, expecting someone to jump out and say *Ha, gotcha!* or something. No one does, though, and after his expensive, leather upholstered Range Rover disappears out of view, I'm left completely alone.

2

The door opens into a vast, majestic hallway, with a black and white checked tiled floor, wide and airy, with a grand staircase in the middle.

Matching grandfather clocks stand on either side, and gilt framed portraits of hunting scenes adorn the walls – men on horseback, wearing red and surrounded by small dogs. In the middle, a big man with ginger whiskers and blue eyes sits on a grey horse. He bears a striking resemblance to Lord Huntington.

I ditch my rucksack and open the envelope to find five hundred pounds in crisp twenty-pound notes. Fuck me. Most places I've worked struggle to buy tea bags with their petty cash.

I head over to an antique-looking telephone desk. A printed sheet tells me a number to ring in case of emergency and more numbers of local tradesmen.

Rooting through the papers on the desk, I find sheets of thick paper with *Huntington House* embossed in gold letters across the top.

Then I hear the hiss he mentioned and glance up to the

ornate brass fitting coming out of the wall, with a Victorian-style glass shade around the end. I've seen gaslights before. Some of the proper old houses in London still had them. But most weren't in use. It is pretty cool, though. I bet they give a really cosy glow.

I head off for a recce. After all, it now looks like this will be my home for the next few months until they sort out the court issues.

I leave the bag in the entrance and start making my way through the rooms, and if I wasn't so bitter and angry at the world, my mouth would have dropped open a little more with each room I entered.

Especially the sitting room and the chaise longues, and leather Chesterfields, and the small tables holding what look like genuine antique Tiffany lamps. Pictures line the walls. Proper paintings and not cheap, printed things. Some of the frames probably cost more than any car I've ever owned.

Then I walk into the dining room and stare at the biggest table I think I've ever seen. A proper dark hardwood thing that could sit fifty people. Matching chairs in neat lines on either side, but the table is bare, giving the room a dark, almost oppressive air.

That pretty much sums the whole place up. Wealthy and amazing, for sure, but empty, and cold, and dark.

The library is nice, though, with floor to ceiling shelves covering every inch of wall, and leather-bound books crammed onto every shelf. Deep red carpet that looks wonderfully worn in places, and red velvet curtains hanging either side of big veranda doors and the windows.

It's the only room so far that looks functional and used. Nice, comfy armchairs next to old lamps.

The view from the French doors takes in the sweep of pasture to the wooded copse.

I can see this being my main room. I love reading.

After the library, the other rooms all looked even more sterile. And while I'm not an expert by any degree, even I can see some of the fixtures and furniture would be worth an absolute fortune. There's no alarm, though. I'm amazed this place hasn't been knocked over by now. It's in the middle of nowhere as I know the nearest dwelling is probably two miles away.

Thinking this prompted me to dig my mobile phone out of my pocket to see an empty signal bar. Which means using the landline to call the police, which would be cut by any self-respecting housebreaker.

At the rear of the staircase, I find the second nicest room of the house so far – the kitchen. A flagstone floor and an old Aga set into one wall.

The big, solid table in the middle looks pitted with generations of use. There was life here. None of the stuffy, overly polite, pretentious tripe with Lord Shithead and his merry fox hunters. This was where the real people worked and lived.

Mild panic does set in when I realise there is no microwave.

I cross over to the back door, which is held shut with a single key lock that could be kicked open by a one-legged, asthmatic child. Heavy duty bolts set in the top and bottom but drawn back and not pushed home. Some people just have no sense of security.

I step through into a square-shaped courtyard, with a high wall running the perimeter, and a thick, wooden gate set into it. On one side is the back of what looks like a workshop or garage. I go over and try the door – locked. Shaking my head, I use my foot to knock a plant pot over and find the key hidden underneath. The key unlocks the door, and I'm in, looking at an old-style, blue-coloured Land Rover four-wheel drive vehicle with a white roof. I climb in, expecting to see the keys in the ignition, but find them wedged into the driver's sun visor instead. Very cunning. One of my chores is obviously to nail a big sign up saying *please come and rob this house, and don't forget to steal the shitty, old Land Rover while you are here.*

The Landy starts first time. I nod with satisfaction, then think that if someone had told me a couple of years ago that I would be pleased at finding myself looking after a stately home and being happy at finding a library, kitchen, and Land Rover, I would have laughed at them.

Now, though? I'll take whatever good fortune I can find.

The thought plummets my mind, and not for the first time, I feel the bitterness start to set in my stomach. I could take some of these antiques in this Land Rover, get a few quid, and disappear. But I know I won't. I might be many things, but I'm not a thief.

I head back into the kitchen and find the kettle next to a glass jar of posh instant coffee. Like something from an artisan boutique store.

No milk, though. In fact, the fridge is empty.

Do I use the petty cash for food, or am I expected to buy my own? There's not much choice, really. I can keep receipts and reimburse them when I get paid.

I head back into the entrance to retrieve my bag and my stash of milk portions pilfered from a café in the train station.

With a coffee made, I fish out my packet of duty-free rolling tobacco bought cheap on the last security gig I worked and head outside. The coffee tastes strong and slightly different to normal brand name instant coffee, but it's still nice, though.

A few smokes. Another coffee, and for the first time in years, I actually feel a slight sense of positivity. That something good has happened for once. A new job, and a chance to be out of the city. A fresh start, and the right time to move on from what happened.

From what I did.

The memory of the incident replays in my mind. The rage I had inside that made me lose it all. I clench my fists. Reliving it like I do every day. What he said to me. What I did, and what I lost because of it.

I snap out of it and tell myself to get a grip and accept my reality. I'm here, and that's all there is to it. I've got months of peaceful living ahead of me. I can read as much as I want. I can even use this time to get in shape again. Get back to the level of fitness I had when I was on the tactical firearms teams, eat healthy, and cut back on the booze and smoking.

Feeling slightly less self-pitying, I head back into the house to continue my unguided tour.

3

I pause at the top of the stairs and look left and right to long hallway lined with doors. A beautiful red carpet down the centre of the floor, leaving enough gap on either side to admire the varnished wooden floor underneath.

I head left to a set of grand double doors, much nicer than the rest, and figure this must be the master suite. I try the handle, and it swings open to a mess inside.

Clothes and items strewn across the floor. The huge four-poster bed unmade, with the sheets all pulled back. Jewellery scattered across the dressing unit, and picture frames knocked over. At first it looks like it's been ransacked, and I stand still from years of experience. Not wanting to trample a crime scene.

But this isn't a crime scene.

It's just messy, like someone left in a hurry.

I walk in carefully, placing my feet to avoid stepping on anything. The jewellery looks to be gold and silver, with precious stones. I pick a necklace up, with a large ruby on a pendant, circled by diamonds, and marvel at the weight. I couldn't tell fake from real, but something tells me it must be worth a fortune. The pictures are in solid silver and gold frames and worth a few quid too.

Any half-decent burglar would have taken those and the hundreds of other antiques in the house. Lord Huntington and who I can only assume is Lady Huntington grace the images within the frames. But where he is ginger and ruddy, she's blond and attractive. A woman like that wouldn't look twice at Lord Ginger in normal life. Money talks. Wealth is attractive. It's a fact of life.

The scene looks out of place, though. The rest of the house is perfectly ordered. I realise the room has more doors leading off, and on checking, I find these are a suit of rooms with a lounge area, bathroom, and walk-in wardrobes. The wardrobes have been mostly emptied, with just a few tweed suits and the odd ball-gown left. The more I look, the more it appears they just left in a hurry. Maybe they had to leave because of the court order, but then they would have been given notice and would know about it if they were involved in the proceedings. Either way, it's not my concern.

I close the door behind me.

I go into the next suite of rooms. Smaller than the master suite but still nice.

It looks like the occupier was a young woman, judging by the feminine furnishings and décor. It's messy too. A few clothes lie strewn about. Hairbrushes. Make-up sets. That kind of thing.

I guess the whole family had to ship out in quick time. I turn to leave and spot a silver picture frame, face down near the door, just waiting to be kicked or trampled on. I pick it up and set it on the side unit. An attractive, young woman with ginger hair in the picture. I figure she's the offspring of the Lord and Lady. It's a good photo too. Professionally done by the looks of it. But then I guess wealthy people don't snap pics on their iPhones and order the prints online with a discount code. They get photographers in to take candid shots. I even spot the copyright symbol in the lower left corner of the photo and snort a dry laugh. Then I frown at the logo for a stock image website in fainter words next to it. Jesus. They used a stock site to get pictures of their own daughter. Not only are they famous enough to be on a stock site, but they're also so bloody tight they downloaded the watermarked picture instead of buying it.

She clearly got ready to go in a hurry too. Unless they were just dirty people.

The bathroom is cluttered but clean, with no residue left round the bath or stains in the toilet. The bed sheets are also clean and not stained.

No, these people left in a hurry, and whatever the reasons, well, that's their business and nothing to do with me. I close the door and move on again. The rest of the rooms down this end of the corridor are immaculately decorated guest rooms. Much like downstairs, they look ready for a magazine photographer or to be used as a film set.

At the far end, I find a leisure room with a bar and a snooker table. A big, old thing that looks antique. Two big, wooden boxes on a side table. I open the lids to see shiny snooker balls inside all neat and tidy.

Double doors at the end of the room lead out onto a balcony looking over the patio and rear lawns.

The bar is well stocked with bottles of fine wine, champagne, and every kind of spirit, including several bottles of vodka, which is my weakness.

I curse myself for finding it because I'll know it's here now. My drinking has got bad since I left the police. No, correction, since I got sacked from the police.

I purposefully didn't bring any booze with me. First, I couldn't afford it, and second, because I wanted to use this time to have a break from it. But now I can't unsee it.

I head out of the room, promising myself I won't go back in.

I find a smaller staircase and head up to the top floor. This seems to be sectioned into two parts – overflow guest rooms, smaller but still perfectly presented, and then, through a door to the area the servants used – small rooms, simply furnished and lacking any of the luxury of the rest of the house, with threadbare carpets and beige walls, with the paint peeling off.

Checking through them, I find a guest room with a normal size double bed all made up and figure this is the one I can use.

Surprisingly, none of the servants' rooms have locks on the doors, which seems strange, but I guess servants in those days didn't have much in the way of employment rights.

The staircase to the attic leads up from the servants' quarters. I head up into the almost pitch dark. No light switch at the bottom of the stairs. I grope around until I feel a twisted wire hanging down in front of me. A couple of bare bulbs blink on, illuminating the massive space. Boxes, crates, and furniture stacked up and covered in dust sheets, casting weird shapes. The floor has been boarded. I walk to the far end, looking left and right at the generations of junk hoarded up. Reaching the end, I make myself jump by not noticing the large mirror propped up and seeing someone moving out of the corner of my eye.

Even in this light, I look terrible. Late thirties, but I look older. A messy beard and wild hair, with deep crow's feet wrinkles and bags under my eyes.

I can't believe they employed me. I wouldn't employ me.

'You're a mess, Humber.' I try to stare myself out to see who will blink first.

I lose.

Recce complete, I go back downstairs into the kitchen and start checking for supplies. I open the first cupboard and find it mostly empty apart from a few condiments. That must be why they gave me so much petty cash, knowing they'd emptied the cupboards. If they're so wealthy, why didn't they just buy more food? Maybe they're like a lot of rich people, and all the money is in the property and estate, with no actual cash in their banks. But then he was driving a brand-new Range Rover, so that at least means he's either got a very good credit rating or cash to spend on expensive toys. Rich people are weird. Strip the food out but leave their antiques with a virtual stranger.

I was going to make a list of things I needed, but there's no point. I pretty much need everything apart from coffee.

Why did they leave the coffee and take everything else?

Like I said, rich people are weird.

4

The double doors on the garage swing open on well-maintained hinges.

I pull the Landy out enough to close the doors behind me, then head off down the mile long drive to the main road. It feels nice to be driving again, even if it is a beaten-up, old Land Rover. We used armoured Land Rovers on the Tactical Firearms Teams, so I'm used to driving them.

The country roads weave through the brown, harvested fields.

It's late afternoon. I hope the village shops don't close before 5 p.m.

I make a decision to rise early tomorrow and explore the grounds. Maybe one of the shops will have an ordnance survey map of the area. The complete lack of security is on my mind.

If any villain got a whiff of the loot in Huntington House, they would be there like a shot, driving a transit van while on the phone to their local fence.

I'm not bothered about them stealing the family jewels.

This is self-preservation because I don't want to be tied to a chair, with dirty socks stuffed in my mouth, and being left for days to sit in my own piss and shit until Lord Ginger comes back round.

A few simple precautions will go a long way – escape routes and finding out the closest point to get a mobile phone signal. I've got my old job torch in my bag in case the power goes out, but it needs batteries. Take care of those few bits; then I can sit back and relax.

The main parking area is in the village square. Leaving the Landy in one of the many empty parking bays, I wander over to the shops, passing an old-style café diner, closed up and dark inside. White net curtains cover half the window.

Equally dark windows of gift shops advertising wares and locally made produce. Butchers, bakers, but looking around, I don't see the candlestick makers.

The obligatory chain-owned minimarket is tucked in the corner, taking the space of two buildings. Big, multi-coloured signs plastered over the inside of the window, offering discounts on kitchen towels.

I head inside and grab tinned and frozen food, a bag of potatoes, and meat from the chilled section. Milk, bread, and some basic cleaning materials. I grab some toiletries as my own supplies are dwindling to almost nothing.

'Just passing through?' the middle-aged woman behind the counter asks when I approach and put my basket down for her to start scanning the barcodes.

'Sorry?'

'You're not from around here. Are you passing through or just moved in?'

She didn't just say that, did she? I thought that phrase was copyrighted and trademarked for films only.

'Oh, my god, did I just say that? You must think I'm a right country bumpkin,' she says with an eye-roll. 'Not from around 'ere?' she mimics herself, and I can't help but smile.

'No, I'm not from here, just staying for a little while.'

'Ooh, anywhere nice?'

Do I tell the truth and therefore expose the fact that Huntington House is empty, save for a lone security guard, which also reveals there is an issue within the Huntington house, and although I have no loyalty to them, they are my employers, and I expect they want discretion.

'Just house sitting for a friend,' I say casually.

'Oh, yeah? Where's that, then?' she asks while scanning my groceries.

'Er, just a few miles out. He's got an old cottage, and I said I'd look after the dogs. You know what people are like with their pets. He won't put them in kennels because of the kennel cough outbreak, so he called me up and asked if I'd mind. Of course, I don't mind, nice to get out of the city for a while, with all that traffic and pollution. Yeah, some nice, clean air for a few weeks will do wonders. His wife wanted them in kennels, though, as she isn't into dogs as much as he is. Let me tell you that. Nice lady, though. She worked in the city too, in advertising, but it ground her down too much, so they moved up here. Always going on about it too, emailing pictures of the woods and things. Tell me, what time do the other shops close?' Speaking fast and smiling all the time, I overwhelm her with information and finish off with a question while staring at her expectantly.

'Er...the, er, what?'

'The shops, what time do they close normally?'

'Between three and four most of them this time of year,' she smiles again, but not so confident now.

I spent years in plain clothes, walking round dodgy

areas, where the local population were always on the lookout for undercover police. Having a quick story and a confident manner was the best defence by far.

'That's great. Well, it was nice chatting with you,' I take the bags and hold my hand out for the change, smiling and walking away while humming cheerfully, which ceases the second the door closes behind me.

I walk back to the Landy, feeling even worse than before. Using the skills I honed for many years on the streets brings back the memories and dampens my mood as I drive back.

It's getting dark when I reach the house. Once parked, I check the double doors and push home the bolts before locking the garage door behind me and heading into the courtyard.

Dumping my bags on the kitchen table, I put the frozen and chilled things away and leave the rest stacked on the side – a clear signal that I'm not making myself too much at home.

Coffee made, and I examine the Aga, trying to figure out where the wood goes in or the coal, or whatever fuel it burns. It takes me about half an hour to work out that it's connected to the mains gas supply.

The big gas pipe running round the edge of the wall gives it away.

Great detective skills there, Humber.

Figuring that if there is a gas supply to the Aga, then there must be a central heating system somewhere. Checking the rooms, I discover that the radiators are all coloured the exact shade of the wall they grace.

I touch several of them but find them cold. They must have turned the heating off.

I go back to the kitchen and make food.

Once finished, I head into the library and flick the light on, illuminating the room in the soft glow of yellow light. Another hiss sounds in here too, coming from a gaslight on the wall, but my eyes are drawn to the French doors and my reflection presented in the glass.

Anyone outside will be able to see me. I pull the curtains before starting to examine the bookshelves and getting lost in the hundreds of leather-bound volumes neatly stacked in well-presented order. My fingers brush along encyclopaedias, volumes on medicine, history, genealogy, and every other subject known to man until I settle on a 1920s edition of Medieval and Modern Times.

Sinking into a deep armchair, I flick an electric lamp on and lose myself in the old pages, leafing through maps with names of countries now long gone.

By half past eleven, my eyes are drooping. Today's events have taken their toll on my body. I head out the room, turn the lights off, and close the door before checking the front door is locked and secure. The kitchen door is locked, and the key removed. On climbing the first step, I stop to think of the French doors all around the property.

I dump the bag and curse myself for not checking them properly earlier. Taking the jailhouse keys, I spend the next hour groping walls for light switches and checking each door is bolted and secure.

As I move through the house, I draw some curtains and leave some lamps on to show any possible intruders that someone is here. It might cost Lord Ginger a few more quid in electricity, but he employed me for security.

By the time I start up the stairs again, I can see my breath coming from my mouth. The temperature is dropping with every passing hour.

On the third floor, I find the door I left open and dump

my bag on the bed. Taking the measly contents out, I stack them on the floor for now and promise myself I will sort them out properly in the morning.

I sit on the edge of the bed and look down at my black police issue boots. Well-made and sturdy, they remind of the hundreds of times I got home from work and sat down to take them off. A feeling of loneliness descends, and I realise that no one knows I am here. My parents are long dead, and I am an only child, with all of my friends still working in the job I lost.

I pull my phone out of my pocket and check the empty signal bar. I flick to the contacts screen and move through the names of former colleagues and associates. The names bring back more memories of incidents, times at the pub, frantic work in offices, and foot chases through grimy streets.

I take my toiletries bag and move across the corridor to the bathroom. A tiled floor and a big tub resting on clawed feet in the middle of the room. A handheld showerhead connected to the taps. An oyster shaped sink with golden taps and a large mirror set into the wall.

I set my bag down, brush my teeth, and start running the hot water tap. Bangs and groans sound out from pipes, but no hot water comes out, only freezing cold stuff that spatters noisily into the sink.

Taking a quick body wash and shivering throughout the whole process, I quickly dart back into my room and close the door. I don't have night clothes, but it's too cold to sleep naked. I dress in a pair of jogging bottoms and a long-sleeved top.

The nagging starts as soon as my head hits the pillow.

I try to ignore it, but before long, I feel my limbs twitching and itching. My frustration gets worse until I can't take it anymore. I flick the light back on and rummage through my bag for the small pot. I twist the lid off and dry swallow two sleeping pills.

The meds only take ten minutes to kick in. Then I'm gone.

Dosed up on sleeping pills like the broken loser I am.

5

Day Two

I wake up, feeling cold and confused.

Weak light penetrates the curtains, so I figure it must be around half past seven if the sun is just coming up.

The cold forces me to get up and get moving. I dart across the hallway to stand in front of the toilet and try to stop shivering enough to aim properly.

While I brush my teeth, I try to avoid looking at the mirror and instead blink, and look twice at the bathroom door.

Which was open when I came in.

I always close doors behind me out of habit. I've always done it. My ex-wife used to get shitty with me for closing every door.

Maybe I didn't close it last night when I was freezing and rushing to get into bed and warm up.

Got to stop with the sleeping pills. They're making me forget things.

Ten minutes later, I'm wearing my coat in the courtyard, drinking another hot, boutique coffee, with the caffeine and nicotine giving me a false sense of well-being.

I feel guilty for reverting to type and ruining my plans for a healthy, new start. I'll do it later, maybe tomorrow. Get settled in and find my way about first.

I remember I was going to tour the grounds today and find the closest spot for mobile phone reception. I get the phone from my room and take the charger down to the kitchen to pump some juice in while I take a trip round the house to open the curtains and turn the lights off.

The weather is overcast and cold as I head back down the driveway in the Landy.

I pull out onto the main road and drive away from the village, and lose myself in the stark beauty of the area. I follow the lane until it winds into a forest, then ends in front of an open five-bar gate, giving access to a parking area in front of an old stone built cottage, with a thatched roof, and a lazy column of smoke coming from the chimney stack.

I pull forward and start to turn, and as I sweep the car around in a wide arc, I see a figure standing in the now open door.

I stop the car and drop out, with a wave of my hand. 'Hi! Sorry for using your driveway. I didn't realise the lane ended here.'

The figure doesn't move. I take a step toward him. Old habits die hard, and I leave the driver's door open and the engine running – a subconscious escape route.

'Said I'm sorry for your using your driveway.'

'Heard you,' a gruff voice replies.

'My name is Mike. I'm–'

'Know who you are. Security from the house.' His tone makes it obvious he does not want to speak with me.

'How do you know that?' I ask.

'Lord Huntington.'

He reminds me of a soldier being asked questions by an officer. Not wanting to answer but required to due to the nature of his position.

'Is this Huntington land?' I ask.

'It is.'

'Thank you. What's your job?'

'Groundsman.'

'Is this the groundsman's cottage?'

If it's a Q and A session you're wanting...

'It is.'

'How big are the grounds?'

'Big enough.'

I stand still and let the oppressive silence do the work for me, but he doesn't rush to fill it like most people would.

'Which way is the house from here?'

'Back the way you came.'

'What's your name?'

'Cooper.'

'Is that your first or last name?'

'Last.'

'First name?'

'Stanley.'

'Who lives with you, Mr Cooper?'

'Just me.'

'No children?'

'Just me.'

'Thank you for your time today, Mr Cooper. I guess I will be seeing you soon.' I turn to leave.

'You won't see me.'

I turn to look back as he steps inside his cottage and slams the door.

I curse myself for slipping into police mode. I'm not a policeman anymore. I'm just a security guard, and that's it. Still, I can't help replaying the conversation over in my head as I drive back down the lane. He could just be a grumpy man, who doesn't like new people.

No, it was more than that. He was acutely unhappy with my presence. Maybe he thinks it should be him living there and enjoying the big house and not some paid stranger.

But you know what? I don't care. It's not my problem. He can be as rude and surly as he likes. I'll do my job, get paid, and that's it.

Back at the house, I sit and stare at the wall in the courtyard, counting the bricks going left to right, then the bricks going up and down, then the plant pots.

No sounds anywhere. No birds. No traffic.

The hostel I was in before here was always noisy. I hated it. I thought I couldn't wait to get away and have peace. I thought this would be perfect.

I tell myself it is perfect.

But I also drum my fingers on the patio table and tap my foot simply to have some sounds.

The dark thoughts soon come. Pulling me down into a fug of blackness that seems to eat my energy and motivation to do anything.

I promised myself that if I got this job, I'd use the time to take stock of my life and make improvements. Get fit again. Stop drinking. Stop smoking. I visualised it in my head like a montage from a shit movie.

Doing crunches and push ups and running. Drinking

water and reading books. Eating leafy green veg and slowly transforming into a handsome, rugged hero.

What a twat.

Seriously.

It makes me cringe, knowing I actually thought that I could ever be anything again. I already had that life. I was super fit and smart, and popular.

I bend forward on the seat. On elbow on my knee. My other hand pushing into my messy hair and rubbing my bearded jaw and face. Images in my head. My fists pummelling the guy's face. Breaking his nose. The rage I felt inside. I couldn't stop. They had to drag me away.

It was less than a minute.

Now I'm here, working for what's probably minimum wage. Jesus. I didn't even take notice of what the salary is. I just took the job to be out of London as if it would be a magical, fresh start.

I think back to Cooper's surly attitude, which doesn't help. That was the only interaction I had with another person today, and it was negative and unpleasant. I used to have interactions like that all the time when I was a police officer. But it was balanced by the fact I was working in supported teams, and I had a positive life.

Now I'm sitting in silence, in the courtyard of someone else's house, thinking only of bad things. What I did. How I lost it all. Cooper.

The despair wells up inside, and it's a terrible feeling. A sense of utter hopelessness. That there is no future or anything good around the corner.

I start sighing and fidgeting. Blasting air through my nose. Tutting and shuffling in my seat.

I need motion.

I need sounds.

I can't just sit here.

But this is my job. I have to be here.

What have I done?

This was a stupid idea.

I'm a stupid man.

A loser.

A sad, broken loser with no hope. No family. No friends.

Everyone hates me.

I hate myself.

Maybe I should end it.

Whoa.

I stand up with another blast of air and shake my head. That impulse was too strong. It scared me.

Gotta do something. I need a distraction.

I head inside to find the TV, figuring to at least have some sounds and pictures.

Except there isn't one.

Who doesn't have a TV?

Wealthy people that have functions and parties, and connections, and rich social lives.

That's who.

Or they took the TV with them.

That makes sense. Most modern smart TVs hold the access account details for the streaming channels.

Logging in via another TV is a pain.

I head upstairs into the messy bedrooms and spot the places where the televisions were in both sets of suites.

'Bollocks.'

I step out into the corridor and stand in silence. I hear myself swallow. I hear myself breathe. I hear the hiss coming from the gaslights on the walls.

Music, then?

There must be a radio somewhere.

I head into the leisure room with the snooker table and purposefully avoid looking at the bar and the rows of booze, and spot the jukebox over to one side.

What a gorgeous, old thing it is. Curved sides and big, chunky buttons to press to make the selection. A list of tracks in nice font just inside the glass, but it's powered down and dark. I find the cable and then grab the plug to push into the socket as a loud bang comes from downstairs, making me jump.

I move quickly out of the room to the stairs and stop to listen in case the noise comes again so I can get a sense of the direction.

Is someone breaking in?

It was a distinct, loud noise of something impacting something else.

I find my hand reaching to my belt as though to check for my baton or Taser, but of course, I don't have anything now. Not even a working phone.

Downstairs is where someone would make entry. I go down and check the front door to find it locked and secure. Then I head through the downstairs rooms. Wincing when I turn the lights on from knowing they'll illuminate me clearly to anyone outside. I check the patio doors all the way around but find no signs of entry.

The last place is the kitchen back door, but that's not likely as the kitchen door leads to the enclosed courtyard, and those walls are high.

Mind you, if the assailants came through the garage, they'd gain access to the courtyard, and that would keep them out of sight from the gravel parking area and the drive.

Shit.

I should have checked that first.

I set off at a jog and rush in to see one of the big, heavy wooden kitchen chairs lying on its back on the stone floor.

Bloody idiot.

I must have left it leaning against the side of the table.

The back door is locked and secure, so I head over and lift the chair most of the way up, then let it drop, and roll my eyes at the same sound it made that I heard from upstairs. Albeit louder.

Which is when I jump again from the music blaring out, coming from the jukebox upstairs.

'Fuck,' I say with a gasp, feeling my heart thumping in my chest. I know I just plugged the machine in, though, which suggests there is an auto play setting, hence why it was unplugged in the first place.

Ah, well. I wanted noise.

It's creepy, though. Hearing it coming from upstairs like that. Especially from it being a slow, old-time song.

I head out into the hallway and cock my head. Recognising the melody and lyrics.

'Danny Boy?'

It is. That's Danny Boy.

I start up the stairs. Listening to the haunting voice and simple piano keys.

> *But come ye back when summer's in the meadow,*
> *Or when the valley's hushed and white with snow,*
> *It's I'll be there in sunshine or in shadow,*
> *Oh, Danny boy, Oh, Danny boy, I love you so!*

Something about it creeps me out again, especially when I reach the top of the stairs and start down the long, straight corridor lined with closed doors, and hear the music growing steadily louder as I near the end room, but when I step inside, I can see it's just a simple jukebox playing an old song. Nothing more.

I let my breath go, and only then realise I was holding it in. I'm too jittery. That coffee I had was strong, and I haven't eaten enough. Everything else that's happened too. I'm on edge.

I head over to the jukebox and flick the switch on the socket, cutting the music off and instantly regretting it from the sudden silence that now seems more pronounced.

But it's not my house, and this jukebox could be an antique or something.

I've just got to get used to being out of the city.

I rub my face as the bang sounds again. The same one I heard before from downstairs. I jump again, with my heart missing a beat.

'Fucking hell,' I say, then tell myself it's an old house.

I must have not put the chair back up properly when I heard the music.

Christ, though. I'm too wired.

I need a stiff one to calm me down.

I head behind the bar, knowing my brain was just looking for an excuse to justify having a drink. But even knowing that doesn't stop me. I grab a glass and pour a big shot of vodka, and knock it down in one. Feeling the burn as it hits my throat and slides into my stomach.

It makes me close my eyes and brace my hands against the bar, with a fresh surge of self-loathing while also feeling an instant buzz from the alcohol.

Oh, Danny boy, the pipes, the pipes are calling
From glen to glen, and down the mountain side.

'Jesus fucking Christ!'

I snap my head up at the music blaring out and see the lights shining on the jukebox. I bloody switched it off. I know I did.

I stomp over to see the switch is off on the socket. That being the very old switch on the very old socket on the very old wall of the very old house. Which clearly doesn't work.

I pull the plug out and head out the room; then with a grunt of frustration at my willpower crumbling, I turn back and grab the bottle and my glass.

Vodka is my friend.

I head down to the library and read the Medieval and Modern Times book while taking big gulps of vodka and munching through the bags of crisps I bought from the minimarket.

Books are my friends too.

Books don't betray you. Books don't take your soul and spit you out to live alone and unloved. Books are truth and filled with the words that someone created.

I stare at the cover, marvelling at how someone thought they would compile a condensed overview of this time period. They thought it out, researched the material, then put it all together, and presented it to be printed. No matter what that person did after that, they are forever immortalised.

I wonder in amazement at the history of the world. Of all the people that have ever lived, are living now, and will live in the future. All those souls filled with sadness, regret, and loneliness. Every one of us striving for a meaning, to be loved, to give love.

Silly twats. It's all bollocks.

I giggle drunkenly and curse the fools for what they are. They're not like me and my vodka, and the books. They don't see the truth like we do. They're not in on our secret, are they?

They don't know that we're just a bunch of organisms, running about, trying to pretend that we're special just because we can think.

Emotions? They're just the result of chemicals pumped into the system, designed to make us horny, angry, happy, sad, jealous, and all just so we can procreate and make more organisms.

'We are all empty vessels,' I impart my wisdom to the books, raising my glass to toast them.

'Empty vessels, yearning for a higher meaning, but you know what?' The books stare back at me, trying to look nonchalant, but I can tell they're listening.

'You know what? It's all bollocks.'

My insight startles them, and they whisper in surprise.

'That's right. It's all bollocks. There is no higher meaning, nothing. There's nothing. NOTHING,' I shout so they understand. It's important they understand. They need to understand me. They stop whispering and go sullen.

'I'm sorry for yelling.'

I feel guilty now.

'But you must understand this is very important.'

I'm on my feet so I can present my lecture with dignity and poise. But my glass is empty, and I can't just stand here with a dry mouth, so I take the vodka bottle by the neck and position the wine glass on the bookshelf in front of me.

'There you go, little wine glass. You can listen so when you grow up, you'll know just how shit it is. Now, listen carefully for I shall say this only once.' I take a big swig. 'Maybe more than once, but I shall tell it until you listen, and listen you shall.' This vodka tastes very nice. It must be weak because I hardly feel drunk. I stare at the label, trying to see the alcohol volume, but the numbers are hidden or too small.

'Sneaky, little numbers, where are you?' I twist the bottle, but those pesky numbers keep running away.

'I shall deal with you later. I have a lecture to give,' waggling my finger at the vodka bottle, I warn the numbers that this isn't over, and I will be back to sort them out after my teachings.

'Now, where were we? Yes, thank you, geography section. We know we are in the library in Cuntington House.' The other books giggle at my witty comment, so I give them a wink.

'Anyway, so there's no higher meaning.' Another swig. 'And if anyone tells you there is, then they're full of shit. No, no, listen to me, religious section. I know you have faith in God, Allah, Hare Krishna, and Buddha, and, and...and the other ones, but let me tell you something. Let me ask you something...eh? Let me ask you. Where is your God now?' I look round so they get the point I'm trying to make.

'He's not here, is he? He's not here. No, he is not. He is not here because he does not exist. There. I said it. I denied the existence of your supreme being, of your entity. Ha! So what do you think of that?'

More vodka pours into my mouth while I listen to their learned responses.

'No, no, no, you've got it wrong. Jesus did not die for our sins. He was a man, who lived a very long time ago and got nailed to some wood, and the bible is a collection of stories written over a long period of time and then found in some cave or something. No, wait... That was the Dead Sea Scrolls, wasn't it? History section, you are needed here. Please tell the rest of the room all about the bible and those Dead Scrolls things... While I sit down for a minute.' I slump down, then spring back up quickly.

'Right, you lot discuss that for a minute while I go for a smoke. Thank you, medicine section, we all know the dangers of smoking, and we don't need your pompous input now.'

Shaking my head at the cheek of the medicine books trying to lecture me, I head outside, pulling my coat on as I go. The urge to urinate comes on strong, so I head over to the corner of the wall and start pissing on a plant pot, then realise that all the plants must be thirsty, so I work my way along, trying to get a bit of piss on all of them. A job well done, and I stagger backwards, upending the bottle and downing the glorious liquid. My fingers stumble to roll a cigarette, and it takes several attempts. Eventually, I am victorious, and we are three. Me, the vodka, and the cigarette. I introduce them, but they're shy and don't really speak to each other.

I take a big swig, but I lean back too far and nearly topple, and drop the bottle on the ground. Then I'm feeling sad at losing such a good friend. I salute my fallen comrade and flick my cigarette down to join him, knowing they were close friends and would want to be together. Inside the kitchen, I realise I must be getting sick as my legs feel all wobbly, and my head is spinning. I close the door and wrestle with the bolts until they ram home.

'Ha,' I jump back in triumph, slamming into the table and falling to the floor. 'You thought you bested me, didn't you, but I won the day,' I stagger back up and give two fingers to the bolts, and start working my way up the stairs. Someone has put more steps in as it takes me a long time to get to the top, and I eventually crawl onto the first floor and work my way down to the bar room.

'Is there another vodka here? Hello, looking for Mr Vodka.' I stagger into the room towards the bar.

'I am terribly sorry to inform you of this tragic news, but the vodka bottle leapt out of my hand and committed suicide on the floor... It was very sad.' I take another bottle and commiserate the passing of a true friend.

6

Day Three

I wake up, feeling like shit, with a hangover, and start to yawn, but it cuts off when I look at the bedroom door.

The *open* bedroom door.

I clamber out of bed too quickly and get a headrush. I lean against the wall until the swirling vision settles back to normal, and I can stand unaided.

Stepping into the hallway, I see the bathroom door is closed, and so is every other door that I can see. Just my door is open.

I know I closed it when I went to bed. It's a habit for me. I always do it. I figure I must have got up in the night and used the toilet.

On checking the bathroom, I find the toilet seat down, and the water in the bowl is clear, with no signs of urine, and no splashing on the sides or floor. That's worrying that I don't remember getting up for a pee. That's one step away from sleepwalking.

I'm also bloody freezing. It's so cold in this house. I can see my breath.

How much did I drink last night? I don't even remember coming up to bed. Did I take sleeping pills? It feels like I did. That's dangerous, taking sleeping meds while drunk. It can slow your heartrate down so much you die in your sleep. Or is that a myth?

Whatever. I've got to change my life.

I vow to keep busy today and make myself tired, and avoid caffeine in the evening. And no vodka.

I get dressed while feeling woozy, and with my teeth chattering from the cold, and head down to make coffee, and go into the courtyard for a smoke, and once again, almost jump out of my skin, but this time from the shrill warble of the phone in the hallway.

'Mike? Its Charles Huntington here. Just calling to see how you are.'

How I am? He should be more worried about his house being left in the care of an alcoholic idiot.

'Fine, sir, everything is fine.'

'That's marvellous. So you're settling in okay?'

'Yes, sir, no problems at all.'

'That's wonderful. So no problems at all?'

Second time he's asked me that.

'No, sir, no problems. I've been putting different lights on in the evening, drawing curtains, and making the place looked lived in, which will hopefully put anyone off trying to break in.'

'Yes, Cooper said about the lights being on at night. He said you met. His family has worked for our family for generations.'

The sneaky bastard has been snooping around, then. I suppose that's only natural, and anyone in that position would do the same, but still, I don't like the thought of it. And I also can't help but note how his voice dropped slightly when he mentioned Cooper.

'Yes, I did meet him. To be honest, though, sir, he didn't seem all that pleased to see me.'

'Ah, yes, the Coopers have always been an abrupt sort. His father and grandfather were the same. Things are a bit different in the country, Mike. Complicated too. Especially things like employment law when they've been indentured for generations.'

'He's indentured?' I ask.

'God, no! Not now, but his family were going back. And that cottage he's in comes with the role, but again, they've had that for generations.'

Why is he telling me this?

'Reason I mention it, Mike, is I think Cooper is probably a bit freaked out because of the whole probate wrangle. That could end it for him, you see. The cottage and the job, I mean.'

That makes sense now. Cooper's worried about the sudden changes, and what they mean for him and his future.

'Right, got it. Just so I know, does Mr Cooper need access to the house?'

'He's got keys. His family have always held them. We've had a running joke for years that the Coopers see it as their house and land, but there's no reason he should be entering now. Everyone has been told to keep out of it.'

'Got it. So if I see him inside, I can ask him to leave?'

'Yes! God, yes. Far too much at stake with this whole thing. If one side thinks the other side is getting people in or allowing access, they could argue *business-as-usual,* which will cause bloody carnage.'

'Got it. Did you ask for your keys back from him?'

He hesitates, with a huffing noise, for a second. 'Like I said. His family has some very strong connections to the house and the grounds.'

And Cooper is a big, angry man. He's also very intimidating, which means Charles Huntington didn't want to ask for the keys back.

'Could you ask your lawyers to make contact and get them back, sir? Make it look like a legal thing.'

'Well. Yes. That is an option. But honestly, Mike. Half the village have probably got the keys, and even changing the locks causes issues. Like I said, that house is listed. The hoops we had to jump through just to get the heating installed–'

'Heating!'

'Eh? What was that?'

'The heating. Sorry. I was going to ask. Can I put it on?'

'Is it off!? Oh, dear god, you poor sod! You must be frozen. Yes, of course. In the basement. Boiler on the side. Can't miss it. Must have tripped. Big button to restart. Oh, and there's a bar upstairs in the snooker room. Help yourself to a drink.'

'That's very kind,' I say in a voice that comes out several notches higher than normal while also remembering pissing all over his plant pots in the courtyard and raiding his bar.

'Not at all! Glad to have you. And I mean it. Have a drink and relax in the evening. And the old Landy is in the garage. Did you find it? Use it if you need to pop into the village.'

'Okay, sir, thank you very much,' doffing my cap again and sucking up to the rich employer.

'Well, Mr Humber, if there is anything you need, just call. Bye for now.'

It now makes sense why Cooper was so hostile yesterday and also why he'll be snooping around. First, because he probably feels a sense of propriety and entitlement and is therefore pissy that he's not allowed free run of the place, but my presence also signifies a big change to his status quo. Especially if some probate judge rules for a division of the house and lands, which will most likely result in the end of Cooper's house and job, which would pretty much be his whole life.

I find the cellar door concealed in the wall at the back of the entrance hallway, cleverly constructed so that only the outline of the door is visible. Even the keyhole has a small metal plate hanging over it, matched perfectly in colour to the rest of the décor.

Retrieving the jailhouse keys, I work through them until I find the right one and detach it from the loop to leave it in the keyhole. There are several more keys on the metal loop, so there must be more doors somewhere.

I push against the cellar door, but it stays stuck. It must open outwards, but there's no handle. I try twisting the key and pulling the door that way, but it remains shut. Finally, I figure it out – a spring-loaded lock.

I push the door firmly once, and it pops open to be pulled.

Very clever, but why go to all that hassle when you can just have an inward opening door?

The stairs lead to a large square room, with a modern-looking boiler situated on one side, with a red button marked *press and hold to reset*.

I press my finger into the button and hold it down. Nothing happens for a couple of seconds; then a loud clunk sounds out, followed by the machine spurring noisily to life until it settles down to a steady purr.

While down here, I have a look around. It's a modern basement. Painted white, with good lights. A big, industrial size washing machine against the side. Workbenches and tables. Big ironing boards and irons. Shelves filled with spare light bulbs, cleaning materials, bedding, spare pillows, and such like.

An old desk against a wall, with a worn chair pushed under it. Sheets of papers on the top and clipped to the wall in front. Wipe clean calendars. Health and Safety at Work notices. Cleaning material manuals. This must be the manager's desk for the house staff.

I find a clipboard hanging from a hook, with dozens of sheets of old cleaning rotas printed out. They clearly employ a small army of people to keep the house running.

Where are they now? Laid off or given paid leave while the court proceedings are sorted?

It does make sense for a totally independent person to be brought in, but then it's only Lord Huntington that met me, and he called me. What's to stop him trying to offer me a bribe or financial incentive to assist them in some manner?

What could I do, though?

More doors lead off from this area.

I open the first door, which leads into a wine cellar, with a bottle rack running the length of one wall. Bottle tops poke out of every hole. I pull a few out to read the labels.

Several of the bottles are over a hundred years old. This lot must be worth a fortune. It's not just wines either but boxes of whiskey, vodka, brandies, rums, and crates of imported bottles of beer.

As I go to leave, I see another door set into the end of the far wall held closed with a clasp and a combination padlock. The door is solid metal and hardly moves when I thump it.

I figure it's probably where they've housed the firearms cabinets.

People in the country love shooting things, so it stands to reason they would have shotguns and rifles.

I head up to find my coffee has gone cold and put the kettle on to make a fresh one, then step over to the table to roll a cigarette. But the papers aren't in the pouch. I glance down at the table, then at the floor while I check the pockets of my jeans.

No sign of them.

I check the kitchen worktops, then the drawers, and cupboards.

I head into the courtyard and check the patio table, the chairs, the ground, then work my way back into the kitchen, and check all the same places over again.

I made a smoke before the call came in, so I definitely had them.

Basement, then.

Idiot.

I head back down, but I still can't see them. 'Fuck's sake,' I mutter and stomp back up, and check around the area near the phone. Nothing. I charge up to my room on the third floor and pull my bag onto my bed.

Still nothing.

Back in the kitchen. I tip the bin contents out in the courtyard, but still no cigarette papers.

I literally had them ten minutes ago.

Fucking sleeping pills and booze. I'm putting things down and losing them now. I get angry at myself and bite my temper down, wondering where the hell I left them, and pull my boots on, and stomp over to the garage.

The village square is a lot busier than last time, but then it's only just gone ten in the morning.

I slot the Landy in a row of other four-wheel drive vehicles. First stop is the minimarket. I'm glad the nosey woman I met last time isn't working behind the counter.

Outside, I roll a smoke and go to light it, stopping when I notice a few chairs and tables outside the now open café. The weather is cold, but it's dry and still, and I'm sorely missing that first caffeine hit of the day.

I enter the café and take in the view, with a quick, sweeping glance. Farmers and farming types sat across two tables, ploughing through huge plates filled with cooked breakfasts. An old couple sitting in silence, eating toast, and sharing a pot of tea. Another old man sat alone, eating a bacon sandwich, with a small, white dog at his feet, staring up hopefully. The farm hands glance over, hardly breaking stride with their eating and conversation.

'Good morning. Do you have cappuccino?'

'You must be the Londoner, then,' a woman in an apron says bluntly when I reach the counter. 'My sister-in-law works in the shop. She said there was a Londoner in the other night. That's her husband there, my brother John.'

I pick up the sudden drop in conversation behind me and can almost feel the farm workers boring into the back of my head. I glance back to see them staring quietly.

'Wendy said you're looking after some dogs,' John says. 'Only the Huntingtons ain't got no dogs, and that's their Landy outside.'

'And Stan said someone's at the house now,' another one of the men says.

Two choices immediately present.

I can stick with my story from the shop the other night, but there's no point since they've clocked the Landy, and

Stanley Cooper has told them who I am. Or I can say who I am and why I'm here, but that in itself is dangerous, given the amount of high value property within Huntington House. Making friends with locals isn't wise with a gig like this.

I think all of that within a second as I frown at the men. 'Is this when you get the banjos out?'

'Eh?' John asks.

'Maybe stick a twig in your mouth. *We don't like no locals in these parts,*' I say in a mock sinister country accent.'

'No, hang on. I didn't mean it like that,' John says awkwardly.

'*And that be their Landy out yonder, and they ain't got no dawgs...*'

'Alright, mate, you've made your point,' John says.

'And don't put a twig in your mouth, mate,' one of the other men says earnestly. 'Bovine TB around here. Fucking badgers.'

'Fucking badgers,' another mutters.

'What's wrong with badgers?' I ask the woman behind the counter. She doesn't reply. Or smile. Or make eye contact. 'Can I have a cappuccino, please?'

She starts clattering about, making the coffee. A moment later, I hear cutlery scraping plates as the men go back to eating.

'On the house,' the woman says, sliding the coffee cup over. 'Don't want no trouble.' She disappears into the kitchen to talk to someone else out of my sight.

I think to ask why or offer to pay again, but she's out of sight, and the energy in the room is still weird.

I'm still too thick-headed from the pills to give it more thought, so I head past the now sullen farmers to go outside and roll a smoke while wondering why they don't like badgers.

I start thinking about the bedroom door being open and losing my cigarette papers. Any dedicated smoker always knows how much tobacco and papers they have left, and most will be able to tell you roughly how much gas is left in their lighters too.

I know I was on my last packet, but it was only about halfway through, so I wouldn't have chucked it out. Sipping my coffee and smoking, I confront the possibility that I moved them myself during the night, but what, when, or how is beyond me.

Jesus Christ. I need to get a grip. And what was all that about in the café?

Then I clock the name on the convenience shop. Huntington Stores.

Which is next to Huntington Post office.

Which is next to Huntington Bakery.

I twist around to see the sign on the café. Huntington Diner.

I'm guessing the Huntington family own this whole area. Which would make them the landlords to the people running these businesses. And if those people think I'm working directly for Huntington, then they figure to be nice and give me free coffee.

Except they weren't very nice.

Or maybe that was their way of trying to be nice, and I shot them down by comparing them to the yokels from *Deliverance*.

A moment or so later, the farmers come out and head off to their vehicles without a glance in my direction.

I chastise myself that maybe I reacted in the wrong way, but I argue back and remind myself that I don't give a shit.

'Penny for them?' a soft voice breaks my concentration, and I lose the ability to speak as I look up into the beautiful face of a woman staring down at me. Blond hair and beautiful, blue eyes.

'Penny for what?' I ask, thinking she's collecting for charity. 'I haven't got any change.'

'Your thoughts? It's a saying. You looked a million miles away.'

'Eh? Oh! Yeah. Penny for your thoughts. Sorry, I was zoned out completely.'

'Would you like another one?' she asks and motions at my almost empty cup. She must be the other staff member that was in the kitchen.

'Yes, please. Hang on, I've got a fiver.'

She looks puzzled for a second before smiling. 'It's okay. On me.'

'Two in one day? Wow, that's hospitality.'

She keeps that same puzzled expression before heading inside the café. I settle back down, with all thoughts of my worries gone at the sight of the beautiful woman, and the thought that at least not all the staff here dislike me.

Yet.

Dislike me *yet*.

She returns within a couple of minutes, pulling the door open while holding two mugs in one hand. She smiles and sits down at my table.

'On a break?'

'From what?'

'From here.'

'Here? I don't work here. Oh, you thought...'

'Yeah. I mean...' I start to say as she takes a sip, then licks the froth off her upper lip in a way that makes me glance somewhere else. 'So. Like. You just offer coffee to random people, then?'

'Totally my thing,' she says as I clock the confident tone of her voice that speaks of a good education.

'That's a good thing.'

'What can I say? Addicts need to stick together.'

'Addicts?' I ask with a rush of worry.

'Coffee addicts.'

'Oh, coffee! Right. Yeah.'

'You're still not convinced, are you?' she asks.

'God, no.'

'Londoner,' she says with a knowing nod. 'People being nice means either you're about to get stabbed by a crazy person or offered sex for money.'

'Right. So?'

'No knife,' she says, holding her hands out.

'What the fuck!'

'Joke! Oh, your face. Sorry. My humour. Rein it in, Tessa,' she says as though admonishing herself.

'Hello, Tessa. You don't look like a prostitute.'

'Why not? What do prostitutes look like?'

'You know. Prostitutey.'

'And that's based on your intimate knowledge of sex-workers?'

'It's based on my working knowledge of them.'

'Wait, what? Are you a sex-worker?'

'No!'

'Oh! I thought. Cos you said working knowledge.'

'Fair point. So?' I ask.

'So, what?'

'So why did you offer the free coffee if you're not a crazy person with a knife or a sex-worker?'

'I never said I wasn't crazy, only that I didn't have a knife.'

'Not helping, Tessa.'

'Not fair. You can't say my name in our witty retorting banter like that if I don't know yours. How can I volley back?'

'It's–'

'Don't tell me!'

'Jesus. Why?'

'Jesus?'

'No! Jesus. Like *why?*'

'So I can guess.'

'Oh. Alright, then.'

'Is it Jesus?'

'It's not Jesus.'

'Jerry? James? Jim!'

'Doesn't start with a J.'

'Urgh. Too hard.'

'Mike.'

'Mike!' she says a fraction of a second over me. 'Nice to meet you, Mike. I'm Tessa.'

'Hello. Mind if I smoke?'

'If you want to die early with tubes down your throat. Crack on.'

'Judgy,' I say and roll, and light a smoke.

'You not offering me one, then?'

'You're not a smoker.'

'I might be.'

'You're not. Your fingers aren't stained, and your teeth are really white, and your skin is literally glowing.'

'Aw, get you, flirty. I don't smoke. I used to think it looked cool, though. Now I don't. You know. Cos I'm a grown up.'

'Are you?'

'Touché. How's your free coffee?'

'Ain't nothing free.'

'Ooh, said the wounded man,' she says with a pursed look. *'Ain't nothing free in this world, Tessa. Everything has a cost.'*

'Good mockery.'

'I thank you. Londoner? You must be. I'm a Londoner. That's why I offered the coffee.'

I blink at her. Not getting it.

'It's been a long time since I spoke to someone who doesn't work on a farm or in this diner, or in that shop.'

I nod at her. Getting it.

'How long you been up here?' she asks.

'Only a couple of days. No. Three. No. Four.'

'Pick one, Michael.'

'Four. It's blurry.'

'Why is it blurry?'

'Long story.'

'Long, blurry story. So? Why are you up here, Mr Blurry?'

'Can't say.'

'Is it a secret?'

'Yes.'

'Don't tell me, then. I can't keep secrets.'

'Okay.'

'Are you that guy looking after Huntington House?'

'Awesome secret.'

'I know, right,' she says with a wan look. 'Can't break wind here without everyone hearing it. I was in the shop yesterday, and Wendy was telling Maggie.'

'Maggie?'

'Maggie,' she says, nodding at the door.

'Oh. I don't think Maggie likes me.'

'She doesn't know your inner beauty,' she says with mock sincerity. 'And they don't like anyone who can't drive a tractor.'

'Who said I can't drive a tractor?'

'Can you?'

'No. Can you?'

'Duh. Yeah. Totally got my tractor licence. I can't drive a tractor.'

'What do you when you're not offering free coffees?'

'We already established that. I'm the village sex-worker.'

'How's that working out?'

She pulls a face. 'A lot of sweaty farmers. Sorry!' she says with a laugh when I pull a face and burst out laughing.

'Rein it in, Tessa.'

'Rein it in, Tessa,' she says with a delighted grin at me while I try and avoid her captivating, blue eyes.

'So, what do you do?' I ask again.

'Ooh. You just got all serious.'

'Did I?'

She nods as though understanding why with a wry smile. 'Research, mainly.'

'What's the field?'

'About two acres. Ba-dum-tss!' she says as I choke on my coffee. 'Sorry! I'm too excited at seeing a new person. It's for a book I'm working on. You look familiar, though,' she says with a sudden frown.

I stir my coffee. It's been two years. I'd hoped everyone would have forgotten me.

'I can't place it. I know we've never met, so that must mean you've been in the papers or on television. But you don't look much like a celebrity, so...maybe a wanted criminal?'

'Something like that.'

'Something like that? No, you don't look like a criminal, and I doubt any rich bloke is going to trust a criminal to look after his house.' She gives a mock gasp and puts her hand to her mouth. 'Unless he's a criminal too.'

'Maybe.'

'Hmmm, I will have to peruse this mystery,' she looks comically serious, with a gentle frown.

'Well, you peruse away while I drink this coffee you bought for me.'

'Yes, I did buy that coffee, so you are indebted to me. You know, don't you?'

'Know what?'

'How I recognise you. You know, but you won't say.'

'Tell me about your book.'

'That was the worst deflection ever!'

'What's it about?'

'It's about deflecting.'

'Sounds interesting.'

She frowns again. Narrowing her eyes at me. *'Tell me about your book,'* she repeats my words back to me. 'Most people would say *what's your book about* or *what's it called*, thereby inviting a single answer. You, however, asked me to tell you about my book, which means you have knowledge of open and closed questions, which suggests you have worked in an industry where the use of open questions is important.'

'That works both ways.'

'Does it?' she asks lightly.

'Most people would say they are *writing a book*. You said researching, which suggests the book is a thing of a factual nature rather than a work of fiction. Moreover, with the use of the question style and the ability to pick up on it,

I would say you had experience in journalism. So you probably worked as a journalist in the city and have either quit and relocated to the countryside, or more likely, the subject material for your book is here.'

'Very good,' she says genuinely. 'Wow. Blimey. That's impressive.'

'Am I right?'

'Maybe.'

'Oh. Well. Then I shall have to peruse this mystery,' I say and repeat her words, making her laugh again.

'Well, you peruse away while I finish this coffee that I bought for myself.'

'Fair point. Can I get you another one?' I ask.

'I would love another one,' she smiles as I feel a rush of pleasure inside.

Which vanishes the instant I stand up and catch the sight of my haggard, unkempt reflection in the window behind me. Shame hits me, bringing a blush to my cheeks that I'm sitting here, trying to be suave and clever with an intelligent, beautiful woman.

'Are you okay?' she asks with genuine concern at the sudden change in my manner.

'Yeah. Er. Sorry. I just remembered I'm due back at the house. I'll have to go.' I start picking up my tobacco pouch and lighter.

'Okay. Abrupt. Something I said?'

'No. Just... I didn't realise the time.'

'It's an empty house, isn't it?'

'Yeah, but... No, I have to. Do rounds and... Sorry. Maybe see you again?'

'I guess,' she says with a shrug.

I rush off with a growing sense of humiliation and clamber into the Landy, and drive onto the main road.

She stays at the table outside. Watching me go. I lift my hand.

She nods but doesn't smile.

I drive off, feeling like an utter fool, playing flirty guessing games while I look like a fucking axe murderer.

Why would a woman like that stop and talk to someone like me? Pity, that's why. She must have thought I looked manically depressed or close to suicide, or something and showed human kindness, which I immediately mistook for flirting. What a creep.

I drive back to the house and park the Landy in the garage, and sit for a while in a sinking state of despair until it gets too chilly.

I head over to the house, with my head down. Feeling sorry for myself.

Which is how I spot the wet boot prints on the otherwise dry stone step immediately in front of the door.

I freeze and look closer, seeing two boot prints facing in.

I lean over to unlock and push the door open, and peer inside the grand hallway to see wet boot prints going towards the cellar door.

Charles Huntington?

No. That doesn't feel right. He was waiting outside for me when I arrived, so why would he risk breaching the family agreement now?

Someone else then, and the tread marks are big, with a rugged pattern. Meaning it's someone with big feet, wearing working boots.

I twist around on the step to look at the parking area, but gravel doesn't leave prints.

The stone path does, though. I spot a few wet smudges and track them to a point coming from the lawns, where two feet have left nice, clear indents going all the way across the lawns.

My sense of direction is hopeless at the best of times, but I get an instinct where they might lead and set off to follow them.

I keep going until I reach the treeline and find a wooden style built into the fence, with the path on the other side heading through the woods.

I clamber over and keep going.

It feels good to be walking, though.

I remember going out for long runs when I was training for the firearms teams. I started off on the armed response vehicles. Driving in response to whatever incident was going on, then either dealing with it on scene, or we'd set up a containment and watch with envy when the tactical firearms teams arrived in their armoured vehicles, wearing black coveralls and black NATO helmets.

I became one of those officers later. The training was brutally hard. We were the closest thing the UK had to SWAT and a non-militarised civilian police unit, but the tactics we were taught were mostly drawn from Special Forces. A lot of our instructors were ex-Special Forces.

I loved those years.

But it's in my nature to never be satisfied and always push for more. Within a few years, I was switching roles and going into investigations, which ultimately led to my downfall when I caught that fucking bastard.

It cost me everything.

Now I'm a loser, feeling humiliated when a pretty stranger shows kindness in a café.

The treeline ends abruptly, and I'm facing the back of Coopers cottage, watching him lift a large axe and slam it down into a piece of wood resting on the flattened stump of a tree.

He's a big guy. Wide shoulders and strong legs, and he moves fluidly like he's well used to hard, physical labour.

'What do you want?' he asks without a glance back.

'I was following a track. It led here.'

'Follow it back, then,' he slams the axe down harder than he needs to as it sticks into the tree stump. He leaves it there and rests his hand on the wooden hilt.

'Did you go in the house?' I ask.

He doesn't reply but stands still with his hands resting on the axe.

'Did you go in the house?' I ask again and take a few steps into his garden, crossing the boundary into his territory, which prompts him to turn and glare. 'What's your problem, Cooper?'

'Said I had one?' He jerks the axe out with a violent tug and bends to stack another log on the tree stump.

I feel angry and jarred, but I force myself to try and at least sound calm and controlled. 'Look, mate, I'm being paid to do a job, and they said to keep people out of the house.'

'And?'

'So stay out of the fucking house!' I snap at him, making him turn again with a flash of anger, gripping the axe with both hands.

'You'll fuck off back to London if you know what's good for you.' I blink at the cliched warning like something from a cheap movie. I even find myself looking for a joke or a punchline, but he's serious and clearly angry. He grunts and starts towards me. 'Leave.'

'Make me.'

He wasn't expecting that. He comes to a stop, like he's not quite sure what to do now. I can see his hands are trembling slightly, which tells me his adrenalin is already pumping, which also tells me he's not used to physical confrontation.

But that doesn't make him any less dangerous. And up close, I can see how bloody big he is, especially the way he's gripping that axe.

'Stay the fuck out of the house and stop telling everyone the owner is away.'

I walk off while resisting the urge to glance back, and when I look back from the treeline, he's gone from sight.

I didn't even hear him move.

7

I stomp back in a foul mood made fouler.

Thoughts in my head. Shame when I replay my conversation with Tessa and create an image in my head of my bearded, scruffy, haggard self trying to be witty and smart.

Speaking to Cooper hasn't helped my mental state either. He obviously knows he shouldn't be in the house.

So why go in the house?

Cos he didn't think I would know. That's why.

I might be a drunken mess, but I was still a detective and a bloody good one. Until I messed it all up. But I can still read signs and see things like wet boot prints. Which Cooper was obviously not expecting.

I tell myself to calm down. This isn't a case, and Huntington House isn't a crime scene. It's involved in a probate dispute, and I don't know anything about probate law. Crime, yes. Not wills, though. That's civil law, and it's complex.

And I tell myself it's nothing to do with me.

Cooper has been told to stay away. End of. Forget it. It

was a tiny infraction, and in all honesty, I didn't even need to go charging across the lawns to confront him like that. The guy grew up here. His ancestors too.

No wonder the guy is going inside to check the place over.

Guilt and remorse start gnawing away at my insides. I should have stayed quiet and kept a low profile. This is the best gig I've had since getting sacked.

You're an idiot, Humber.

A world-class idiot.

But then just for a few minutes this morning, I felt like a real person, sitting at the café with Tessa made everything okay just for that tiny period of time.

I can feel my mood plummeting and the depression threatening to take over. If I don't take action now, I will sit here all day, feeling sorry for myself and counting bricks while I think of more inventive ways to kill myself. Pity there's not a gym here. I could exhaust myself with hard exercise, but who needs a gym?

I change into jogging bottoms, running shoes, and a sweatshirt, then scoop all my dirty laundry up, which is pretty much everything apart from the clothes I'm wearing now.

I head down to the basement to put my clothes into the washing machine, but when I go back up the stairs, the door at the top is closed.

I push it to get out before remembering the door must be pushed in from the outside. I look for a hand grip, something to tug on, but the inside of the door is smooth, with nothing to grab.

There must be something I'm missing. The basement looks like the heart of the working household. The staff would be coming and going all day. They wouldn't risk letting themselves get locked in like this. But no matter how closely I examine the door, I find there is nothing to grip.

I step in close and run my hands all over the surface and down the edges, where the door meets the frame. Nothing, not even a slightly bevelled edge.

Back downstairs, I search through the cupboards and drawers, looking for anything I can jam through. A wire coat hanger gets unwound, and I manipulate it to make a right angle at one end. I stick it through the gap at the bottom, twist, and pull back, but when I pull to try and push the door against the spring lock, the wire bends back, too weak to create enough force.

I bend the wire on itself to make it stronger, then try again. This time it catches, but it takes several attempts until I can generate enough of a quick pull to release the mechanism. It works, and the door swings open. I charge out, looking for any reason why the door would close behind me. Everything appears the same.

I look closely at the cellar door, positioning it at various angles to see if it will swing closed on its own. It remains as I leave it and neither closes nor opens any further.

Then I spot the tiny screw holes on the inside of the door and the outline of a bracket that must have been for the handle the staff used to open the door from stairwell.

What the fuck?

Why would that have been removed?

I start getting creeped out again, and the hairs on the back of my neck stand up.

Then I tell myself there will be perfectly normal reasons. The interior handle could have broken, and they never got round to replacing it or something equally plausible. As for the door closing, it's an old house with high ceilings and wide spaces. A draft or breeze from outside could set off a chain reaction.

I head into the courtyard to have a smoke, and the music comes on.

> *Oh, Danny boy, the pipes, the pipes are calling*
> *From glen to glen, and down the mountain side.*

'Fuck!' I jolt again, visibly flinching from the sudden noise even though it's faint and coming from upstairs. 'Fucking jukebox.'

I head inside, with the unlit cigarette between my lips, and pass into the hallway to go upstairs when the loud bang of the same kitchen chair tipping over makes me jump again.

I spin around. Feeling a shiver run up my spine like a sensation of cold dread, with my heart whumping in my chest. 'Just fuck off!' I shout, but I don't know why. There's clearly no one here. I left the jukebox plugged in, and the kitchen chair must have been propped again.

No. I unplugged the jukebox, and the chair was not propped.

Was it? Were they?

I go upstairs to the snooker room and pull the plug out, plunging the house back into silence, then back downstairs to right the chair.

Then I try again and light the cigarette in the courtyard while trying to ignore the tremble in my hands.

It's an old house with uneven floors, and Cooper probably plugged the jukebox back in earlier to freak me out.

Could it have been him shutting me in the basement?

Fuck. I'm stressed and not thinking straight, and the most likely reason is that I closed the door behind me when I went down.

◊

A few minutes later, I set off with a light run along the driveway. I'd already worked out that the drive must be a mile long, so a nice two-mile run will be a good place to start my new fitness regime. Within a couple of minutes, my legs feel weak and jelly-like.

Another couple of minutes, my lungs are bursting, and my chest heaving, causing my diaphragm to get out of whack. I slow to a steady walk until my breathing recovers; then I try again. That's all I manage to do for the two miles. Run, then walk. It takes ages to complete the route. On the last few hundred metres, I force myself to keep running, desperate to prove that I'm not an entirely washed-up alcoholic junkie.

Back at the house, I collapse on the step of the front door and lean back as I really struggle to draw air into my body. I knew I was unfit but not this bad, and for the thousandth time today, I berate and detest myself for what I've become, with depression threatening to plunge me down. I force myself to my feet and through the house to the kitchen. I drink cold water and head out into the courtyard.

Ten press-ups followed by ten sit-ups, then ten squats followed by ten star-jumps.

I lift one of the patio chairs. It's heavy wrought iron, so I add a few sets of arm and shoulder exercises into the mix.

Telling myself I can do at least three rounds, I drop down and commence the press-ups. I reach eight before my arms start shaking, and the tenth is only just achieved. The sit-ups are messy, the squats are relatively easy, and the star-jumps could have been done better by a one-legged, blind man, and by the time I reach the wrought iron chair, I'm again gasping for breath and feeling weak and dizzy.

Being the stubborn idiot that I am, I drive myself on and finally finish the last set before slumping down onto the chair I was just pressing overhead.

I feel like shit. I can't believe how bad my breathing has got. If I'd known just how unfit I was, there is no way I would have almost picked a fight with Cooper.

Something spurs me on, and I do the circuit again until I'm almost crying from the pain signals being sent out by my muscles.

Sweat pours off me, stinging my eyes. I stagger into the kitchen and stick my head under the cold water tap, feeling the sharp bite as the freezing water hits my neck. I'm going to suffer for this tomorrow, probably the day after too, and quite likely for the next few weeks, but at least I've done something positive for a change.

I cling onto that tiny nugget of hope in my otherwise-ruined life.

By the time I reach the bathroom, I've stopped sweating, but my face is red and patchy. I head over to run a bath and find my toothbrush lying in the middle of the tub.

Slightly confused, I bend down to pick it up and hear a door slam shut.

I rush out into the corridor to see my bedroom door is now closed. With my heart hammering in my chest, I rush to the door and burst into the perfectly normal room that isn't full of bad guys waiting to jump me.

I stand in the corridor for a few minutes, listening, and then check a few of the other rooms, but find nothing untoward.

I head back into the bathroom, still feeling creeped out, and run the bath, adding a dollop of some fragrant bubble bath stuff I find on a shelf.

With the taps thundering behind me, I take a good, long stare at myself in the mirror before heading to my room and come back with a pair of scissors and my shaving kit, and start hacking at the weeks of growth. Cutting it back until I can get a razor through it.

I don't look any better when I finish. I look gaunt. I think about cutting my hair, but honestly? My arms are hurting too much, so I give up and sink into the bubble bath, and figure I can try and find a barbers.

At which point, I start taunting myself that the sudden spurt of exercise and shaving my beard, and the promise of getting my hair cut is only because I met Tessa.

I tell myself to piss off and leave me alone, but I don't, and I keep goading until a full-blown argument develops. Eventually, it stops after some nasty things are said, and we fall into a sulky silence.

Once done, I chuck some minced beef and frozen veg in a pan, with a jar of Bolognese sauce, then figure I'll get my clothes out of the machine and spread them on radiators.

I limp back down into the basement, but not before I take the kitchen chair that keeps tipping over and push it firmly against the cellar door.

I also make sure my wire hangar is still on the top step.

The wash finished some time ago. I start taking them out, then stop, and check the machine again. Sure enough, the washing machine has a setting for drying, so the clothes are put back in to dry while I head up and eat my food in the kitchen.

An hour later, I slump in one of the comfy armchairs in the library and reflect over the day. The bad points are that I woke up to find my bedroom door was open and my cigarette papers were missing. I was rude to the locals in the diner and almost got into a fight with Cooper, and then got locked in the cellar. Another bad thing was the shame I felt at myself when I caught my reflection when I was talking to Tessa.

The good points: well, I went for a run or at least tried going for a run, and I did some exercise, and washed my clothes, and of course, I met Tessa.

Which again fills me with shame. I keep reliving the conversation with Tessa, but in my head, I get worse each time, and I turn into a leering, filthy, haggard, old man.

She almost recognised me too. It was years ago now.

Well, no, she did recognise me, but she didn't place me, which meant I didn't have to go through the whole subject again and how it felt, and then the obligatory judgement that follows, and then, of course, *So what have you been doing since you left the police?*

Well, I've been drinking a lot and chain smoking. Oh, and I have this addiction to sleeping pills, and I'm also pretty much homeless after spending the last few months in hostels, so yeah, things have been great. Never looked back if I'm honest. Wish I'd got out a lot sooner. By the way, how's the child rapist doing that walked free cos of what I did?

That single thought plummets me down even worse than usual. The self-loathing hits me hard. I stare into my soul and see nothing worthwhile.

Ten minutes later, I'm sat at the bar in the leisure room, drinking neat vodka. My resolve gone the instant the dark thoughts hit me while also reminding myself that Charles Huntington practically told me to have a drink and relax.

Half a bottle later, and I remember I haven't turned any lights on or drawn the curtains, so I head back downstairs with the bottle in my hand and work my way slowly through all the rooms, trying to remember which ones I did yesterday so I can do different ones today.

Who cares?

Who gives a shit?

It doesn't matter what I do. If someone wants to rob this house, they can fill their boots because I won't be able to stop them. I can barely walk after trying to run about like an idiot.

I drink more, trying to chase that numbing buzz that helps me forget everything. With the last room done, I head back to the library and trip over my own feet on the way through the door. Righting myself with a grunt in front of the books.

'He was unsteady on his feet, yer honours! His speech was slurred, his eyes were red and glazed, and he smelled of intoxicating liquor.' I reel it off. Remembering the old wording we always used in police statements or when giving evidence in court to describe drunk people. I can hear the books chuckling. They think I'm funny. I am funny. Even Tessa laughed with me earlier.

No. She laughed *at* me. Not with me. I shrug it off and drink more vodka, and imagine myself in court, presenting evidence to the books all dressed like judges.

'I was proceeding in a northerly direction when I came upon the villain, your honours. He was dressed in black and white, striped, long-sleeved top, with a black mask and carrying a bag clearly marked with the word *swag*.'

That sets me off, and I'm chortling away to myself, remembering the good old days when arresting a petty shoplifter seemed the most important thing of the week.

I lapse into silence and keep glugging away at the vodka until I pass out.

8

Day Four

I WAKE UP TO A FIGURE STANDING IN THE DOORWAY AND scream.

I sit bolt upright to see my bedroom door is closed and realise I was dreaming. It takes me a few seconds to gain coherent thought, at which point I become aware of the urgent need to pee.

I scoot the covers back and rush out and into the bathroom while wincing at the agony in my legs from the exercise yesterday. Which is nearly as bad as the pounding throb in my head.

Why did I drink so much again?

What is wrong with me? Why can't I do anything right? It's like I keep pressing the self-destruct button inside my head.

I start brushing my teeth to rid the taste of decaying

sewers; then I frown as my foggy brain catches up with what my eyes saw a moment ago.

I step out into the hallway, with my toothbrush in my mouth, and look down the corridor in both directions.

Every door I can see is wide open.

The hairs prickle on my neck again.

They were all closed. I know they were.

I peer into a couple of the rooms, but nothing seems to have been touched or moved.

Why the hell would I open all these doors? I try and think back to last night. The last thing I remember was being in the library, drinking neat vodka. God only knows what carnage awaits me. Puke. Piss. I wouldn't be surprised if I've shat on the kitchen table or something.

I'm too hungover to think straight. I head into my room to get dressed and stare stupidly for a second because my clothes aren't in my room.

Jesus. I must have stripped off and walked around the house opening doors while naked.

Actually. That is the kind of thing I would do. Especially if I was drunk and got it into my head that Cooper was watching me.

'Fuck's sake.'

That means walking down to the basement in the buff to get my clothes out of the dryer. I could grab a towel from the bathroom or cover myself with a blanket from my bed, but honestly, I can't be bothered.

Naked, hung over, and very confused, I head down the stairs to the next floor and find all the doors are open on that level too.

At least the jukebox isn't playing Danny Boy. I give thanks for the small mercy and start down to the ground floor.

. . .

Oh, Danny boy, the pipes, the pipes are
  calling
From glen to glen, and down the mountain
  side.

I jump out of my skin again and once more feel that horrible sense of dread and fright while reminding myself that ghosts don't exist.

I go into the library, thinking I probably stripped off in there, but my clothes aren't there.

I move to the cellar door and find that wide open too. The kitchen chair is still there. I wedge it against the door and head down into the basement, and come to a stop on the bottom step, staring in shock as the haunting tune of Danny Boy drifts down from upstairs.

At least I've found my clothes.

The ones I was wearing *and* the ones I left in the dryer.

They're all here. On the basement floor. Laid out in human form. Or to be precise, they're laid out to make the shape of human forms.

I look at my boots. Each one is positioned at the leg of my jeans, with a pair of socks showing from within the bottom hem of the jeans, which, in turn, are beneath the pullover I was wearing last night, all of which is laid out flat and perfect.

Next to them is another pair of jeans, again, with a pair of socks, but this time resting over my running shoes.

Another top is laid out in the right position above the jeans.

Next is my one pair of black work trousers, with a black jumper above them, and black socks poking out the legs.

Three figures laid out in clothing on the basement floor.

The rest of my clothes are staged around them, almost framing the figures.

*But when ye come, and all the flowers are
   dying,
If I am dead, as dead I well may be.*

I stand there for long minutes, trying to take it in while listening to Danny Boy.

Trying to process what my eyes are seeing.

Trying to understand what it is I'm doing when I'm drunk.

I approach the clothes like a crime scene, trying to see if any clues have been left as to why I did this.

Then something hits me.

The way they've been laid out is so neat.

This is not the work of a man drunk on vodka.

But if it's not me, then who did it?

And how did they get in?

Cooper has keys.

But why? What's the point?

Too many questions. Not enough answers, and my brain is too unwilling to even try and make proper sense of it all. Well, I'm up, with nothing to do, so I should go to the village and get some painkillers.

Yep, that's what I need, some painkillers.

They might have some here, but it would be wrong to keep using their stuff.

I should buy my own and maybe get a cappuccino while I'm there.

Ah, I see what you're doing.

Subtle as a house brick, Humber.

✤

I park the Landy in the square and head into the shop, not before glancing at the café and feeling a sense of disappointment at not seeing Tessa there.

Bloody idiot, what did I expect after running off yesterday?

After buying and dry-swallowing the painkillers, I walk into the café without bothering to see who is inside.

Which is a mistake as Cooper is sitting with the other farm people, eating breakfast. All of whom fall silent as Cooper gives me a hard glare.

I volley it back and walk past while half-expecting to get a chair wrapped around my head. But nothing happens, and after a few seconds, the conversation resumes, albeit quietly.

'Back again?' the same woman mutters while still avoiding looking at me.

'The other café was closed.'

'What other café?' she asks, then rolls her eyes when she realises I was being sarcastic. Mousy, brown hair. Brown eyes. Name badge saying *Maggie*. She just stares at me expectantly.

'Can I have a cappuccino, please, Maggie.'

Her eyes narrow just a touch when I say her name, and

I wince inwardly, hearing how it sounded when I said it. 'I didn't mean it the way it came out. Sorry. I'm Mike, by the way.'

She shoots me a look this time. I guess looking for mockery, but I stay sincere and smile again. She starts making the coffee, with that same god-awful racket as I slide a fiver onto the counter. 'No charge,' she says.

'I pay my way.'

She tuts and presses the button for the machine to commence pouring the coffee. She glances again. I figure I look pitiful or something because she seems to soften a touch. 'Settling in alright? Must be rattling around that big house.'

'Yeah. Could say that. Couldn't even find my own clothes this morning,' I reply in a voice meant to carry.

She frowns while steaming the milk. 'How'd you lose your own clothes? You on another bender or something?'

Another bender. Not *a bender.* Which means Cooper must have told them he's seen me drinking in the house.

'Found them alright, though?' she adds, nodding at me.

'In the basement.'

A pause while the steams billows out of the milk jug. 'In the wash, then?' she asks as I realise Maggie doesn't like silences. That's useful to know. 'Used to work up there a few years back. They do the laundry in the basement.'

I nod again when she glances in a way that's seeking reassurance that I'm still actively participating in the conversation.

'That bloody door, though,' she adds to fill the silence again. 'You got stuck inside yet?'

'I did, actually,' I say with a smile and a sudden sense of relief.

She twists the steamer off, then does that thing coffee

makers do and smack the base of the milk jug on the counter while my hungover head winces with each impact. 'Old Hunty.'

'Sorry?'

'Old Hunty,' she says in a louder voice. 'One of the old lords. Lucky you're not a woman,' she says, then glances while still swirling the milk jug in what has to be the world record for the slowest coffee ever made. 'Groping old git.'

'Who is?'

'Just said. Old Hunty.'

'Yeah, I heard, but who–?'

'Just said! One of the old lords.'

'Fuck me. Are we stuck in a loop?'

I rub my face and catch her giving me another pitying look.

'Ghost, love. Old Hunty is a ghost.'

I splay my fingers to peer at her through the gaps. 'A ghost?'

'Are you bloody deaf or just really hungover?'

'I'm really hungover,' I admit as she finally slides the coffee on the counter.

'Stop bloody drinking, then.'

'Easier said than done. Thanks, but... So, like, what were you saying?'

She rolls her eyes, but her whole manner seems less harsh. 'You heard bumps and bangs?'

I nod.

'Chair tipped over in the kitchen?'

'No way. Really? Thank fuck for that.'

'Poltergeist, they call it. The house is famous for it. Look it up. He'd slap your arse if you were a woman. Mind, the current Lord is the sa–' she cuts off with a clear self-adjustment to what she's saying. 'I mean. Nice family, though. But yeah.'

It's pretty obvious she just remembered she's talking to someone privately and directly employed by Lord Huntington.

'And that bloody jukebox,' I say to try and put her at ease and keep the chat going.

'Eh?'

'Danny Boy?'

'What is?' she asks.

'I keep turning it off and unplugging it, but it keeps coming on with that bloody song.'

'Yeah, that ain't Old Hunty,' she says, giving me another look. 'Least not when I was there. Arse slapping maybe and that bloody chair, and the basement door.'

I take my turn to frown. Wondering about the jukebox, which is before I remember that I didn't believe in ghosts. Which it would appear I now do.

'Hang on. Arse slapping.'

She nods.

'A ghost?'

She keeps nodding.

'No,' I say slowly, shaking my head. 'No.'

She shrugs, as though she doesn't care if I believe her or not.

'He hasn't slapped my arse,' I tell her.

'Well, he's not a gay ghost, is he? Anyway. Get your coffee,' she says, pushing it closer. 'And stop drinking.'

I head off towards the door and pause next to Cooper as I look back to the counter. 'Does it arrange clothes?'

'What does?' she asks.

'The ghost man thing. Does it arrange clothes?'

'Course it bloody doesn't!'

'Oh. Cos I was thinking it's got great taste if it did. You know. The way it did the outfits was very stylish. Must have missed his calling in life.'

'Are you alright, love? You having a stroke or something?'

'Don't think so,' I say as I glance at Cooper. 'Hello, Mr Cooper. Nice outfit. Choose it yourself?'

He scowls all angrily as I head outside and light a smoke, and wonder if things could get any weirder.

While also looking up like an eager spaniel every time a car goes past.

And then looking like a depressed spaniel when it's not Tessa.

Then I try and look like a mean and moody spaniel when the farmers pile out and head off to do hearty farming things. Cooper is the last one out. I call him back. The other farmer men glance but don't say anything. Cooper just glares at me.

Or rather, he glares *down* at me.

Seeing as he's massive.

'I told you to stay out of the house.'

'You're that copper.'

That catches me out. Why is he bringing that up? And how did he know?

He walks off without a single glance back.

'What the fuck?' I mutter, wondering what the hell he was going on about.

Weird people these country folk. Can't bloody read them as well as city dwellers. At least you know where you are with city criminals. They'll run or try, and stab you, but I've never heard of one breaking into a house and rearranging a man's wardrobe before.

'Penny for them?'

'Jesus, fuck!' I say with a yelp and turn to see Tessa standing close behind me with a grin. 'How did you—?' I start to ask, wondering how on earth she sneaked up or where she came from.

'You look better, though,' she says brightly while looking at my chin. Then she glances down and frowns for a split second. 'Nice clothes too.'

'It appears I now have my own personal stylist.'

'A shocking development. I want to hear all about it, but I am also very thirsty,' she says with a mock dry cough and sits down, then hands me my empty coffee mug.

'Coffee?' I ask.

'Obviously. I wasn't sure you'd come back,' she says when I get to the door. I look back at her. 'You looked like you'd seen a ghost yesterday.'

'Don't even joke,' I say and head inside to the now empty cafe. I return with two mugs and place them down on the table, positioning one in front of her.

'Thank you, *Mr Humber*,' she says, and for a second, I lose myself in noticing that she's applied some discrete make-up. Then my brain finally clocks that she just used my surname. Which I didn't give to her.

Fuck it. That's her *and* Cooper that know, then.

'I remembered yesterday after you'd gone,' she says. 'I knew I recognised you from somewhere.'

'Yeah. I should have said,' I say and brace myself for the questions that always follow and the inevitable judgments too.

'The beard threw me off. I was on the papers when the story broke. I didn't cover it, but I knew a lot of the journalists who did.'

I look down at my coffee, feeling a sense of shame.

'Shall we change the subject?' she asks gently. I look.

She smiles back at me, and I swear something inside of me melts.

'It's alright. We can talk about it.'

'Hang on. Let me get my tape recorder out. Your face! Oh, god. Sorry. I don't have a recorder. Sorry! Rein it in, Tessa.'

I smile back, feeling somewhat stupid for falling for it.

'I'm wearing a wire instead...' she leans forward, thrusting her chest at me. 'So, Mike Humber, tell me everything.'

I avert my gaze from her chest area, and she laughs again.

'Sorry, I didn't think that one through, did I? Second date, and I'm already thrusting my boobs at you.'

'Date? I'm just here for the coffee.'

'Oooh! He shoots and scores a point,' she says and holds her hand up for a high-five.

'I'm not high-fiving you. We're British.'

'What do you want to do, then? Shake hands?'

'I'd rather shake hands than high-five,' I say as she rolls her eyes and lowers her hand for a shake, then pulls it up, with a cross-eyed look, when I reach over.

'Oh! She shoots and scores a point.'

'One all, then,' she says. 'Seriously, though? Is it okay to ask about it?'

I shrug and wait for the internal flinch I get whenever it's mentioned. Except it doesn't come this time. But then it's been a while since anyone asked about it, and she's looking at me all serious, with those big, blue eyes.

'I remembered it. Plus, I googled it last night and refreshed my memory. Honestly, though? And I'm not just saying this, but it must be one of the worst things I've ever heard off.'

'In what way?'

'Catching a monster like that and having him in your hands, and like, you know, knowing what he did. I think anyone would have reacted the way you did. He was goading you, right?'

'He was.'

'Your tone has dropped,' she says with sudden concern and even reaches out to touch my hand. 'If this is too intrusive, just say.'

It is intrusive, and normally, I'd clam up and change the subject abruptly. But right now, the only thing I can think about is her hand on mine.

'Sorry! I'm tactile with people I like,' she says and draws it away. I want to say it's fine and that she can leave it there, but thankfully, even I've got enough sense to *not* say that.

'It's okay. I don't mind you asking. And yeah, he was goading me.'

She frowns, with a nod for me to keep going.

I shrug and take a sip of coffee, figuring she was a city journalist, which means she can handle it. 'Yeah. He, er. He told me exactly what he did to those children.'

She scowls in horror, shaking her head as I continue.

'And he told me how it made him feel. And how he was going to do it again.'

'Jesus,' she murmurs, with genuine disgust showing on her features.

'Then he kept going.'

'What did he say?' she asks.

I rarely talk about what he said next. I skirted over it in the interviews I did after. But I don't know. Maybe time has passed, and there's a weird sense of safety in talking to a stranger. 'He kept telling me I should try it. I told him to stop. And I got triggered and told him to shut the fuck up.

But he was smart, and he saw the reaction he was getting, and he'd planned for it. He'd set it up and knew what he was doing. So he kept on. *You want to try it, don't you, detective Humber? You want to. I can see it in your eyes. You're getting turned on, aren't you?'* I hate the words in my mouth. I hate the memory of his face saying those things to me. I hate the anger it provoked.

'Oh, my god,' she whispers and puts her hand on mine again. 'I didn't know it was that bad.'

'That bit never got leaked. But yeah. I bit. I lost it and saw red. And well. You know the rest.'

I take a sip of coffee. She squeezes my other hand and sighs heavily while shaking her head.

'It might not have been so bad if I just hit him once or even just a couple of times. I could have taken him to the floor and... And, you know, made it look like a normal restraint or something. Nobody would have raised an eyebrow at that. But I didn't. I went for him.'

'And you didn't know the cameras were there?'

'No, but that's not a defence. Every copper knows there are cameras everywhere and most phones have got video cameras built into them. But I just flipped. I'd met some of the victims and their families, so it was personal to me. And I just couldn't *not* react. But that second. Man. I replay that every single day of my life. If I'd just *not* reacted. *If.* He'd be in prison. That was my fault. All of it. Vanity led me to him. I could have waited for an arrest team, but I wanted the glory...'

She squeezes my hand again. 'It wasn't your fault.' She leans forward, speaking earnestly. 'He was quite badly injured from what I remember.'

'I beat him unconscious. Broke his jaw, a few ribs. A lot of bruising that looked great in full colour, high-definition pictures.' I can see the question burning away behind her eyes. 'You can ask me.'

'Ask you?'

'How it felt.'

'Was it that obvious?' she asks with a gentle smile.

By now, I'd normally be creeping in my seat, desperate to get away or change the subject. Anything to avoid going through this again. But Tessa is a trained interviewer, and whether or not she's using work skills now or she's genuinely interested, I can't tell, but I know it feels different for some reason. It feels nice to be talking. 'So? How did it feel?'

'I didn't do it to achieve an aim or objective. I wasn't in danger, and he wasn't trying to get away. He was already in detention and not struggling or resisting. He was overweight and out of shape, so running away wasn't a fear. My entire reaction towards him was based on anger. Anger at knowing what he'd done to those children. Anger at how many lives he'd devastated. As clichéd as it sounds, those children lost their innocence and would be affected for the rest of their lives. Did you know that one of the fathers later committed suicide?'

She nods grimly. 'Yeah, I heard that.'

'He thought he'd failed as a father. That he wasn't there to protect his child. He hung himself.'

'You can't blame yourself for that, Mike. You didn't make him do those things.'

'But to answer your question? How did it feel?' I pause and think back to fighting with Cooper and all the other violent confrontations I've dealt with in my life. That one was different. I wasn't in control. 'I didn't feel anything at the time. Just rage. Just this absolute instinct to kill him. Which I guess means I did feel something, but not on a conscious level. It wasn't like I had coherent thought.'

She nods, staring into my eyes. 'Animal instinct.'

I frown at her. Not quite getting it.

She shrugs. 'It's pure animal instinct. I think we all knew that. You sensed he was a predator that had to be killed to protect the species or the children. Jesus. Anyone would have done that. And most would have actually killed him.'

'I wish I did,' I wince at the words coming out of my mouth, thinking she'll be repulsed. But she doesn't show any adverse reaction at all.

'Hmmm. Well. I can tell you the feeling in our office was that you were a hero, and the funny thing is, it was the only time I can remember that everyone was in agreement. Not one person thought you'd crossed the line.'

'But I did, and here I am... With an empty coffee mug.'

She gives me a sudden, bright smile and squeezes my hand one final time before pulling it away as she stands up. 'Another cappuccino?'

'I was joking. Let me get them,' I say and start to rise.

'No. Sit down. It's my shout.'

She disappears inside, and I realise I haven't smoked since she arrived. I roll one now, light the end, and sit back, feeling strangely calm and content.

Tessa arrives back with two more mugs and settles down, making a subtle change in her seating position to face me more directly.

'You okay?' she asks, with what appears to be genuine concern.

'Yeah, fine,' I nod back, and I mean it too. I can't help but smile, and my heart warms when she returns the gesture.

'So, Miss...Tessa,' I say as she laughs, 'you have twice now successfully evaded the topic of your book, but ve have vays of making you talk.' She laughs again at the crap joke.

'You're too good for me, copper. I'll cough the lot... Where do I sign?'

'Come on. Before I start cautioning you.'

'Can you remember it?'

'Bloody hell, I could write it with my eyes closed.'

'Go on, then.'

'Seriously?' I ask as she nods eagerly. 'You do not have to say anything. But, it may harm your defence if you do not mention when questioned something which you later rely on in court. Anything you do say may be given in evidence.' It rattles off my tongue with long-practised ease.

'Very good. I'm impressed.'

'Now, you've been cautioned, so you have to tell me about this book.'

'But what about my free legal advice? Surely, I'm entitled to that?'

'Nope, this questioning is being done under the Terrorism Act, so therefore you are not entitled to legal advice.'

'I'm a terrorist now?'

'This is very serious,' I try to show my most serious policeman face, but she just laughs.

'Hmmm, okay, but not here.'

'Wow, sounds secret, or are you just trying to lure me back to your house?' I narrow my eyes and look at her suspiciously, causing her to laugh again. I like the sound of it.

'Oh, you've seen through my dastardly plan, and I was going to hold you captive too.'

'Really? Hold me captive and force-feed me home made cakes with coffee... Sounds awful.'

'You've not tried my cooking.'

'Okay, so not here?' Intriguing. There's no one about or nearby, and I wonder what her reluctance is.

'We could meet up later?' Her eyebrows rise as she asks the question, making me think she's a bit nervous. 'I could come to you?'

'Er, yeah. I think that would be okay.'

'Why wouldn't it be?'

'They've got some court proceedings going on. A dispute between the family or something, and no one can live there until the court ruling.'

'Ah. I see. So that's why they have a security guard staying there.'

'Yeah. If any of the family gains access, they could claim possession. Then the other members would face a lengthy court battle just to get them evicted. I think they've all agreed to stay away until it's resolved.'

'How did you get the job?' She seems overly casual now, trying hard to act normal.

'Answered an advert online. They invited me up for interview and asked if I could start that day if I was successful.'

'So you don't know them?'

'The Huntingtons? No, never heard of them until I got here. It's just a job.'

'It's meant to be a beautiful house,' she says, and the intent is clear – she wants me to invite her round.

'It's very beautiful. The rooms are amazing. You should come round and see. Then you can tell me about your book.'

'Is it okay? Would the owners mind?'

'They never specified about visitors or anything. They can't expect someone to stay there for that length of time and not have a visitor.'

'Okay, well, if you're sure, then I'd love to see it.'

'Sure, what time? I'll make sure I hoover first. I was joking about hoovering; it's too big.'

She smiles back at me and bites her bottom lip as she thinks, and I have to look away from the alluring expression.

'Well, I'm free all day, so...' she shrugs lightly.

'How about now, then? Do you want to follow me back?' I ask.

Please say yes. Oh, please say yes.

'Sounds great. One thing, though... Do you have coffee?'

She said yes! Best day ever.

'I do. Where are you parked? I'm in the blue Land Rover there.'

A couple of minutes later, I pull out and watch as she follows me.

I turn up the volume on the radio and lose myself in the music. My mind, however, has other ideas and keeps flitting back to Tessa, the way she looks, and the expressions that cross her face.

I can't help myself from continually glancing in the mirror, thinking she will change her mind and turn off. Waiting at a junction to pull out, she must know I'm looking as she gives me another big smile and waves. My arm's out the window, and I try to casually lift my hand as though I'm some cool truck driver.

Idiot.

9

'Wow, this is amazing,' she says, standing next to her open car door and staring up at the front of the ivy-covered house. 'And that driveway. Can you imagine owning a house with a driveway like that.'

'Try running up it,' I say as I limp stiff-legged to the front door.

'Are you okay?'

'Yeah, fine, overdid the training yesterday,' I say while thinking I may have destroyed every muscle in my body.

We step inside, and I guess having been here a few days, the impact has worn off a little. But Tessa's reaction reminds me just how majestic it is, and I watch the way her eyes sweep over the room, taking in the details of the fixtures and fittings.

'Yeah, so. I worked very hard to get it to the current standard, but you know how it is trying to find expert craftsmen these days,' I say with a mock serious expression.

'Oh, of course, I have exactly the same trouble with my stately home. One can never get the chaise longue cleaned the way one wants them, and the gold bath taps are never buffed up properly.'

'You joke, but this house has lots of both of them.'

'Yeah, I've seen the pictures.'

'Pictures?'

'Online. They're on some sites for stately homes and décor of the rich and stupidly wealthy or something like that. I had a look when I first moved up here.'

'Oh, right. How long have you been here?'

'Few months. So are you giving me the guided tour then or what? And I want running commentary, giving a detailed history and description of each room.' She fixes me with a serious gaze – eyebrows arched and mouth pursed. I would tremble at the knees if I wasn't already.

'Follow me, please.' We enter the first room – a long room with comfy armchairs and sofas arranged around small tables. 'This room dates back to the, er, Pre-Raphaelite era and was used for, er...sitting in. Yes, they used to sit in here all the time. It was all the rage back then, sitting.'

'My god, this is beautiful. Look at the detail on the armchairs and the table legs.' She moves forward, closely examining the intricate carvings and designs on the wooden furniture.

We enter the next room, with the huge dining table that could seat fifty people. 'And here we find the dining room, where they would also sit, but this sitting would be accompanied by food.'

'That table is huge.'

'Yes, it was the law back then. You weren't allowed dinner unless there was at least fifty people. Fear of wolves and bears, you see. '

'Lions and tigers, and bears,' she singsongs as I smile, and we move on from room to room. It's also somewhat reassuring to see that she has the same reaction I did. Jaw dropping at first, but then it gets repetitive. I notice she looks closely at the walls in each room, running her hand along certain parts as if feeling for something. Eventually, we're back in the entrance hall, facing the wide staircase.

'Fancy going upstairs, love?' I wink suggestively and am very relieved that she laughs.

'Thought you'd never ask. Do you want a hand, old man?' she says as I wince on the first step.

Reaching the first-floor landing, she takes in the red carpet and the exquisite colouring of the walls. Every shade blended perfectly to compliment the next.

'These are the Lord and Lady's rooms. They left them in a right bloody mess, though.'

Pushing the door open, I step back so she can enter first. 'What mess?' she asks.

'Eh?'

'I thought you said it was a mess. Jesus. Don't come to my house if you think this is messy.'

'It's a bloody pigsty–' I start to say, but my words cut off as I take in the perfectly made-up rooms. The bed sheets all pristine and tucked in. The jewellery back in the boxes. Picture frames upright. I check the other rooms in the suite and find them all the same – clean and tidy.

'Mike, what's wrong?' she asks with a concerned look at my reaction.

'These weren't like this... I mean this morning, there was stuff everywhere.'

'Someone must have cleaned up.' She shrugs, puzzled at why I'm making a big deal out of it.

'Yeah, but he said no one is allowed in. None of the staff and none of the family. That's why I'm here.'

'Maybe one of them forgot, or they remembered how messy the rooms were and sneaked back in to tidy them?'

'Yeah, yeah, you're probably right. Sorry, it just threw me off for a minute.'

'That's okay,' she says and holds her gaze on me, with that slightly puzzled expression again. 'You sure you're alright?'

'Yes. Honestly. I just... Big, old, spooky house and... Ignore me. Yes! I'm fine. I'll show you the rest.'

We move down, and I unlock the teenage girl's room to step in, which has also been tidied.

Tessa steps in beside me and scans the room. Her eyes coming to rest on the girl's picture. She steps forward to examine it closely before turning back to smile at me.

We move on through the house, and I unlock each room in turn. First, so Tessa can see them, but more, so I can see what else has been moved or touched.

'Stunning house,' she says softly as we reach the door to the leisure room. I unlock the door and step in. Scanning the room quickly, I see the snooker table is laid out ready for play, with all the coloured balls positioned where they should be.

But it wasn't like that.

The balls were all in the boxes on the sides. That are now both open.

Cooper knew I was at the café. It must be him.

'Nice room, though, and look at that view,' Tessa says. I join her at the doors, and we take in the lawns and the meadows, and forests in the distance. Well, Tessa does while I stare down at the rear lawn and the fresh tracks leading across it.

Fucking Cooper. It is him, then.

We head on, with Tessa laughing again at me wincing

on sore legs up the stairs. She even offers to help and takes my arm like I'm an old man. 'Come on, duckie. Take your time.'

'Cheeky shit,' I say with a laugh, feeling her bump my side, and we reach the next floor up and continue the tour through the smaller guest rooms.

'This is my room,' I say as I push the door open. Which, I note, is still closed. 'They didn't specify what room I should use, and none of the servants' rooms were made up with bedding, so I picked this one.' I'm relieved to see it's the same as I left it earlier, and at least there's no dirty boxers lying on the floor.

'Nice work luring me into your room already.'

I feel myself blushing, which she picks up on immediately and starts laughing again. 'Honestly? I'm in way too much pain for any hanky-panky.'

'Hanky-panky! I haven't heard that in years. Okay, fair enough. No hanky-panky, then. Where's the bathroom, though?'

'In there,' I point to my bathroom opposite. She smiles and walks in while I step back into the bedroom to avoid standing in the corridor and listening to her pee.

'Er, Mike,' she calls, with a voice that sounds worried.

I rush out to see her standing in the open doorway, staring at the bath. 'You were right about the gold taps,' she laughs again, and I roll my eyes before moving back to my bedroom.

My nerves are frayed to the hilt. Those rooms being tidied, and the snooker table laid out. Is it Cooper? Or like Tessa said, maybe someone is employed to pop in weekly or something and clean up. I'll have to call Lord Huntington later and ask him.

'You there, Mike?' Tessa calls out, closing the bathroom

door behind her. We move into the servants' rooms, and Tessa picks up on the basic décor throughout this area and the much smaller sized rooms.

'No locks on any of the doors,' I say and nod at the plain, wooden doors.

'No human rights back then,' she replies.

'That's what I thought.'

'Different times, different rules,' she says with a sad sigh.

'*Sad but true*,' I say.

'Yeah. I suppose back then *nothing else matters*,' she says and shoots me a look.

'Well, for *whom the bell tolls*, then they shall have no locks,' I reply and see the glint of mischief and fun in her eyes.

'Ah, but no locks makes it easy to for the *sandman to enter*,' she says with a nod of victory at scoring a point.

'Must be dark up here at night. I guess it *fades to black* quickly.'

'Nice! Poor servants, though. They must have thought they were *unforgiven*.'

'Oh, good one! Yeah, the lord must have treated them badly, like a *master of puppets*.'

'You shit! I was going to use that one,' she says and swipes my arm. 'Well. It's hardly *paradise city*.'

'That's Guns N' Roses.'

'It's not.'

'It is.'

'It's not. It's Metallica.'

'Guns N' Roses. It was their best song. Axl Rose... *Take me down to the paradise city, where the something, something isn't shitty.*'

She frowns at me comically, then bursts out laughing. 'Yeah, fair one. You win, but please don't ever sing again.'

We finish the tour and head downstairs to the library, where she spends a few minutes pouring over the books. She even bends over to look at the lower shelves, with my eyes drawn to her shape for a second before I realise what I'm doing and look away.

'Are you looking at my bum?' she asks without turning, but I can tell she's smiling from how she says it.

'Er, no… I was looking at this book.' I quickly flip open Medieval and Modern Times to peruse a random page.

'You were so checking me out,' she says. 'S'alright. I was checking you out earlier,' she adds, looking over her shoulder to smile wickedly at me. 'I've got a thing for old men that struggle to walk upstairs.'

'Oh, that was low!' I say as she grins and bumps into my side again when we walk out, showing she's being playful and not mean.

We head into the kitchen, and Tessa makes coffees while I toast some bread, and the chat flows easily. Without awkwardness or any weird silences, and we sit down at the big kitchen table to munch on buttered toast.

'So, about this book,' I ask, prompting her again before she can start on a new subject.

'You are relentless, Mr Humber,' she says with a mouthful of toast. I stay silent, watching her with an expectant gaze. 'Okay, but first…'

'No more but firsts.'

She laughs and covers her mouth to hide the food she's eating.

'Seriously, I need to be sure of a couple of things first.' Her expression changes, and she looks around the kitchen to the door leading out to the entrance hall.

'Tessa?' I ask at seeing she looks worried.

'This toast is lovely,' she winks at me strangely and seems desperate to avoid the subject. 'The grounds look amazing. Have you walked round them much?'

'Not much really. Would you like to see them?'

'That would be lovely. It's a beautiful day for a walk.' She keeps staring straight at me.

'So, what do you think of the house?' Changing the subject, I see a look of relief, and she smiles gratefully.

We make idle small talk about how quiet the area is compared to London. I play along, adding comments here and there but wondering how much weirder this all wants to get. This was meant to be so easy – stay in a house and get paid for it. That's it, and nothing more. A chance to repair my body and mind, but instead, I find the whole thing getting stranger with each passing hour. Either I'm going mad and doing things in the night that I have no recollection of or someone is getting into the house or is already in the house. And on top of that, I now have a beautiful investigative journalist eating toast and giving me cryptic messages.

It's too much for my frail mind; it really is. I want to just lie down in a dark room and forget everything. But then I glance over and see her chatting away, and everything just seems to slide into the background, and I slip into a strange sense of peace, listening to her voice.

10

'So what's all the secrecy about?' I ask once we're outside and walking around to the back of the house.

She loops her arm in mine and gently guides me off the path, onto the lawn, and out towards the meadows.

'Where do these tracks go?' she asks with a frown at the clear footprints in the grass.

'I expect they'll lead to the groundsman's cottage.'

'That's the Cooper guy, isn't it?'

'Yeah. So, what's all this about?'

'So, you really don't know the Huntingtons, then?'

'I already said. I saw an advert online.' She nods, but I can sense she needs more reassurance. 'I don't know anyone here at all,' I add.

'Have you spoken to anyone else since you got here? Like, anyone?'

'Right. Okay. So, I spoke to the woman in the mini-market and cocked up by spinning her a yarn and failing to realise that everyone round here is married or related somehow. Then the woman in the café. Maggie, who I think is related to the woman in the shop. Her husband or brother, maybe both? Anyway, he was one of the farmers in the café, and they kind of asked where I was staying, but it turns out they knew anyway. That's it. Oh, and Cooper.'

'What's Cooper like?'

'Er, strange bloke if I'm honest. I think he's got an issue with me staying in the house. Maybe thinks it should be him or something like that. He was all like, *Go back to London!*

'Did he say anything else?' she asks. 'I've heard he's a weirdo,' she says after a pause. 'Like really chopsy, and he can get obsessive.'

'That's comforting,' I say with a mock groan. 'And he's got a big axe.'

'Is that a euphemism for a big willy?'

'What? No! I meant an actual axe. Like a...like an axe murderer axe. Willy? Where did that even come from?' I ask as she bursts out laughing.

'Oh! No, stop,' she says suddenly and comes to an actual stop. 'Do you think Cooper broke in and tidied those rooms up?'

'Well. I did think it... And the tracks are leading that way but...'

She nods with wide eyes. 'That's so creepy.'

'Yeah, but... I don't know. He doesn't seem the type.'

'I just said he's obsessive.'

'Yeah, not to break in and tidy rooms, though. He's like this massive, wood-chopping man, and that's not another euphemism for a big willy,' I add as she smiles, then frowns.

'Who else would do it, though?'

'A cleaner?' I ask with a shrug.

'Yeah but. What if it is him?'

I rub my chin and shrug. 'I think if it is him, he's got

some serious skills because he's already laid my clothes out in a colour-matching outfits, *and* then he's breaking in and tidying rooms like an actual professional cleaner? Honestly? I think he'd be a good catch. I might even invite him for dinner.'

She bursts out laughing again and swipes my arm, and we set off walking again.

'People went missing from Huntington,' she says without warning.

'What the fuck? Where did that come from?' I ask, looking for humour but seeing none. 'Is that what this secrecy was about?'

She pulls a face as though thinking hard while I study the shape of her lips and the tone of her skin, and the blueness of her eyes when she finally looks at me like she's made a decision. 'I want to tell you something, and it may sound weird, but hear me out, okay? I answered a call in the office one day a few months ago. The caller was a man, and he said that people are going missing up here. Anyway, I took it to the editor, who told me to report it to the police and carry on with what I was already working on.'

'Did you call the police?'

'Yes. I called the Met Police. They took some details and said they would get in contact with the local force here.'

'I can see where that went,' I say in a tone that makes her frown.

'What do you mean?'

'An anonymous, vague call about missing people?'

'I wasn't anonymous.'

'No, but the source is. The person who told you. Which then makes it third-hand anon info.'

'So they wouldn't have acted on it?'

'In a place like this, if people were actually going missing, they wouldn't need an anonymous intel report to tip them off. They'd know. Which then works the other way, cos if they got that report, and people were *not* going missing, then they wouldn't do anything with it. But thinking about it, if it did link to an active case, then the SIO would have...' I trail off at her blank look. 'The SIO? The Senior investigating officer?'

'Oh, god. Yes! SIO. Totally zoned out for a second. Sorry, keep going. You've got beautiful eyes, Mike. No. Sorry. Totally unprofessional, but I got lost in them for a second there.'

I lose the power of speech for a moment. She detects my awkwardness and touches my arm lightly, and only then do I realise we've come to a stop again. We carry on walking, with her bumping into my side once more.

'Er, yeah, so, the SIO would have made contact with you if there was something in it. Assuming that *you* gave your details when you passed the intel,' I say while mainly thinking about what she said about my eyes.

'Wouldn't they have at least looked into it?' she asks as I realise that she hasn't handled criminal matters and doesn't have an in-depth knowledge of day-to-day policing.

'Look into what? It's a rural area. The population isn't that big, and everyone knows everyone else. Someone going missing would be noticed.'

'Hmmm,' she says thoughtfully. 'But maybe the police don't know about it.'

'Yeah, but one vague tip off isn't enough to start an investigation unless it has credibility. Is that why you came up here?'

She nods and bites her lip thoughtfully. 'I wish I met

you before,' she says before glancing to the treeline with a sudden, worried look. 'I feel like I'm being watched.'

'We probably are,' I say.

'What if he is breaking into the house? You might be asleep or something,' she adds as I shrug.

'Huntington's too scared to ask for the keys back, and he said the house is grade one listed, so they can't change the locks.'

She pulls a horrified face while shaking her head. 'He might be actually watching you sleep.'

'Don't,' I say with a shudder. 'Anyway. Go back to the missing people. Tell me what you know."

'Right. Okay,' she says, changing mental gear. 'So, it started with that call. This goes back a long time, but my editor didn't want to know. I started doing some digging. I'd already quit. No. Not quit. I was freelance, but I didn't say anything because I didn't know you. And the SIO never called me so... And but the man seemed sure.'

'What the fuck. I didn't get a word of that,' I say with a smile at the gibberish and how she says it.

'Alright! We're not all detectives,' she says with a flash of irritation that quickly morphs into humour as she smiles at me, with her blue eyes holding onto mine. 'Sorry. I was gabbling. It's you, though!'

'Me?'

'Yeah. Being all like *rarrr*.'

I blush again at the compliment. Not quite sure how to take it while my brain goes into meltdown, and my belly turns flips.

'Anyway. So I left my job and went freelance, and started to look into it.'

'Okay. Big step.'

'What is?'

'Going freelance based on one call.'

She blinks at me for a second. 'I didn't go freelance just to do this. I mean. I meant. You know. I do other jobs and stuff.'

'What like?'

'Just like some articles and writing things for adverts.'

'Copy.'

'I don't copy!'

'I thought it was called copy? When you write content? Isn't that called copy?'

'I mean. Like a hundred years ago,' she says with an eye-roll. 'Anyway. Shush. Stop interrupting me and being all smart. Which is like insanely hot, by the way. Shush, Tessa! God. I can't believe the things I say sometimes. But you must get that all the time, though.'

'I honestly don't.'

'Yeah, alright.'

'So? Who went missing?'

'Oh! Yes. Right. So. I need to get this right. So, one was like Chinese, and the other was Eastern European. Like Estonivia? Was that it? Is that a country? God. I'm useless at geography.'

'Estonia?'

'That was it!'

'Or Latvia?'

'Yes.'

'Which one?'

'Aren't they the same?'

'No.'

'Oh. I thought one was in the other? No? I said I was rubbish at geography. Er, I'm going to say Latvia. And the other was like, yeah, Vietnamese.'

'You said Chinese.'

'Or Chinese. I meant *or* Chinese. It was never fully ratified.'

'Ratified?'

'Yeah. You know. Like when you check something.'

'Ratify is when you get approval. Verify is when something is checked.'

'That's hot,' she says with such a comical smile it makes me laugh. 'Listen. Don't judge me. I know I'm not smart like with words and things.'

'You're a journalist!'

'I never said I was a good one! But listen. So, two girls really did go missing. And that man said they went missing from here.'

'In Huntington?'

'No. Here, here. The house.'

'This house?' I ask, glancing between the house and her. 'You never said that.'

'I was *verifying* you weren't a spy.'

'For who?'

'For whoever did it.'

'Hang on. My brain is melting. Go back to the start. This anonymous man phones the newsroom and says two women are missing. Is that right?'

'Yes,' she says decisively.

'And he said they were from Latvia, and one was Asian? Is that right?'

'Not Indian. He meant like Chinese.'

'China is in Asia. So is Vietnam.'

'I said I wasn't good at geography.'

'Okay. No. That's fine. It's actually normal now. With phones and the internet, you know, people don't study and retain information like they used to,' I say to make her feel better after getting the impression she was feeling a bit stupid. 'So, he says one is Chinese or Vietnamese?'

'Yes.'

'Try and think back, Tess. Did he say Chinese or Vietnamese? Details like that are important.'

'No. He said both.'

'Oh! Okay. So *he* said both. That's why you said both. Right. Got it. Got it. Sorry. Okay, so that suggests *he* saw this woman and concluded she was Chinese or Vietnamese. And the other one was Latvian. Did he say Latvia, or did he also say she might be Estonian?'

'Yes. He said that,' she says with a nod.

'Okay. So the caller probably heard her accent. But that's unusual, though. I mean. Most workers in this country were Polish, and to most people the accents are very similar. I wonder why he said Latvia or Estonia. Anyway. So. How are they connected to here?'

'I said. They went missing.'

'No. I mean. How do you know they went missing *from* here.'

'The man said.'

'No. I mean. How does *he know* they went missing from Huntington House?'

'Oh. They were working here.'

'As what?'

'House cleaning maids.'

'House cleaning maids?'

She nods but stays fixed on my eyes, and although it's like wading through mud, I can't help but get lost in her gaze. 'It's just, that's, you know, that's a weird way of saying it.'

She shrugs. 'It's what he said.'

'He said they were house cleaning maids?'

She nods again.

I take a second and engage my brain while figuring for a journalist she's pretty shit at passing information. But journalists come in all shapes and sizes just like cops, and a lot of cops I know are just as bad at relaying details.

'Sorry, Mike. I got all that garbled up. Let me start again. So, this man calls the newsroom and said two women, one Vietnamese or Chinese, and the other from Latvia or Estonia, and he said they worked here in the house, but they'd gone missing. And I did call the police, but they never called me back. And I was leaving my job anyway, so I came up here and thought I can do freelance and look into it.'

'Got it. Okay. How far have you got?'

'Can I tell you something else,' she says with a comical grimace. 'I was actually a fashion editor. I did home furnishings and stuff.'

I get it now. The lack of knowledge and experience in this area.

'Sorry. I realised when I was telling you, you know, cos you're like this smart copper, and I'm way out of my depth.'

'It's alright.'

'Are you angry with me?'

'Angry? Why would I be angry?'

'Do you think I'm stupid now?'

'No! Of course not,' I say as she looks crestfallen and embarrassed. I reach out to touch her arm without realising what I'm doing. 'Sorry!'

'What for?'

'Touching your arm.'

'Why are you saying sorry?'

'Unwarranted touch is like a *big* thing in the police.

Probably everywhere, actually. They must have had rules like that in your offices.'

'In fashion?' she asks with a laugh. 'We're all over each other, darling!' she says in a posh voice. 'You touch away.'

I try not to dwell on the images flitting through my mind when she says that.

'Sorry, though,' she adds and steps in to kiss my cheek. 'That's for not being a dick about it. You know. For me being thick and not knowing countries and policey words. So. Yeah. Er. What would you do then?'

My brain goes into meltdown again but for entirely different reasons this time, which is even worse when she takes my hand, and we start walking. I shake my head and try to focus. 'Er. Okay. So, you called the police, but they never got back in contact. Right?'

'The Huntingtons own the whole area. So they probably own the police.'

'Yeah, it doesn't work that way. Not in the UK, anyway. I mean. I know movies and things make it look that way sometimes. But modern police forces have anti-corruption squads and checks in place.'

'You're telling me you don't get bent cops?' she says with a bitter laugh.

I take her point because she's right. It does happen, and more than it should.

'Okay. So that aside, you called the police and heard nothing. Have you done anything else?'

'I got hold of some names of people that worked here, and then contacted them, and said I was a homes and fashions editor, and I was doing some pieces on Huntington House, you know, cos I was doing period articles. And I just got them chatting and managed to find out two women like that did work here.'

'Fuck. Really? Why didn't you say that? That's brilliant.'

'Shush. Don't put me off. So, one was from two years ago. The Chinese woman. And the other was last year.'

'That recent?'

'Yes, but it took hours, Mike. I mean *hours* of just chatting shit about curtains and colour schemes, which I quite like actually, but then they also waffled on about dinner parties and famous people, and everyone I spoke to I asked who else they worked with so I could build a full picture.'

'That's impressive.'

'Patronising.'

'I didn't mean–'

'I said I was a fashion writer. Not a cop.'

'I mean it genuinely. That was good thinking.'

'Oh. I thought you were mocking me.'

'No. So that took a while, then?'

'What did?'

'Talking to all those people.'

'God, yes. Forever. And it was all by phone too. I didn't want to meet any of them in person, and get this, I called some other big, fancy places and did it with them too, just to make it look convincing.'

'Okay. Not patronising, but that's a very nice touch.'

'Yeah?' she asks with a big smile and holds her hand up for another high-five.

'Really?' I ask, feeling awkward at doing something so un-British. I go to slap her hand, but she grabs my fingers and yanks me closer to body-bump me.

'Say it again,' she says with a delighted laugh. 'Tell me I'm a genius.'

'I wouldn't go that far.'

'Oh, touché! Two one to you. But that was really bitchy, though.'

'I didn't mean it,' I say at her mock hurt look while she still holds my hand, and in so doing, keeps me in close, and looks up at me while biting her bottom lip.

'Anyway, anyway, anyway,' she says suddenly, with a shake of her head as though making herself focus. 'Right. So. You were telling me what you would do.'

'I haven't got the full picture yet.'

'I just told you everything.'

'Go back to the other staff you spoke to. Did they give names of these women? They must have at least known first names. And did they speak good English? Why were they in the UK? Did they have family? How long did they work here for? And how did they end up working here? Was it through a temp agency? A website? And how long did they work here for? Weeks? Months? Did they overlap and know each other? Did they have any troubles? Were they dating anyone? Did they have kids or families back home? Did they work hard? Did they live in the house? Did they get on well with the other staff? And when they left, did they give notice? Or were they just suddenly not here one day? And how did everyone else react to that? I mean. Suddenly not turning up would be weird and prompt questions.'

She stares intently at my mouth as I speak. 'You must have been a really good copper.' Her words hit harder than she probably meant, and I think it shows on my face. 'Sorry,' she adds with a wince and touches my arm again. 'Didn't mean to hit a nerve.'

'It's alright.'

'That was... I mean. Wow,' she says earnestly. 'Did you do all that stuff to catch Edward Scoble?'

I can't help react at the name. It's been over a year since

I heard it, and before that, the name Edward Scoble dominated my life.

It did more than that.

It ruined my life.

'I guess,' I say while trying to push the memories down.

'Shit. Sorry. Bad Tessa,' she says with a grimace and rubs my arm. 'God, I am so clumsy with what I say. Come here.'

'No, it's okay,' I try and say as she pulls me into a hug.

'Your face, Mike. I'm so sorry. I shouldn't have said his name. Are you okay? God.' She rubs my back, and I can't help but scent her perfume and feel her body pushing into mine. 'Good hugger, though!' she says, breaking the tension as I give a small laugh. 'Come on. Let's get you back for a cuppa.'

'I'm okay, honestly.'

'Your face said otherwise,' she says and takes my hand.

'Anyway. So. What did the staff say about all those things?'

'Shush now,' she says, giving me a concerned look. 'Bless. You looked absolutely heartbroken when I said his name. Is it still that raw for you?'

I didn't think it was *that* raw. But maybe it is. I mean. If she saw such a strong reaction.

'We'll chat about the other thing later. No. I mean it,' she says. 'Enough for today. You've got enough going on with creepy Cooper.'

I snort a laugh. 'Is that his name now?'

'He is a bloody creep. Sneaking around and arranging clothes, and tidying rooms. And the thought that he's in the house watching you sleep.'

I think back to the bedroom door being open, but I'm

still not sure that wasn't me. And I'm still not fully sure Cooper would arrange clothes and tidy rooms.

'I know what you're thinking. You're thinking Cooper wouldn't do that. But that's what he *wants* you to think,' she says as we get back on the path next to the house. 'People like that are unpredictable.'

She cuts off with a wave of her hand to signal we need to be careful when we reach the front door. 'Cuppa?' she asks lightly.

'Love a coffee. I'll just check the house.'

I head off to check the rooms, but everything seems the same. When I get back, the coffees are done, and she's by the open back door, holding out my rolling tobacco and papers.

'Thought you'd need a smoke after my stupid comment.'

'Cheers,' I say, touched at the thoughtful gesture.

'Oh, and I don't know if it's a smoker's thing, but your ciggie papers were in the coffee jar.'

I look back at her holding the packet of rolling papers I lost yesterday. 'They were where?'

'In the coffee jar.'

'That coffee jar?' I ask, nodding past her to the posh artisan coffee.

'Do you have more than one open coffee jar?'

I shake my head and murmur a thank you.

Why would I put my cigarette papers in the coffee jar? And I made a coffee then too. So I would have found them. Or did I make coffee first, and the papers fell from my hand? But then I've made coffees since then. Even when we got back here.

'Are you okay?' she asks, coming out into the courtyard to once again rub my arm with a look of concern.

I shake it off. Feeling embarrassed. She'll think I'm some needy twat with loads of baggage if I keep this up.

'Turned the house upside down looking for them,' I say with a laugh, shrugging it off. 'But... If I hadn't lost these, then I wouldn't have gone into the village and had that coffee and...'

'Go on. Finish the sentence. *And I wouldn't have met you, Tessa.* Was that it? It was, wasn't it? Oh, you're blushing! That is so cute. How are you even single?'

'Yeah. What a catch.'

'Oh, piss off. Hang on. Weren't you married when that thing happened with Edward... Whoa! Almost said it.'

'It's okay. And yes. I was.'

She tuts sadly. 'What happened?'

I shrug. 'We split up.'

'Split? Like mutual?'

'I mean. I think.'

'That's a no. then. So basically, she ditched you in your hour of need. Great wife.'

'No, but. What I'd done. And I was a mess.'

'Defensive. Are you still in love with her?'

'Eh? No! I haven't even spoken to her in like eighteen months.'

'Hmmm,' she says, giving me an arched eyebrow. 'God. Get me. I'm terrible when I like someone. I'm like *you can't like anyone else. Just me!* It's a flaw. I'm working on it.'

It's a hot flaw from where I'm standing. And she just said she likes me. God, she's beautiful, though. Those eyes and the way she keeps bumping into me and touching my arms.

'Anyway. Right. I'd better be off,' she says. 'I've got company tonight. I need to have a bath and pick some nice clothes. and maybe choose a nice bottle of wine... And then get the dinner on.'

'Sounds nice,' I say lightly and try to hide any show of disappointment or reaction.

'So. You okay, then?'

'Yep. Fine. All good. Well. Enjoy your, er, evening.'

'I shall! And I hope you do too. Time?'

'Time?'

'Yeah. What time?'

'For what?' I ask.

'For coming round mine for the dinner I'm making,' she says with a delighted laugh. 'Oh, your face was so trying so hard not to look disappointed. Bless. At least I know you like me now.'

I stutter a few nonsensical words and clear my throat.

'You are so cute. Seven? Put your number in my phone,' she says and presents hers as I try and summon enough mental aptitude to unlock my own phone. 'Is there anything you don't eat?'

I shake my head and hand her phone back. 'I'll prank you,' she says, pressing to call me.

'No signal.'

'Oh. Right. I'll text you then so it comes up when your signal comes back. Right. Seven.' We step outside. She kisses my cheek. 'Thank you for letting me gabble on today, and sorry I cocked up and said his name. And for being thick and not knowing countries. But we can go over it more later if you want.'

'Okay,' I say, having lost the ability to talk properly. I watch her walk to her car and get in. She gives her hand a kiss and blows it at me before closing the door. 'Hang on! Where do you live?' I call.

She grins and winds the window down as she starts the engine. 'I left you a clue, Detective.'

'What clue? Where?'

'Check your papers!'

'My papers?'

'Seven!' she calls and drives off. I frown after her, wondering what she meant, then dig the packet of cigarette papers she gave me out of my pocket to see her address written on the inside cover, next to a heart.

And honestly.

I feel like a teenager.

11

I'M TOO SORE TO EXERCISE.

But I do it anyway in the vain hope it will somehow get me toned and buff before I go to Tessa's.

My energy is high, though, and for the first time in two years, I can actually feel a positive rush inside of me, which, perversely, also causes a spike of anxiety because good things don't happen to me anymore.

I have got to get a grip on my emotional reactions.

I can't keep flinching or wincing, or retracting inwardly if she inadvertently mentions that fucker Edward Scoble or my ex-wife, or what happened.

It was all over the national news. The footage had millions of views online. Me beating the shit out of Edward Scoble – the man suspected of kidnapping and sexually assaulting young children in London. He was an aristocrat too, but he also liked snatching children and hurting them.

I was hailed a hero, but anyone with a shred of judicial knowledge knew I was anything but a hero because what I did to him was filmed and released, and it meant Scoble would never get a fair trial.

So he walked.

Not only that, but he was given a big payout too.

Some hero.

It replays in my head again, like it was yesterday. His leering face and posh voice telling me I was turned on by what he did to those children. The way he kept leaning closer to me. Licking his lips and winking.

Even now I get a rush of anger at the thought of it.

I don't really remember beating him. I'd lost it. I just have these images of his nose breaking and spraying with blood and the crack of bones when I fractured his jaw and some of his ribs.

Two uniform cops dragged me off. They'd turned up in a police van for prisoner transport to find the arresting officer pinning the suspect down and repeatedly punching his head and body.

I should have fucking killed him.

I thought about doing that after. When I'd been sacked and my wife left me. I thought about tracking Scoble down and finishing him off.

I'd met some of his victims. Their families. I'd seen the pain and horror in their eyes and the physical marks left on their bodies.

I use the dark energy those memories pulse into my body to exercise harder, and for a while, I even forget how much I hurt until I eventually stop, dripping with sweat, and with my chest heaving.

Leave the bad memories behind you.

Think about Tessa.

I can't believe she likes me. I keep telling myself not to get carried away.

But the way she kept bumping her body into mine and

looking up, and biting her bottom lip. The way she hugged me. And it was her suggestion to go for dinner.

That's a good signal.

I mean. If she just wanted help with her research, she could have arranged to meet at the café or something.

But she said all that about having a bath and choosing nice clothes.

I can't help the smile that feels like it's stretching from ear to ear. I head inside and make coffee, then go up to the end room to plug the jukebox in, and purse my lips while choosing a track. It's certainly a weird collection. Everything from old songs like Danny Boy that must have been recorded before the First World War all the way up to ABBA and more modern stuff.

ABBA, though.

Who doesn't like a bit of ABBA?

I select *Dancing Queen* and watch the mechanism slide the old vinyl record out and pop it onto the turntable. Then the needle comes down, and the air fills with that wonderful, static hiss.

A second or so later, and that jaunty disco opening fills the air, and I groove around the snooker table and give the bar a double set of middle fingers because I'm going to stop drinking and clean my life up.

I dance up the stairs. Well. More like limp, and for once, I'm glad of the faulty issue with the jukebox because it keeps repeating the song, meaning I can sing along to it while I have a bath and a shave.

I even head down to the basement and use the big iron and board to un-crease my one nice shirt.

'*You can dance... You can something, something... Having a time of something...*'

I mangle the chorus out full whack, feeling weird in

clean jeans and a pressed shirt. I even think maybe I should check my bank and see if I can afford some new clothes. And some aftershave.

I wonder if the village shop sells flowers.

Would that be too much?

I mean. It feels right to take flowers. Just like a small bunch of something simple.

I go into the snooker room to unplug the jukebox, then think to leave it on replay. If Cooper's sneaking around, he'll hear it and think I'm home.

I find a button marked *shuffle* and press that. *Dancing Queen* ends, and *Seasons in the Sun* by Terry Jacks comes on as I get downstairs and check the front door is locked.

I go out the back door. Making sure to lock it and pocket the key; then a jiffy later, I'm humming *Dancing Queen* in the Landy, heading up the drive.

A bored, spotty teenager takes the cash for the limpest, half-arsed bunch of flowers I think I've ever seen. It'll be fine. I can make a joke about them to break the ice.

God. I'm nervous.

My heart feels all weird, and my belly is churning a bit.

I thought it might be hard finding her cottage, but she'd put some directions on the cover of my papers.

(Mile out of centre. Left. Half mile. Last cottage)

One mile out of the village centre, I turn left, and half a mile later, I find the row of cottages and stop on the verge just up from the last one. I smile at the lights on inside, making it look all cosy against the dark autumnal night.

I take the wilting flowers and head up the drive, already smiling at the jokes we can make about the awful bunch.

Then I hear Tessa laughing, which is lovely, and it makes me smile, but then I frown and wonder what she's laughing at.

Which is when my phone bleeps in my pocket from an incoming message.

I fumble the flowers as I pull my phone out to see a message from a number I don't have saved.

Laughter inside again. Muted voices.

I come to a stop and open my screen.

> Sorry. Need a rain check. Catch up soon. T

I read it again as she laughs inside the house, but it's not just her laughing. It's a guy too. Motion inside the ground floor window to the front as Tessa walks through a door into her lounge, holding a glass of red wine in her hand. A guy behind her. Big and handsome. Mixed race. Dressed nicely in fitted clothes. A glass of red in his hand.

She sits on the sofa, shaking her head while saying something. He laughs and sits down next to her.

I feel weird and jolted, and odd.

'No, no, no! I just felt sorry for him!' Tessa's voice carries clear, and she turns towards the window right behind her.

I back out of the gate onto the road, suddenly fearful of being spotted, and speed-walk back to the Landy.

I get in and drive off, and curse myself at having to drive past because there's nowhere to turn. I go by as she's drawing the curtains, but I keep my head facing forward and hope she doesn't see me.

A big layby down the road. I turn there and drive past the other way. The lights are still on, but the curtains are closed.

I tell myself not to overreact.

I tell myself that absolutely nothing bad has happened.

I tell myself that I literally only just met Tessa, and that she doesn't owe me anything, and she can change her mind and arrange other plans, and do what she wants. We just met. We're not dating.

I tell myself she had the decency to send a text.

I tell myself all of those things, and I tell myself they are all normal, and that every single one of the eight billion or so people on this planet all have their own shit going on, and one single change of plan by another person is not a malicious act or done with intent to cause harm.

I tell myself all of those things as I drive back to Huntington House and park the Landy, and cross the courtyard, and step into the silent house.

But it doesn't stop me plummeting into despair.

Which only gets worse a second later as I once more flinch in fright.

> *Oh, Danny boy, the pipes, the pipes are calling*
> *From glen to glen, and down the mountain side.*

That fucking song. I hate it.
  Who was that guy?
  That's none of my business.
  Yeah, but... Who was he? He was big, and he looked fit and handsome.
  That's none of your business.
  She looked really nice too. She had a low-cut top on. Was that for him?'
  Stop it! She can wear what she wants.
  And why didn't she cancel him instead of me? And she didn't even put a kiss on the text.
  'Enough! Enough, enough, enough, enough, enough, enough, enough, enough, enough...'
  I keep saying it to blot the bad thoughts out.
  I keep telling myself she can do what she wants.
  But I feel jealous, and freaked-out.
  I was never a jealous man before. I've never been controlling to anyone.
  No, but in fairness, that was a harsh let-down.
  Why was it? I hardly know her.
  But she said she felt sorry for me.
  And the way she said it.
  'No, no, no! I just felt sorry for him!'
  She was emphatic like the idea was gross.
  'Stop it, Mike!'
  But I can't stop it.
  How do you stop it?
  'Maybe an old friend popped in,' I tell myself.
  'Yeah, but that text was like really blunt.'
  'No, it wasn't. It was just a text.'
  'She was flirting and all over me.'
  'Said the defendant to the judge. *She was asking for it.*'

'Fuck off! I don't mean it like that. I just mean... I meant...'

'That's probably just how she is. She worked in fashion. Creative people are expressive and tactile.'

'Yeah. So she's getting expressive and tactile on her sofa with that guy.'

'Enough!'

'Fuck off! I'm entitled to an opinion.'

'Not when it's this dark and self-destructive, you're not. Get a grip. Jesus. A woman you hardly know changed her plans. That's it. And this reaction? This is all that baggage you're so worried about displaying. You're a bloody mess.'

'Yeah, but.'

'So she can't change her mind? Is that it? And what? She has to word things in a certain way on text messages because of your fragile ego? Get over yourself. You're turning into one of those desperate, sad, bitter, middle-aged, divorced men that get triggered by everything.'

'Should I have text her back? I didn't text back.'

There's no signal, though.

Shit. I should have done it on the road.

I get back into the Landy and drive out onto the road, and almost reach the village by the time I get signal. I pull over and type out a dozen text messages.

> Hey! Yeah! Of course! That's fine! (deleted): Er, excuse me? Triggered! Joke! That's cool. No probs! (deleted)

> Hey! Yeah. Actually. I could do with an early night. Speak soon! (deleted)

> Okay (deleted)

> (deleted)
>
> Sure. Did you want to meet for breakfast at the café? I could pick you up? (deleted)
>
> Yep. No worries. Coffee tomorrow? (deleted): Okidoki, cafe tomoz? (deleted)
>
> How very dare you! (deleted)

'Fuck, fuck, fuck.'

I throw the phone on the seat next to me and blast air. Then I make myself reply like it was a work text from a colleague.

> Hi Tessa. Okay, no worries. See you soon. Mike

I click send before I talk myself out of it and then spend another thirty minutes seeing if the word *sent* will change to *read*.

It doesn't

And she doesn't reply.

She's probably busy.

In bed.

'Stop it. Jesus.'

I sit back and exhale slowly, and without warning, the angst and adrenaline disappear, and I slide down into an internal void. Like there is nothing within me. No heart. No soul. Life has no meaning. Therefore, it has no consequences.

Ten minutes later, I'm at the bar, drinking shots of vodka.

On cue, the jukebox comes to life, and the songs start again. Making me flinch and grip my glass.

I stomp over and yank the plug out, then wince when I realise this thing plays vinyl and pulling the plug halfway probably isn't good for it.

'You can break that as well,' I murmur to myself and down another shot. But the buzz I normally get isn't coming. I just feel numb.

And stupid.

And small.

Insignificant.

Useless.

Old.

Pathetic.

I can't stop that voice.

I can't stop the things it says to me.

I can't stop thinking about Tessa.

I pause as the glass touches my lips.

Then I'm off the stool and heading out of the room and down the stairs with my glass of vodka.

I go down into the basement and over to the manager's desk and pull the chair out. I take another gulp of vodka and pull the clipboard down from the hook, and leaf through the rotas for the cleaning staff.

Names of women written into boxes. One for each day.

One sheet for each month.

I leaf through them. Seeing the last two weeks' worth of days are empty, but before that, it looks like it was business as usual.

I find certain days are highlighted in yellow, with more names written in. I cross-reference those dates for the last few months to the big dry-wipe wall planner and can see names of functions.

The highlighted dates on the paper sheets were when more staff were needed to cover extra guests.

I flick backwards from this month.

October. September. August. July. June. May. April. March. February. January.

The previous year.

December. November. October. September. July. June. May. April. March. February. January.

Hang on.

I check again.

Eleven sheets for the previous year.

August is missing.

Maybe they lost it. It could have slipped off the clipboard and got ruined or something.

There aren't any more sheets on the board.

I drink more vodka and read the ends of the box folders, and find *Old Rotas*. I find the rotas for the full year prior to the ones on the board.

December. November. October. September. July. June. May. April. March. February. January.

No August.

I go back through the year previous to that one, which is three years ago.

That does have August.

But the cleaning rota for August three years ago is significantly different to the other months, with a much-reduced work force.

In fact, they've only got someone coming in for a couple of hours twice a week for that whole month.

Why is that?

I glance to the wall-planner for this year and see the month of August is marked in bright pink marker pen.

Summer holidays?

It has to be.

The kids are always off school in August, and that's when posh people go off on their travels to the south of France to polish their yachts or whatever, and working-class people give themselves heart attacks by trying to arrange childcare.

So it looks like Huntington House shuts up for the month of August, and the cleaning staff are given time off, save for one poor sod coming in to check it all over and pick the chair up in the kitchen that Old Hunty keeps knocking over.

On cue, the chair in the kitchen falls over, making me jump.

'Fucking ghost.'

I finish the vodka, having not found what I was looking for, which were the names of either a Chinese or Vietnamese woman or a Latvian or Estonian woman.

Which I figure would stand out from Bev, Deirdre, Janey, Jenny, and all the other very English names.

That's not to say Asians or Eastern Europeans can't have English names or even share the same names as used commonly here.

But it was an idea that popped into my head between the worsening bouts of self-pity.

Which comes back now ten-fold.

I'd even stay down here in this comfy chair if I'd brought the vodka bottle with me.

But I didn't.

And I'm not drunk enough yet.

I go back to find the basement door is closed.

But I wedged it open with the chair.

Maybe I didn't. I use my wire hangar to open it and head out to see the chair knocked over in the hallway. When I pick it up, the chair in the kitchen slams over with a loud bang, making me jump again.

'Fuck's sake,' I snap and stomp into the kitchen, and pick that one up as the music comes on upstairs.

> *Oh, Danny boy, the pipes, the pipes are calling*
> *From glen to glen, and down the mountain side.*

I tense up, with that creeping sensation crawling up my spine. I know I unplugged it. A flash of anger, and I set off charging up the stairs. Ready to brawl with Cooper because it must be him doing it.

Except he's not in there.

Nobody is.

And I question if I even unplugged the machine.

Didn't I go to unplug it, then stop in case it damages the record?

I turn it off properly this time. First, at the machine, then at the plug, and then I detach it from the socket and loop the wire over to remind myself I definitely did unplug it.

At which point, the chair in the downstairs lobby falls over with a loud bang.

I stride out of the snooker room, into the upstairs

corridor to see the wall-mounted gaslights glowing feebly with a soft hiss.

How the hell did they come on?

Then a door slams shut upstairs with a loud bang, making me flinch, but it triggers something close to anger, and I set off, running up the stairs and along the corridor, seeing all the doors are closed.

Apart from the door to my room.

I rush inside. Freaked out and scared, and angry. Nobody inside.

I step out and close the door, then stop at the gaslights glowing on the walls with that soft hiss.

And a door slams downstairs.

I run again. To the middle floor. Seeing all the doors are closed.

Then I head to the ground floor to wedge the chair in the lobby into the basement door, then into the kitchen to pick the other three wooden chairs up and place them seat-side down on the table.

And the music comes back on.

'CUNT!' I scream the word out and run the fastest yet, up the stairs and past the flicking gaslights.

The door to the snooker room is closed.

I fly inside to see the jukebox plugged back in.

I unplugged it.

I looped the wire.

The chairs downstairs tip off the table with a crash.

I yank the plug to the jukebox out and physically pull the machine away from the wall, heedless to it being a priceless antique.

I set off again. My mind racing. My heart beating weirdly. Chills run up and down my spine. The gaslights go off halfway along the corridor, making it seem suddenly dark and sinister.

I start down the stairs and stop midway.

Staring down to my bottle of vodka placed on the seat of the chair now positioned in the middle of the lobby. The chair I'd wedged into the basement door.

'COOPER!' I shout. 'COOPER!'

Into the kitchen. All three chairs now on the floor. The music comes back on. The gaslights flicker and go off. A door slams shut or open somewhere. My mind spirals. 'COOPER!' I scream the loudest yet.

Then silence.

The music stops.

The banging stops.

The gaslights go off.

Silence.

I clutch my head and go out into the lobby to grab the vodka, and drink straight from the bottle.

And in the silence, in that moment, I swear I hear a low laugh.

It sends shivers through me.

I take the vodka upstairs to my room and slam the door closed behind me.

Then I sit back on the bed. In the dark.

I drink from the bottle.

And the gaslight in my room flickers on.

And a door opens slowly somewhere. Creaking until it hits the wall with a dull thud.

Footsteps. Floorboards creaking. Coming closer.

My gaslight goes out.

I squeeze my eyes closed and drink from the bottle.

I drink until I pass out.

12

Day Five

My bedroom door is open when I wake up.

I step out with a raging hangover into the hallway to see every other door is also open.

But the terror of the night seems far off and distant, and not as acute as it was.

I go into the bathroom to brush my teeth and avoid the sorry state of my reflection.

Got to stop drinking.

Then I remember Tessa, and shame hits me at my reaction. It's a deep, burning shame too.

'Fucking loser,' I tell myself.

Not from any sense of self-pity or from internally fishing and expecting a counter mitigation to my woes.

It is a statement of fact.

I am a fucking loser.

I turn the tap, knowing it takes a while to run hot. Pain in my side. My liver probably. The body can't process that much alcohol without issue. I'm turning into one of the alcohol dependant people, who spiral into mental health and end up looping in and out of the police and emergency services' orbits. A&E departments. Rehab. Petty crime. Public order.

A greater sense of shame hits me when I realise I used to look down my nose at people like me.

I believed I'd never become one of them.

I had a life. A career. A wife.

I was balanced, and I had purpose.

But that balance wasn't quite as balanced as I thought it was.

Evidently not from what I did.

And now here I am.

Exactly *one of those people*, with the same sorry story about how *it wasn't my fault. It was the world turning against me.*

I exhale long and slow and give thanks when the steam from the hot tap mists the mirror and blots my view, and in so doing, the words just about become clear.

Words written with a finger on glass now dripping with condensation like watery droplets of clear blood.

DIE HUMBER

DIE HUMBER

HUMBER DIE

Now, I'm no expert on the supernatural, but I'm pretty sure ghosts don't have fingers. And I'm especially sure they don't have fingers covered in sweat that coated the glass to prevent it misting up.

Which means it was a person who did this.

Not a ghost.

I put my finger to the first D in the first sentence and trace it along the first line of *Die Humber*.

Then my head reminds me that I drank a whole bottle of vodka and tailspins off, with a thud of pain that makes me feel nauseous.

When I reach the bottom of the stairs, I spot the chair I used to wedge the basement door open has been left in the middle of the lobby. I drag it back over.

In the kitchen, I pick the knocked over chairs up and push them under the table.

Then I fish my cigarette papers out of the coffee jar.

After that, I make coffee and have a smoke in the courtyard.

'Fucking Cooper,' I mutter while shaking my head and reading the words written on the outside of the back door.

Die
die
Die
Die

I touch one of the letters. Red chalk. I take a picture with my phone and use a jug of water to rinse it off, then go back to nursing my hangover.

I should feel threatened.

But honestly.

I just feel sick.

I'm not even that bothered about Tessa. I think maybe, for once, venting it out last night and running around the house, getting drunk, and chasing ghosts, or rather, not ghosts must have been a bit healthy. Which is massively messed up, seeing as my liver hurts and my head hurts, and my whole body hurts, and I want to throw up.

But the angsty drama stress about Tessa isn't there.

I only met her twice. She flirted a bit, then cancelled a date.

So what?

Good luck to her.

I do know one thing, though.

I'm really hungry.

◊

'Jesus, Maggie.'

'What?'

'I can't eat all that.'

'Get off. Do you some good. And I only did you a regular.'

'What the f–! What's above a regular?'

'Large, obviously.'

'What does that come in? A wheelbarrow?'

'You daft twat,' she says and swipes my shoulder as she walks off after leaving a plate full of enough food to feed a whole shift of cops.

Three eggs. Three big sausages. Four rashers of bacon. Mushrooms. Beans in tomato sauce. A big, grilled tomato. Hash browns. Four slices of toast.

I turn from the mountain of food to flap my hands at

Maggie behind her counter. She calls me a daft twat again while making me another coffee. The first one having been pretty much inhaled when I shuffled in, feeling like a zombie.

'You look like a zombie,' Maggie told me bluntly.

'Thanks.'

'Welcome.'

'Where are all the farmer men people?'

'Doing farmer men people things.'

'Oh,' I said because I really wasn't feeling very bright.

I ordered breakfast and coffee.

I drank the first coffee.

Now I stare at the breakfast, feeling somewhat intimidated.

'Want me to cut it up and feed you?' Maggie asks as she plonks my coffee down.

'I preferred it when you didn't like me.'

'I still don't like you. And I preferred you with a beard,' she adds as I stab a sausage and hold it an inch from my mouth, and look up at her. 'Idiot,' she says with another laugh at my expression. 'Look like you're in a porno.'

'A non-beardy porno,' I say and bite into the sausage.

'D'you shave it for that blond?' she asks as I chew and give her a look. 'That's a yes.'

I wave my hand to say that she should hang on a second while I finish my mouthful; then I take another mouthful. 'Such a dick!' she says, and I get hit with the tea towel this time. 'I was bloody waiting for you to speak, then!'

'No, hang on,' I say when she walks off.

'Piss off!'

'No, I mean it,' I say as she goes behind the counter and rolls her eyes. 'I want to ask you something.'

'Go on, then,' she says.

'Okay. So. Like. I'll just shout it across this massive café then, shall I?'

'Yeah, this really busy café,' she says, motioning the otherwise empty chairs and tables.

Which is a fair point.

'Fair point,' I say and go to bite into the sausage as she calls me a daft twat again and walks off laughing. 'Who looks after the house in August?'

'Eh?' she asks, coming out of the kitchen.

'Huntington. Who looks after it in August?'

'It shuts down in August,' she says and walks over with her coffee to sit down at my table.

'Just sit down, then.'

'Why you asking?' she asks, and this time, I get the tea towel flung in my face.

'Just wondering.'

'No, you weren't. That was a copper question, that was.'

'Wasn't.'

'So was.'

I chew my mouthful. The joke now established as she rolls her eyes and waits for me to finish. 'This is really nice,' I say, motioning at the food.

'Cheers.'

'Just found some old rotas in the basement after Old Hunty locked me in.'

She almost snorts her coffee through her nose at that one. 'Did he? Bloody hell. You would not get me working in that house on my own for all the tea in China. He slapped your arse yet?'

I shake my head and bite into another sausage, making her laugh again.

'Yeah, it shuts up in August. They go off on their travels.'

'South of France?'

'They got villas everywhere. I only been to Benidorm once, and that was half board in a two-star.'

'But three years ago, they had someone going in for a couple of hours a week.'

She narrows her eyes like she's remembering. 'Bev. And she told 'em they can stick it cos she ain't stepping foot inside on her own ever again. If I remember right, she took her fella up with her. I went in a couple of times with her and all. Can't blame her.'

'Ah okay. That makes sense.'

'Why?'

'Cos the rotas for August were missing the next two years after that. So they must have just shut the whole thing up.'

'Probably. And how bored are you if you're reading rotas? Come and play bingo.'

'Bingo?'

'Yeah. It's when they give you a card, and it has numbers, and they call the numbers, and you cross them off, and you can win if you get a line or a full house.'

'Never heard of it.'

'What, really?'

'Of course, I bloody have.'

'You twat,' she says and takes her tea towel back to throw at me again. 'Come up if you're bored. Monday, Thursday, and Saturday. Saturday's the best one. They open the bar up and put some music on after. Bring your fancy lady.'

'What fancy lady?'

'The one you shaved your nice beard off for. Her. Whatever her name is.'

'Tessa.'

'Tessa, then.'

'She's not my fancy lady. I met her twice. What's that look for?'

'Yeah, right.'

'What? What!?'

She snorts and huffs, and nods, and rolls her eyes in a way that makes me laugh while also chewing bacon, which then almost comes out.

'Eat it properly,' she says.

'She lives here,' I say.

'Who does?'

'Princess bloody Diana.'

'Eh?'

'Tessa!'

'What about her?'

'How do you not know her if she lives here? You all bloody knew me on my first day!'

'That's cos you're that copper that was on the news.'

'Oh, god. No.'

'What?'

'Does everyone know?'

'Course they bloody do! Wendy told everyone, didn't she?'

'Who told Wendy?'

'Stan probably. She's about the only one the grumpy twat speaks to. Only cos he shagged her back in the day. How's that sausage?' she asks when I bite into it with a face.

'Please don't talk about Cooper's willy while I'm eating sausage. And I thought she was married to your brother John.'

'Well, she is now. Not then.'

I nod and eat, and completely lose my train of thought.

'You've forgot what you were asking me now.'

'Was it about bingo?' I ask.

'Bingo!' she says with a grin as the door opens to the farm lads traipsing in and making the place seem suddenly very small.

Which is mainly because they're massive.

'I'm on a break!' Maggie says.

'Get off your fat arse!' her brother says, reaching over to scuff her hair as she flings the tea towel at him.

'Padded! Not fat,' she says as the others laugh, and the banter flows easily between people that have grown and lived alongside each other their whole lives. 'All these sausages I keep eating,' she tells me and winks, and nicks the half a sausage left on my plate before heading off to the counter.

She doesn't have a fat arse, though.

Padded. But not fat.

She turns to catch me looking with a cackle.

'Was he looking?' John asks with a laugh as the lads grin, and I hold my hands up in surrender.

'How you getting on anyway?' one of them asks.

'Me? Yeah. I guess,' I say, surprised at the lack of animosity. Then I remind myself it was my own behaviour that caused the awkwardness last time.

'Shit job,' another says.

'Yeah,' John says. 'Wouldn't catch me in that house on my own.'

'Bloody right,' another one says as the rest murmur in agreement.

Which catches me out because they're all physically big men. Broad, with thick legs and arms.

John even shudders at the thought of it.

'Doesn't it give you the willies?' one of them asks.

'We had that chat!' Maggie yells from the kitchen. 'Ask him about his beard!'

I roll my eyes again.

'Yeah, but what he's done, though,' one of the lads says.

'Yeah, course. Forgot about that,' John says.

'Copper in London. Must have seen it all.'

'That's Geoff, by the way!' Maggie yells.

'Who is?' I ask.

'I am,' Geoff says, the one who just said about being a copper in London.

'And that's Pete!' Maggie shouts while still out of sight as Pete lifts a hand in greeting. 'And the thick twat is Derek.'

'We just calls him thick twat,' John says as the lads jostle the last one on the table.

'You did that pedo over, though, didn't you?' Derek says.

'That's why we call him thick twat!' Maggie yells as the others groan.

'It's alright. And yes. I did.'

'I said it was him,' Derek tells the others.

'We all bloody knew it was him. Stan told Wendy,' Pete says as I spot a dark look pass over John's face.

'That pedo had it coming, though,' Geoff says to me as Maggie carries the first two plates out, which, firstly, tells me that she must have had the food already cooked and heated to have them so fast, and second, that she's strong as an ox by carrying two such big plates, each laden with enough food to feed a whole police station.

'His eyes,' she says with a laugh and a nod at me. 'This is brunch for these lads. They had breakfast at dawn, and they'll have lunch yet. Anyway. You lot leave him alone. What he went through. Poor bloke don't want to relive it every five minutes, does he?'

'Only asking,' Pete says.

'Yeah? How about I only ask about old Gilbert getting run over by that harvester? Yeah. Your face now, Pete. Not nice, is it?'

'Sorry, Mags,' Pete says. 'Sorry, Mr Humber.'

'It's fine. It's just Mike.'

'You finished yet?' she asks with a glance at my half empty plate. 'Go on, then. Get it down. Do you good.'

I think to protest, but the last shred of masculinity in me prevents me from looking like a complete loser, and I force the rest down and sit back in a near-on digestive coma.

'You going for a smoke?' Maggie asks as I get to my feet. She grabs a tin from behind the counter and takes a pre-made cigarette out. 'There's a couple of sausages left on the hot plate,' she tells the lads and carries her coffee outside with me. 'See,' she says.

'See what?'

'They're alright.'

'I never said they weren't.'

'Your face did first time you came in.' I can't argue with that. So I don't try. 'They think you're like the dogs wotsits anyway.'

'Eh?'

'The lads. For staying up at that house on your own. Everyone reckons you're like that, you know, that bloke. Him.'

'What bloke?'

'The one from the telly.'

'That narrows it down.'

She laughs again. 'The copper man that Kiefer Sutherland did,' she says as the grin slowly fades, and she glances past me.

'Hey!' Tessa says as I turn to see her walking over. 'Well. Fancy seeing you here? Waiting for me?'

'I gotta get back in,' Maggie says and stubs her smoke.

'Can I get a coffee, please?' Tessa calls.

'Order at the counter!' Maggie says, with the door already closing.

'What's got her goat?' Tessa asks.

'Dunno. She seemed alright.'

'Yeah! I could see you two getting cosy. Well. I'll order at the counter, then. You having another one?'

'Er, no. I'm okay actually. I need to get back.'

'What for?'

'Sorry?'

'What for?' she asks, with her hand on the door, and those blue eyes holding me in her gaze.

I find myself unable to speak or summon a reason to give as to why I can't stay. I only said it because she made that joke about me waiting for her.

'You're not poochy, are you?' she asks.

'Eh? No! God. No. Don't even. I didn't even think... It's fine. You don't need to apologise.'

'I know I don't *need* to, but your face.'

'Why do people keep talking about my face?'

'Okay. It was just a comment. Take it easy.'

'I'm fine,' I say, which doesn't come out like I am fine.

'Okay. Whatever,' she says and pushes into the café.

I suddenly feel bad. Like I've done something wrong, and I should go after her and apologise, except I'm not entirely sure what for.

Then the hangover and the food coma combine forces and sap all energy from my body, and I turn back into a zombie and shuffle back to the Landy and then back to the house.

Which, for once, is how I left it.

Apart from the wet tracks in the grass.

Fuck Cooper.

13

I stopped myself from charging off across the lawns after the tracks.

Partly because it wouldn't achieve anything, and partly, or rather, mainly because the hangover was killing me.

I don't normally get hangovers that bad. But then I don't normally have unsupervised access to my own bar.

But either way. I didn't charge across the lawns. Instead, I pottered about the house and drank coffee.

I went down into the basement a few times too. But I didn't get locked in.

Nor did the jukebox turn itself on, and no chairs were knocked over, and my arse was definitely not slapped.

Not that I particularly wanted my arse slapped.

But you know. I'm just saying it *wasn't* slapped.

What I did do, against my better judgement, was some exercise.

It hurt like hell in places that I didn't even know could hurt, but I figured sweating the booze out of my system would help. I couldn't physically feel any worse.

I set off up the driveway, with my head pounding and

my guts churning. I started sweating quickly, and I was feeling cold and clammy, and weird, and all sorts of not right.

At which point I bent double and puked the nice, regular-sized cooked breakfast that Maggie made for me onto Lord Huntington's nicely manicured verges.

Which was a shame because I really enjoyed that breakfast.

I thought I'd pass out when I puked. I felt faint and dizzy, and actually wondered if I was having some kind of seizure or something.

Then it eased off, and surprisingly, within a few minutes, I actually felt better.

I figured the vomiting had purged some of the booze or something. I don't know. I just know I was able to carry on running up the drive and then down again, which was a bit weird when I passed my pile of spew.

I hoped some night creatures would eat it. Like foxes or rabbits, and then I hoped Cooper would catch the rabbit and eat it, and then he'd be eating my puke.

Which is what got me thinking.

That thinking then carried on while I was doing exercises in the courtyard. I wondered what Cooper had to gain from his attempts to scare me.

What was his motivation?

The cop TV shows and movies always bang on about motivation, as though every offender needs a solid reason for doing something.

Sometimes, they don't.

Sometimes, people do bad things just because they can.

Or because, like Tessa said, they're fucking weirdos and obsessive.

Cooper could be nursing a smouldering hatred of life in

general, and then I come along and tell him he's not allowed in the house he's had access to his whole life, and something goes pop in his head.

That happens a lot.

Undiagnosed bipolar and paranoid schizophrenia, and psychosis are far more common than people realise, and you add any of those conditions to a bleak, isolated place like this, and well...

Or he might actually have a proper motivation.

Tessa did say two women went missing.

Or rather, a man phoned her office and told her that two women had gone missing.

I was going to ask Maggie about them this morning, but what with the food coma and the tea towel flinging, it slipped my mind, and then Tessa turned up. Which also distracted me.

She had tight yoga trousers on and a tight hoody, and her hair was pulled back, and her eyes were so blue. And the way she looked at me from the door. The shape of her lips, and the way her eyebrow arched up.

Her image kept coming back into my mind. I shooed it away and focussed on exercising and thinking about puke and Cooper.

I made some simple pasta after exercise, and then had more coffee and told myself I wasn't going near the bar.

I also told myself I wasn't going to think about Tessa.

I didn't go near the bar, but I failed dismally on the other thing.

Damn. What a shame. I thought she really liked me. The way she flirted and kept touching my arms and hugging me. But I think that's just the person she is, and I totally misread it all because I've been so lonely and isolated for the last two years.

I kept imagining going to her house for dinner last night, and what it would have been like. I even thought about kissing her and got turned on at the thought of having sex, which is something I haven't thought about for a long time.

Then I remembered what she said to the man on the sofa next to her.

I don't feel jealous, though. Well. No. I do a bit. But like more sad-jealous rather than angry-jealous. I'm sad I read it wrong, but I hope she's happy.

> *Oh, Danny boy, the pipes, the pipes are*
> *   calling*
> *From glen to glen, and down the mountain*
> *   side.*

My thoughts cut off when the music starts.

It makes my heart thump harder, and I get that same chill running down my spine.

The day has gone now.

The night is here, and so the house is dark and sinister, and that atmosphere is back too.

But it's different now.

The feeling of acute terror isn't there.

Because I'm different now.

It was what Maggie said. *They think you're like that cop Kiefer Sutherland did.*

That blew my mind.

Those lads are big and strong, but they all said they were too frightened to be in the house alone.

Whereas I'm not.

Because I'm not a farmer, and I used to do this sort of thing for a living.

Hiding in shadows.

Waiting.

Watching.

And sometimes, we'd hide in plain sight and pretend to be prey to lure the predators out.

That's what I did today.

I exercised and made noise.

I walked around the house and went out onto the balcony outside the snooker room to drink coffee and smoke so I'd be seen from the treeline at the edge of the woods.

When dusk came, I put the lights on and opened and closed some of the curtains.

Being seen.

Being prey.

I close the book I'm reading and stand up from the armchair in the library, and walk over to start mounting the stairs.

I reach the top.

I make the turn into the corridor.

Halfway along, and the chair in the kitchen falls over.

When I step into the snooker room, the chair in the lobby next to the basement is knocked over.

I go to the jukebox and bend down as though to unplug it from the wall, and clock the faint smudges in the baking flour I found in the pantry in the kitchen earlier. It was a good find. I sprinkled a fine layer in a few places to detect motion.

While doing that, I look over to the patio doors and can see the thin strand of cotton I found in the sewing kit in the basement is still unbroken across the doors.

Meaning Cooper didn't come into the house through these doors.

The house falls into silence when I pull the plug.

A moment later, I walk back into the corridor.

Halfway along, the gaslights on the walls glow brighter, with a louder hiss.

I keep going and make sure to tread heavily going down the stairs. The chair next to the basement door is in the middle of the floor on its side.

I pick it up and put it back where it was, and clock the strand of cotton across the basement door is still there and intact.

I right the chair in the kitchen and see that the strand of cotton across the back door is also unbroken.

But I do note that both chairs had particles of baking flour on them.

I almost smile to myself.

It feels good to be taking control.

Even though my headache has come back again, and I keep feeling sick.

I breathe deeply for a moment until the wooziness passes, then get myself a glass of water, and head back to the library.

Into the armchair with my book.

'Oh, Danny Boy,' I sing softly, and a second later...

> *Oh, Danny boy, the pipes, the pipes are calling*
> *From glen to glen, and down the mountain side.*

Repeat.

Book down.

Up the stairs.

Halfway along, and I nod a split-second before the first chair is knocked over; then I count the seconds and imagine Cooper running out of the kitchen and grabbing the other chair, which falls over on cue.

I go into the snooker room while Cooper gets into the basement, and by the time I've unplugged the jukebox and made ready for the next time, the gaslights are dimming in the hallway.

I go downstairs and pick the chairs up.

The strands of cotton are all still in place.

Hidden corridors. Hidden stairwells. I'll find them tomorrow.

I go into the library.

Into the armchair.

'Oh, Danny Boy,' I sing, and on cue...

> *Oh, Danny boy, the pipes, the pipes are calling*
> *From glen to glen, and down the mountain side.*

'Predictable,' I mutter.

Repeat.

Up the stairs.

Halfway along, I pause and turn to listen, with a satisfied smile to god-awful racket coming from the kitchen as Cooper tries to knock the chair over without realising I had it prepped with cotton tied to the handles of metal pans on the table.

All of which crash to the floor.

I snort a laugh and flick the switch off on the jukebox, but I don't touch the plug.

Because I smeared it with my puke when I came up before, which I had ready in a plastic bag in a corner pocket of the snooker table.

I'm already back in the corridor when I hear the basement door slamming open from Cooper grabbing the other chair, which I'd tied to cotton through the tiny gap in the basement door to the wire hanger inside. Meaning when he grabbed the chair, it would ping him back and release the lock, and make it crash open.

Which it just did as I reach the top of the stairs.

'Sniff your hand, Cooper! That's my puke. You're lucky I didn't smear it with shit!'

Footsteps going away, and this time the grin spreads as I head back down the stairs and fix the mess he just caused. Picking up the chair in the lobby and the pans, and the other chair in the kitchen.

'We going again?' I call in the lobby and wait for a reply. 'Yes? No? We still playing? And who is keeping scores? That last round was mine.'

Silence.

But it's a heavy silence. I can just sense that fucker is listening to me.

'I'm not a farmer, Cooper!'

I go back into the library. To the armchair. To my book.

My eyes narrow. I look up. Waiting. Expecting it. Almost wanting it.

*Oh, Danny boy, the pipes, the pipes are
   calling
From glen to glen, and down the mountain
   side.*

'Petulant twat,' I say with a laugh, shaking my head and figuring we're in for a long night.

Up the stairs.

Halfway along the corridor.

'And cue chair...' I say and pause as something very heavy smashes through glass, with a clear and distinct escalation.

I turn and run fast. Drawing the tyre iron from my waistband as I reach the stairs and head down and into the kitchen to see he's put one of the chairs through a kitchen window into the courtyard.

He's rattled.

Be careful.

Another loud smash as the chair from the hallway flies into the kitchen and bounces off the table into my back.

I take cover in case of further attack as the basement door slams shut. Then I'm up and moving with the iron raised in case it's a ploy and he's waiting for me in the lobby.

And the power goes off.

Plunging the entire house into darkness.

The music cuts off too.

Silence.

Blackness.

Fuck.

I should have thought about that.

But darkness to me is the same darkness to him.

Apart from the fact he knows the house like the back of his hand.

Including the hidden corridors and stairwells.

Fuck it.

I've been outmanoeuvred.

I take my tyre iron and feel, and grope my way to the third floor, and those terrors of the previous night come back tenfold. My heart hammers in my chest, and I feel sick and cold, and clammy.

I grope my way to my room and go inside. Not knowing if he's already in there.

Waiting for me.

Low cloud outside in the sky.

No moon.

No ambient light coming through the window.

I hold still to try and hear him breathing as a door slams somewhere else in the house.

It makes me jump, but it also makes me realise he's not in this room.

I go for my bag.

For my torch I keep inside.

That isn't there.

'Wanker,' I whisper again. He'd planned for this. He's taken my torch.

I push a chair I left in here up against the handle and retreat to my bed with the tyre iron.

Doors slam open and slam close in the house.

It goes silent for a long time. Then something thumps the wall directly behind my head in the room on the other side.

Silence.

Something thumps my door.

I was expecting it.

But I still flinch.

And this time I don't have any vodka to drink, so I stay awake, gripping the iron and staring into the darkness while imagining Cooper stalking the dark house with a shotgun or a knife.

14

Day Six
Saturday

I wake with a start, not realising I slept, and snatch the tyre iron up, thinking I heard a bang from Cooper forcing himself into the room.

But I must have been dreaming. The chair is still wedged under the handle, and I can't hear anything.

My head, though. That hangover is still lingering. Unless I've picked a bug up from my immune system being so low because of my awful lifestyle.

Thirsty too. Really thirsty.

I pull the chair away and open the door, figuring the shenanigans of the night are over.

Or he could be right outside, waiting to stab me.

Thankfully, he isn't, and I go across the hallway and through the open bathroom door and groan audibly at seeing my puke smeared over the mirror.

I guess I had that coming.

I gulp cold water from the tap, then empty my bladder as the banging I thought I heard comes back again.

But it's not chairs being thrown this time. It's someone at the front door.

I lurch back to my room, thinking to get dressed, them remember I already am from sleeping in my clothes, and head off down the stairs, seeing all the interior doors have been left open.

I also narrowly miss stepping in the faeces left at the top of the stairs leading down to the ground floor.

Actual human faeces.

Right there on the top step.

Dirty bastard.

It stinks something awful too.

I veer around it as the banging comes again.

'MR HUMBER!'

'I'm coming!' I yell with my voice still thick from sleep. I clear my throat and yank bolts back, and pull the door open to see the ruddy cheeks and blue eyes of Lord Huntington staring at me.

'What's happened?' he asks.

'Happened?'

'The window!'

I blink at him.

'The kitchen window, Mr Humber.'

It takes me another second to remember Cooper threw a chair through it. 'Sorry! The window. Just woken up. Yes. Er.'

'I'll meet you in the courtyard,' he says and marches off towards the garages.

'Just come through this way.'

'I can't cross the threshold!'

I go back through the kitchen, with a grimace at seeing the pans still on the floor and handprints of flour here and there, along with slick, glistening smears of my puke that must have been on Cooper's hand.

By the time I get the door open, Huntington is in the courtyard, staring at the chair, then up to the broken window it went through. 'And how do you explain that?' he asks.

'The chair went through it.'

'I can bloody see that, Mr Humber.'

He shoots me a look, but I'm too foggy headed to decipher it. 'How did you know?' I ask. 'You can't see this window from the road or anywhere.'

'Cooper.'

'Cooper?'

'Said he heard a smash last night and came looking, and could see you drunk inside.'

'I didn't drink last night.'

'Your eyes say otherwise, Mr Humber.'

'I didn't bloody drink.'

He looks over to the nearly empty bottle of vodka on a table nearby.

'I didn't put that there,' I tell him and almost sag at being outmanoeuvred again. 'Cheeky fucking prick,' I mutter with such a filthy look even Huntington raises his ginger eyebrows, then steps closer to the open back door, and peers inside to the disarray.

'Explain.'

'Nothing,' I say sullenly. Figuring I'm about to get fired. Which will then warrant a visit to Cooper's house with that fucking tyre iron.

Huntington grunts. 'Never seen him this bad.'

That gets my attention. 'Cooper?'

He nods again. Looking grim, with thin lips. 'This is a problem, Mr Humber,' he says quietly.

'I can leave today,' I say with a sigh.

'I don't want you to leave. I want you to fix it.'

Again. That gets my attention.

'Fix it?' I ask, which is all I can just about manage, with my mind churning so slowly. I really need a coffee. 'The window? Have you got any ply anywhere?'

'Not the bloody window!'

He shoots me another look, as though I'm way more stupid than he thought.

'That I don't believe was you,' he says quietly while pointing to the window. 'That, however, I'm not sure about,' he adds, with a nod to the vodka bottle.

'I said I didn't drink last night.'

'Then I would suggest someone is making it look like you did. Anyway, old chap! Accidents happen,' he adds in a cheery voice. 'I'll get a glazier booked in. In the meantime, there are some wooden boards in the garages. Pop one of them up, would you? But don't overdo it on the screws or nails. The conservation officers in the council are utter shits. Walking me back to my car, are you?'

Apparently, I am.

We go back through the garages and out towards the big gravel driveway. He waits until our feet are crunching noisy stones before he speaks quietly. 'He's been a problem for a long time.'

'Cooper?'

He nods grimly.

'Sack him, then.'

'Not that simple.'

'Why not? Go through solicitors. Or pay some of those big farm lads to go round with you. Or both.'

'Can't.'

'Why not?'

'Because of the legal issue, Mr Humber.'

'What's Cooper got to do with that? He's a groundsman, isn't he? Oh. Oh, shit. Oh, that's fucking messy,' I say as my brain finally shifts gear, and I make the connection, to which he once more nods grimly.

'Cooper's mother was very attractive, and my father, God rest his soul, couldn't keep his prick in his trousers.'

'Is Cooper your brother?'

'No. Thank God. But he had a sister. Or rather, his mother had a daughter.'

'Is that the other claimant to the estate? Yeah. That's messy.'

'Messy isn't the word.'

'Where's the sister now?'

'My father paid her off a long time ago on the proviso she went away and stayed away. She'd be in her fifties by now. Born the same year as me.'

'Is she ginger as well? I didn't mean it like that. Not like, you know, gingers stink of piss or anything.'

'Stop talking, Mr Humber.'

'Okay,' I say, figuring that's good advice.

We near his expensive Range Rover left by the front of the house, with Huntington slowing to keep making noise underfoot. 'This house has been in our family for nearly half a millennium, so I am sure you can understand we are desperate to avoid it being sold off for the spoils to be shared.'

'Just tell the courts he's breaching the agreement by entering the house.'

'Which will delay proceedings for a very long time.'

We reach his car. He pauses to look me in the eye for a

long second. 'You're a smart man, Mr Humber, and clearly not frightened of being here. Which are attributes we need right now. Along with discretion and understanding.'

He gets in the car and closes the door. A second later, the engine starts, and the electric window glides smoothly down. 'It's an old house, Mr Humber!' he calls cheerily. 'These things will happen. Glad we've got you here, though. Any problems, give me a bell.'

He drops his voice again before pulling away. 'Keep that house in my family, and I'll change your life.'

Then he's off while I'm left wondering how my world just got so bloody complicated.

Then I sag because dried puke and shit don't clean themselves up.

That all takes a while. Finding yellow rubber gloves, which are two sizes too small and pinch like hell, but no way am I manhandling Cooper's turd with my bare hands.

Then I have to find buckets and spray detergents, and brushes, and cloths.

I find a hoover in the basement and vacuum the flour up, and clean the kitchen.

Then it's out to the garage to find wood and a saw to cut it with, then tools to fit the board over the window. By the time the broken glass gets swept up, I've had two coffees and starting to feel more human.

I run what Huntington said through my head while I work.

What does he think I can do?

I know what it felt like he was asking me to do. Or rather, what was being implied.

But that can't be right.

Was he asking me to kill Cooper?

I'm not a bloody hitman.

I was a cop for god's sake.

Keep that house in my family, and I'll change your life.

I used to get offered bribes a lot. Especially when I worked on the major crime teams as a detective. Fraudsters. Money launderers. Gangland bosses. They use cash as a way of avoiding prison. It works too. Coppers don't earn a lot.

I never took a bribe, though. I loved the feeling of taking bad guys out and being honourable. It made me feel I was above them. Like untainted or something.

Until Edward Scoble.

I grab a smoke in the courtyard and try to imagine what my future would look like if I had life-changing money.

What would I do with it?

Where would I go?

Could I kill Cooper for money?

And how would that resolve these issues?

Cooper is obviously trying to exert pressure and control over the situation by intimidating Huntington to keep him away from the house.

That might also be why the Huntingtons were so willing to accept the agreement and stay out of the house.

Was Cooper doing tactics like this to them?

Jesus. That would be terrifying for any family, having to face someone as unhinged as Cooper sneaking around your own house at night. Knowing the place was so big that he could be anywhere.

Speaking of which.

Time to do some mooching around.

I finish my coffee and smoke and head back into the house.

The cotton strands were all intact across the exterior doors. I put them across yesterday evening.

Which means there is another way into the house, and it also means there are other *secret* ways to move *around* the house.

Damn it. I should have asked Huntington.

My bloody head, though. I'm still not right. I keep getting woozy spells, with my mind going blank.

Got to stop drinking and sort my life out.

What was I doing?

I stand in the lobby for a second, trying to remember why I came in here. Then I spot the chair next to the basement door, which reminds me.

I head downstairs into the cellar after checking my wire hanger door release tool is still at the top of the steps.

The basement is nice, though. I like it. It's functional and lived-in, and used, and not a sterile, ancient show home like the rest of the house. Old, worn chairs and the battered desk the head housekeeper used for paperwork. An old sofa wedged against one wall, with a coat rack next to it.

I can picture the staff down here having a break and gossiping about the family. Eating cheese sandwiches they made at home and slurping tea.

That's made me feel hungry.

Mind you, I did puke my breakfast up yesterday.

Which then also means it would be okay to have another today, seeing as I didn't actually fully consume it.

I'll do this first, then go for food.

But where would it be?

Cooper was able to get from the snooker room into the kitchen and then down into the basement without using the main stairs.

Dear God. I am so thick sometimes.

That's why the bloody door in the lobby doesn't have handles and is a bugger to use.

Because the house staff didn't bloody use it.

I find the electrical board, which Cooper used to kill the power last night. He must have put it back on because it was flowing when I woke up.

Right next to it are the levers to increase the flow of gas to the wall lights, which is how he made them come on and go off.

It's like seeing behind the curtain to how the magician does his tricks.

What I don't see, though, is a door or anything leading to another stairwell.

But I do know someone who *will* know where it is.

♦

'There he is!' John says when I walk into the diner.

'Survived another night, then,' Pete adds.

'Survived what?' Derek asks.

'You thick twat. Being at the house on his own,' Geoff says as I nod a greeting and smile at the friendly banter between them.

Which cuts off when Cooper comes out of the toilet.

'That killed the atmosphere,' I say as I come to a stop and watch him. He spots me instantly and stands taller. Which he doesn't need to do, seeing as he's bloody massive anyway. 'Did you need another shit?' I ask and nod to the toilet.

I expect a comment back. Something witty that will hint at the events of the previous night.

But Cooper isn't the bantering sort, and so he doesn't say anything.

He just glares at me like he wants to eat me.

So I glare back.

Because fuck him.

'You off then, Stan?' Maggie says lightly from the counter.

He grunts and walks past me.

'See you tonight, sweetie,' I say as he goes by and spot the filthy murderous look on his face.

Which suggests I shouldn't be taunting him.

But again.

Fuck him.

He goes out, with the farm lads staring from the door back to me, with a mixture of awe and something that suggests I might be the stupidest person they know.

'You seeing Stan tonight, then?' Derek asks.

Well. Maybe not the stupidest.

'You wanna watch him,' Maggie says when I head to the counter. 'He ain't right. Is he, John?'

I look back to see a dark look on John's face and remember there is history between him and Cooper.

'Cooper dated Wendy, then?' I ask quietly when the farm lads go back to eating and chatting.

She shakes her head while making coffee. 'Not dated. She slept with him once when she was drunk, and he gave her a lift home.'

'How drunk was she?'

'Very. Apparently.'

'Did she consent?'

She shrugs with all manner of nuances as I realise me asking that from the clear lines of law and order don't quite marry up to the reality a lot of people live in. Most drunken incidents like that go unreported for lots of reasons.

'Anyway. He didn't take it well when she said it was a one off,' Maggie says with a glance past me to check John isn't listening. 'He got weird,' she mouths, 'like stalking her.

Then John went and had a word, and Cooper turned on him instead. Went on for a long time. Still ain't right now. He don't let grudges go.'

She slides the cappuccino on the counter and takes the money for the coffee and a breakfast. 'You sure you know what you're doing?' she asks.

'I had one yesterday.'

'Not the breakfast, you pillock. Winding Cooper up and being up there on your own.'

'Oh. And no.'

'Didn't think so. Large breakfast?'

'God, no!'

'Kiddies' breaky it is,' she says with a wink and a smile to show she's teasing. 'He said you were out of it.'

'Eh?'

'Stan. He told everyone in here you were pissed and rampaging around the house, and you threw a chair through the kitchen window. And he said he went in to check it, and you'd done a shit on the stairs.'

I snort a laugh. Shaking my head. 'Okay. Yeah. That was me.'

She gives me a puzzled smile as I spot how pretty her brown eyes are.

'You're brave. Or stupid. I'll give you that.'

'Definitely stupid.'

'Go on. I'll bring it over.'

I take a seat and say bye when the farm lads head off to fling hay bales and sheep around or whatever it is they do.

They still seem alright with me, though. Considering they were just told I was in a drunken rage, breaking windows and doing poos on the stairs.

Which means that not only is Cooper disliked, but people don't believe what he says.

Keep that house in my family, and I'll change your life.

But getting rid of Cooper wouldn't solve the inheritance issue.

His half-sister must have made the claim. Killing Cooper wouldn't resolve anything at all.

And I'm not a killer. No way.

A hand touches my shoulder. I look up, expecting to see Tessa from the familiarity of the touch, but it's Maggie, leaning over me with the food.

'Plate's hot.'

'Thanks,' I say as she flumps down on the chair opposite me. 'Do you eat here?' I ask.

'Have you seen the size of my bloody thighs?'

'Padded. Not fat,' I say as she grins at me. 'Ask you a question?'

'No.'

I roll my eyes.

'You sure you didn't have a drink last night?' she asks before I can ask my question and leans closer to peer at me.

'No, I didn't. But I think I'm getting a bug or something.'

'Keep it to yourself, then,' she says and makes a point of sitting back.

'I'll get some meds from the shop after this. So. Listen, the basement.'

'I don't trust meds,' she says over me and gets up. 'I'll make you something.'

'Eh?' I ask as she turns and goes back towards the kitchen, and clamps her hands on her own bum cheeks.

'Stop checking me out!'

'I wasn't!' I say as she turns and winks, and laughs again.

I tuck into the food.

'Cor. Check you out,' she says a few moments later when I'm nearly finished and eyeing the last half a sausage.

'Not having that, then?' she asks and uses my knife to skewer it, and takes a bite, and sits down all at the same time as placing a mug of some steaming concoction next to my plate.

'Yes. I was going to have it. And what...on god's green earth...is that?'

'Medicine.'

'Medicine comes in pills,' I say and lean in to inhale the aroma, and immediately cough with my eyes smarting.

'Poison comes in pills,' she says with a mouthful of my sausage.

'Alright, flat earther.'

'Who says it isn't?' she asks.

'Astronauts. Am I meant to drink this?'

'No. Pour it in your socks.'

'What is it?'

She shrugs. 'Some stuff. Lemon. Ginger. Turmeric. Bit of this. Bit of that. The lads swear by it. Stop being a wuss. You just bloody stood up to psycho Stan.'

I take a sip. Which makes my eyes widen and fill with moisture.

Which, in turn, makes Maggie burst out laughing from my expression.

I egg my reaction and gag for comic effect. It's cool hearing her snort and laugh.

'What did you want to ask anyway?' she says, reminding me that I'd completely forgotten again.

'Basement. Is there another staircase door or something?'

'Yeah. At the end,' she says, as though it should be obvious. 'Didn't they show you around?'

'Can't. Cos of the legal issue. They're not allowed inside.'

'Could have bloody got someone else to show you. Tight as a duck's arse that lot.'

'You volunteering?' I ask.

'You can piss off, am I going in that house,' she adds with a shudder. 'Go to the end room. You can't miss it.'

I frown while thinking about the basement. 'What end room?'

'How many bloody ends have you seen?' she asks. 'Past the wine racks and down there.'

'It's locked up.'

'What is?'

'The bloody door to the end.'

'Locked?' she asks, taking her turn to frown. 'Locked how?'

I shrug and pull a face, making her laugh again. 'With locks.' I let the joke play out for a second, then shake my head. 'But hang on. So, you're saying that door isn't normally locked?'

'I don't even remember there being a door.'

'It's got a padlock on it.'

She carries on shaking her head as the realisation dawns on me.

'Fucking prick,' I mutter.

'Who? Oh. Let me guess. Stan?'

I nod grimly. 'That's how he's sneaking around. He's locked it up with a combination padlock to keep me out of the back stairs.'

She pulls a face, looking instantly concerned. 'Sneaking around? Is he in the house? Jesus. That's dark,' she says with a serious expression.

'Was last night when he cut the power, which was after he put the chair through the window, and before he took a shit on the stairs.' She looks horrified. Wide eyes and her mouth hanging open. 'I thought maybe the shotgun cabinets were in that end room.'

'Lady H won't have them in the house,' Maggie says, still looking horrified; then, she grimaces again. 'Stan has them all at his place.'

'Wonderful,' I say and finish my herbal drink, which is actually very nice. 'This is actually very nice.'

'That'll be the rum.'

'Oh. Am I safe to drive?'

She waggles her hand. 'Yeah. Probably. Maybe have another coffee. Mike, though. I mean. God, that's awful. What you gonna do?'

I shrug. 'My job.'

'You staying there!?'

'I'm kinda, you know, between jobs. And places to live.'

'Bless you,' she says earnestly.

'Be alright. I don't think he's used to people standing up to him.'

'I told you. John did, and he suffered for it for years.'

'No disrespect to John, but I'm not a farmer.'

'Christ, though. I don't know which one's worse. Old Hunty or Stan. You coming up for bingo tonight, while I think of it? Do you good to get out. But going back to the stairs, though. There's a door behind the bar in the room with the snooker table and at the end of the corridor on the top floor. They all link up. And do me a favour and take my number. If it gets really bad, you can always pop round mine for a cuppa or call me if you can't find the doors.'

'I haven't got my phone. It's on charge, and there's no signal anyway.'

'There is,' she says, as though again someone should have told me. 'End of the corridor. Top floor.'

'Fuck's sake,' I say and think back to Tessa sending me a

text and that I could have avoided going there. I give Maggie my number, and she writes hers down and her address on the back of some till roll.

Half hour later, after another coffee to offset the rum in the concoction, I set off back to the house.

15

I go down the spiral stone stairwell to a door at the bottom held locked with a thick bolt.

The door swings open, and I stare into the basement, shaking my head at my own stupidity because it was never locked from the other side.

The clasp holding the padlock wasn't fastened to the frame. It was just made to look like it was.

I found the door behind the bar when I got back to the house. Just as Maggie said I would.

She told me during my second coffee that it was the same as the door in the lobby and hidden from view, as were all the doors to the servants' corridors.

But once I knew it was there, it was just a matter of finding the gap in the shelving and swinging it open.

It was cleverly done, with shelves holding bottles, fixed to the actual door, disguising it completely.

I saw the flour particles on the floor as soon I stepped through, and I also saw the marked difference between the wealth and opulence of the house to the bare walls and floors of the back corridors.

Old, twisted wires hung from the ceiling with bare bulbs. Thick cobwebs high in the corners, and the walls were all scuffed and marked from generations of use.

I follow it down to the basement and shake my head at the fake clasp on the outside of the door.

So this is how Cooper was moving around so easily.

Then I notice something else.

A bigger area at the base of the spiral stone staircase. I go round to the rear and spot an arch leading into a long, dark corridor that seems to go beyond the outside wall of the house.

I use the torch on my phone and follow along. Cold and damp, but not musty or stale. Which means air is circulating through here.

It also stands to reason that a house built in the fifteen or sixteen hundreds would have escape tunnels. The Civil War and all the religious stuff going on meant rich people might need to hide or get away quickly.

It leads to a set of stone steps going up to a modern fitted trapdoor in a stone-built mausoleum that you can see from the house. An ancient, crumbling, gothic-looking thing.

Now I know how Cooper is getting into the house.

I go back through the tunnel and up the stairs to the top floor of the house and come out just where Maggie said I would. At the end of the corridor. It also feeds to another narrow service corridor running to the back of the rooms.

Which is where I find the peep holes.

I get another woozy spell and stumble against the wall, which causes a second's worth of light to flit across my eye.

For an instant, I think I'm having a stroke and seeing bright dots. Then I realise it's a hole, and I'm staring into the room on the other side.

'Dirty fuckers,' I murmur and go back to the door and out into the main hallway, and into the first guestroom, but finding the hole in the wall is hard, even knowing roughly where it is. The wallpaper is heavily patterned, and the walls hold mirrors and shelves.

I eventually find it.

A tiny dot that nobody would ever see.

Then I go back into the service corridor and work along.

Every room has a peep hole.

Every bedroom.

Every bathroom.

Some have more than one.

So the viewer can see the bathtubs.

And the beds.

I find two sets looking into my room. One near the bed. One near the end, where someone would get changed. I use the torch on my phone to see tiny particles of flour on the wall either side of the peep holes.

Meaning Cooper stood here last night, watching me, with his hands pressed to the walls.

It was pitch dark, though. Unless he was using night vision goggles. You can get them quite cheap now.

I step away and come to a stop with the revulsion magnifying by the factor of many from the sight of the plain white toilet roll tissue on the ground all bunched up.

I crouch next to it and pick it up by the corner to see something has made it stiff and crusty. I was a detective long enough to know what it is without needing a forensic analysis.

Cooper masturbated.

Which is a worrying escalation.

It means he's not motivated just by money from the prospect of the inheritance.

Being a voyeur is turning him on.

If I was still a cop, there would now be enough grounds to arrest him. Being a voyeur for sexual gratification is a criminal offence.

He's also left forensic evidence behind.

But it wouldn't be enough to get him remanded.

He'd get arrested, but he would get bailed pending a court date for a trial.

Which could be months. Sometimes years.

They might put bail conditions on him not to come to this house, but it's quite evident Cooper wouldn't adhere to those rules.

The police would, however, remove all the shotguns and firearms from his cottage. Anyone arrested and released on bail has their firearms seized.

That certainly reduces the risk of Cooper going nuts with a shotgun.

But then again. Someone like Cooper isn't likely to declare every firearm they have.

Firearms laws in the countryside used to be loose a few years ago. Which meant people traded and gathered guns without the authorities ever knowing. Who is to say the Cooper family declared them all when the legislation came in?

Many didn't.

I leave the tissue in situ and work along, checking the peep holes and feeling more disgust when I realise even the servants' rooms at the end have them.

That's awful.

Imagine being forced to work and live here for a pittance of a salary, knowing the landed gentry could peep on you whenever they wanted.

I reach the end of the back corridor to see an old chest

of drawers beneath a dusty laminated sign pinned to the wall saying *here*.

'Here what?' I ask, not understanding it.

Then two things happen.

I look around to see what *here* means and spot the corner of a bit of paper poking out from behind the chest of drawers.

I pull it out to see spidery handwriting on one side. A few sentences, but not in any language I can understand. It's a western *Latin* alphabet, but some of the letters have accents over the top or underneath.

At which point, my phone buzzes from messages coming into my inbox from the one bar of signal I now have.

I read the first one from a number that seems familiar with three 4s.

Maggie.

Her number had three 4s in a row. I smile before I even open it. Feeling pleased that she messaged me.

> Cheking ur alive?? Did u find the coridors?

I save her number and send a reply.

> No, I'm dead from that drink you made me 😂

> Yeah, I did. Cheers!

> Oh! That's what "here" means. I just got it!

I tell myself I'm a silly twat for not realising what the sign meant and swipe to read the next message as a photo slowly loads of Tessa in tight yoga bottoms and a very tight, low-cut sports top. Posing at an angle while taking a selfie in a full-length mirror.

> TESSA
>
> Hey! Guy's opinion. Is this too much? I'd wear it in London for a run, but here??? Waddya reckon? Don't wanna give any farmers a heart attack 😊 😉

Jesus. She looks good. I swipe to the next message, with another picture loading. This time showing Tessa smiling into the camera while outside running. No words. Nothing said.

Then another picture message comes through.

Tessa at home, looking stunning, with a light sheen of sweat from the run.

> TESSA
>
> I'm so ugly when I sweat. 😢

Then the next one showing her pouting.

> TESSA
>
> Stop sulking! Are you cross about the other night? It was
>
> a guy I used to work with. He just split from his HUSBAND!!!

That guy was gay? Oh. That changes things, which I immediately forget about when the next picture comes through. This one taken in the bedroom. Her top clearly off, and showing the top of her chest, with a suggestive smile and wink.

> **TESSA**
>
> Gonna be so funny when all these pics come through!
>
> Your face will go soooooooo red hahahaha! 😈

'Fuck,' I mouth and rest against the chest of drawers, staring at her shoulders and the shape of her neck.

At which point the phone beeps again.

With another picture.

Tessa having a bath. The view taken from her head, looking down. Bubbles cover her boobs and her groin, but her stomach and legs are clear.

> **TESSA**
>
> Feeling a bit lonely....

I swallow and blink, and check the times and dates to see these messages were all sent this morning.

Then my phone beeps again from another incoming text.

> **MAGGIE**
>
> Ur noT dead if u texin back! 😂😂

Maggie again. I smile and think to reply as another picture comes in from Tessa, making me swipe quickly to see her sitting on the edge of the bath, wrapped in a clinging and also very thin, wet towel while taking a selfie in a full-length mirror.

> **TESSA**
>
> Fancy dinner tonight? 7? Won't cancel this time. Promise! 😊

Then another text.

> **MAGGIE**
>
> U coming to bingo? Top prize 2nite is a tray of eggs 🥚😋🔍 EGGS! Who don't luv eggs??? 😋 if u win i make u an omlet

Two invites in two years, and they're both on the same night.

But as Maggie said, it would do me good to get out.

As to which one, though?

That's a no brainer.

Because when a woman like that comes into your life, you don't hesitate.

16

I pull up outside the cottage just before seven. I don't have flowers this time. I didn't want to jinx it.

I get out and head through the garden gate and remember seeing Tessa and that guy in her front room and how it made me feel.

The front door opens before I knock on it, and she's right there. Giving me a huge smile while also looking surprised.

'Didn't think you'd actually come!'

'I want those eggs.'

Maggie laughs in that way she does. Unashamed and loud. She's put some make-up on. She looks lovely in jeans and a shirt.

She grabs a jacket and closes the door. I catch a glimpse of her front room. It looks cosy, with a log burner.

I step ahead to open the passenger door to the Landy. She pulls a comical, impressed face and gives me a look. 'No one ever opened a door for me before.'

I walk around the front of the Landy and think about *the door test* from the movie A Bronx Tale, where Chaz

Palminteri gives advice to a younger man taking a woman out on a first date. He tells the young man to open the car door for her, and if she doesn't lean over to open his door as he walks around, then she's selfish.

It's a hard line to take, but then it was a hard movie about gangsters.

I reach the front and make the turn as my door is shoved open from Maggie leaning across.

'What's that grin for?' she asks as I get in.

'You ever seen A Bronx Tale?'

'No. What's that?'

'Movie.'

'Is it old? Like black and white from when you were a teenager.'

'I'm not that old,' I say as she grins, and I pull out.

'Where you going? Community centre is that way,' she says and thumbs behind her.

I laugh at the faces she pulls. It's easy to laugh with her. I slow and start to reverse into the drive of another cottage.

'*No-no-no!* Not here. That's Angry Alice's house. She goes mental.'

Too late. The cottage slams open, and a thin, old lady comes steaming out.

'Can't you bloody read?' she shouts.

'Oh, god! I said don't turn!' Maggie says with a groan as I wind my window down, and she slides down the seat as though to hide.

'Hi! I'm so sorry. I didn't see the sign until it was too late.'

'Right. Well,' Angry Alice says, coming to a stop. 'Just bloody remember it next time.'

'Of course. It's very nice to meet you, though. Your

garden is beautiful. What are those?' I ask, nodding at a big cluster of pretty, pink flowers.

'What, them? They're my Japanese anemones. Cos of the weather, isn't it?'

'Is that climate change, then?' I ask.

'No! Seasons just get wonky sometimes, don't they? Bloody climate change. Folk think too much of themselves.'

I get what she means. It's a common view that humans assume they are the sole contributors to climate change, whereas it might just be the fluctuations of the planet.

'It's beautiful, though. I don't know anything about flowers. Are those roses? I think those are the only ones I know.'

'Aye. Roses over there. They're blooming late an' all.'

'Oh, wow, look at all those bees.'

'From the hives, ain't they?'

'Hives?'

'She's got beehives in her back field,' Maggie says next to me.

'Who's that? Is that Maggie?'

'Hello, Alice!' Maggie says, leaning over to offer a wave.

'You should bloody know I don't have no turning!'

'She did tell me. It was my fault entirely,' I say, holding my hands up, then catching a whiff, and leaning out the window to inhale the aroma. 'What is that? Oh, my god. Can you smell that?' I ask Maggie as she leans over me to sniff out the window.

'You making apple pies, Alice? Alice makes the best apple pies.'

'My mouth is actually watering.'

'She puts honey in them from her beehives.'

'Stuff bingo. Can we just stay here?'

'You like that smell, do you?' Alice asks, giving me a hint

of a smile in a way that makes Maggie blink. 'Where you from, then?'

'London.'

'What you wanna live there for?'

'I was born there, and I worked there.'

'Mike was a police officer, Alice. He's staying up at Huntington.'

Alice's face darkens instantly. 'That bloody lot. None of my beeswax, but I heard they had troubles. Bloody good. I don't wish bad on anyone, but they're fuckers.'

'Jesus,' I say at the strong language.

'Mike's having to stay there on his own,' Maggie explains.

'On his own? On your own? Well. You wouldn't catch me in that house on my own. I won't even go inside when they do the summer fete. You going to bingo, then?'

'We are. Are you coming? I can put you in the boot?'

'Get off with you!' she says with a toothy grin. 'And no bloody turning!'

'I will turn. Every day until I get an apple pie.'

'You sod!' she says with another grin. 'I'll throw one at you!' she shouts as I drive off and wave out the window.

'Oh, my god,' Maggie says, shaking her head at me. 'She bloody loves you! Alice literally hates everyone. Best pies ever, though. Way better than mine.'

'Should do a taste test.'

'Alright!' she says with another laugh. 'She'd probably give you one if you go back and turn in her drive again.'

'I will.'

'Look at you. Coming up here and charming all the singles.'

'You single, then?'

'No. I asked my husband could look after our five kids

while I played bingo with a weird ex-copper who can't handle–'

'Don't say it!'

'Who can't handle a normal breakfast!'

'They're not normal!'

We pull up a few minutes later outside a square brick building, which, I'm told, doubles as the community centre and the cricket club, and the football, bridge, bingo, book group clubs, and yoga every other Tuesday.

Seeing the yoga sign on the way in makes me think of Tessa.

Who is insanely hot.

And very clearly a narcissist.

'Still can't believe you came,' Maggie says, giving me another smile that reaches her brown eyes. 'It's not much, though. I mean. You're probably used to posh places in London and all that.'

'You should see me in a ballgown.'

I love it when Maggie laughs. I think it's the nicest sound I've ever heard.

'There he is!' John calls from a table of the farm lads when we walk into the main room. It's busier than I was expecting, with a lot of big men in soft cotton, checked shirts holding pint glasses of golden ale. Women too, in jeans and boots, and shirts. Wooden tables and wooden chairs. A trophy cabinet on one wall. A small, low stage, where another guy is setting up the bingo machine and tapping a microphone that gives a big squeal, making everyone shout good-natured abuse.

'Alright, Mike!' John says, crushing my hand as he gets up. 'Mags said you might be coming. Saved you a seat.'

'Thank you.'

'Alright, Mike,' Pete says, shaking my hand. Then Geoff.

'Do you have bingo in London, then?' Derek asks.

'No, mate. Never been invented there.'

'What really? You should take it back and make a fortune.'

'Thick twat,' John says, rolling his eyes. 'Pint, Mike?'

'I'm driving. I'll get a coke. What you having?'

'They only do one beer here,' Maggie says as I spot her grin stretching from ear to ear. She nods for me to follow and checks behind a couple of times as though still not sure I won't run off. 'Stop looking at my bum!' she says the next time to make a joke of it.

'Padded.'

'Not fat!' she says.

'Ah. You must be that copper, then?' another older, farmer type man says.

'You say hello. I'll get the drinks,' Maggie says.

'Hang on. Money,' I say, pulling a note from my pocket.

'S'fine!'

She heads off as my hand gets gripped and crushed, and dwarfed by lots of men wearing checked shirts and clutching beers and a few of the women too.

'Make sure he bloody pays you,' one of them tells me.

'Who?' I ask, not getting what she means.

'Lord Charlie!' another man says.

'They're shits for that,' another guy says, with a shake of his head. 'Can't get a penny out of them.'

'Who's that?' Maggie asks, bringing me a big glass of coke over.

'Huntingtons,' the man says.

'Tighter than a duck's arse,' Maggie says. 'They want their bloody rent on the dot, though.'

That sets everyone off as I figure that most of the village live in places owned by the Huntington estate.

'What's that anyway?' the man asks, nodding at my drink.

'Coke. I'm driving.'

'We're all bloody driving!' someone says, holding a beer as the others laugh. 'Eh, mind though. He's a rozzer. Might breath test us.'

I brace myself for the comments and questions as I look at the ruddy faces around me.

Except that doesn't happen.

'Maggie told us all to wind our necks in,' the first older man says as he pats my shoulder with a big hand. 'Good effort, though. He had that coming. Fucking pervert. Here's to you.'

'Here's to you, Mike,' the others chorus and take a drink, and nod, and pat my arm or back. Then it's done. Over. No questions. No awkwardness. I spot Maggie behind the bar pulling pints and can't help but feel deeply touched at the thoughtfulness of her actions.

Then I realise she's actually behind the bar pulling pints, and something about it makes me laugh.

'You work here?'

'No! We all volunteer. Just thought I'd jump in and get the drinks out before the bingo starts. Go and sit down with the lads. Be right over. Here, take my drink. Sure you don't want a beer?'

Of course I want a beer.

I want more than beer.

I want vodka.

'It's fine,' I say and take a tray of drinks back to the table, with Derek rushing to take two off while the other men berate him.

'Wait till he puts it down, you bloody pillock,' Geoff says.

'I'm only trying to help!' Derek says.

'We been through this,' Pete tells him. 'You have to apply force to hold the tray, so when you take the drinks off, the tray shoots up unless it's balanced.'

'Yeah. No. I know,' Derek says, who clearly doesn't know. 'That's what I was doing.'

'You took the drinks off the tray!' Geoff says.

'Yeah! To counterweigh the thingy.'

'Thick twat,' John groans, taking his beer from the tray now slid onto the table. 'Forgive Derek. A bloody sheep's got more common sense than him. And sheep ain't got no common sense at all.'

'They're thick as shit,' Pete tells me. 'Cheers, though.'

The others do the same. Offering cheers and taking sips. 'Strong, though,' John says to me, with a nod at Derek. 'Cor. Bloody hell.'

'Who is? Derek?'

'What is?' Derek asks.

'You is. Mind your own,' John tells him.

'One of my ewes got stuck in a ditch,' Pete tells me over the table.

'Was it alright?' I ask.

'Told you. They're thick as shit. Happens all the time. Anyway. So I called the lads up and said come and give me a hand, and Derek gets there first, don't he? And he gets in and puts the bloody thing over his shoulder and walks up the bank with it. She was what? One twenty?'

'Hundred and twenty pounds?' I ask, thinking that's about eight stone, which is impressive.

'Kilos,' John says.

'Are you being serious? That's like eighteen stone,' I say in awe and look again at Derek's short and stocky frame.

'What is?' Maggie asks, coming over to place a hand on my shoulder as she sits down and takes her drink.

'Telling me how Derek picked a big sheep up,' I explain.

'Couldn't bloody spell it, though,' she says as they burst out laughing, and she reaches over to smack Derek's arm and ruffle his hair. 'He's a good lad, though. Hard worker.'

'He is a hard worker,' John says as they lift their glasses to toast Derek, who grins widely at the attention and praise.

'He ain't your normal type, though, Mags,' John says as the lads laugh, and Maggie pulls a warning face. '*I kissed a girl!*'

'*And she liked it!*' the others join in singing the famous line.

'I said don't bloody tell him!' she says, throwing place mats at them. 'So embarrassing.'

'What is?'

'I had a phase,' she says, giving me a sheepish look. 'Just shush!' she tells the others.

'With a woman?' I ask, then shrug. 'It's really normal. Don't worry about it.'

'See! From the city. Not like you, close-minded twats,' she tells the others.

'*Alright! Settle down, you noisy lot!*' the host calls through the microphone, instantly prompting another barrage of abuse, which he clearly enjoys. '*Behave! We've got the law in here with us. Copper from London. Everyone, say hello Mike!*'

'HELLO MIKE!'

'Ex-copper!' Maggie calls after they chorus the greeting.

'Once a copper, always a copper!' someone else shouts.

'Best hide them bloody plants you growing, then!'

someone else shouts at the first guy as the place erupts in laughter and jeers.

'I ain't got no plants,' the man tells me quickly. 'I ain't!'

'You smoked it all then, Gilbert?' John asks.

'You lot can piss off. We all bloody smoked it,' Gilbert says, with a touch of panic while shooting me worried looks.

'You snitch!'

'Grass!'

'Don't tell him that!'

I can't help but laugh at the way they do it and can sense the lifetimes of familiarity these people have with each other. 'It's fine, mate,' I mouth to Gilbert, who grins with relief and lifts his drink to toast me.

'You ever want any, just let me know,' he says, which just sets them off again, with banter about selling drugs to coppers.

Until the host taps his microphone, and the bingo gets underway.

'Don't worry, Mike. I'll show you how it's done,' Derek says earnestly.

'He knows!' Maggie says. 'Don't you?'

'I mean. I know what it is, but I've never played it.'

'One and eight. Eighteen!'

'We ain't bloody ready!' John says as they scrabble to get the wipe clean playing cards and marker pens.

'All the twos. Twenty-two!'

'Fuck's sake. What was the first one?' Geoff asks.

'Er, this one,' Pete says, leaning over to flick his card away.

'On its own. Number 6!'

Geoff scrabbles for his card while Pete moves his chair; then, John flicks Geoff's card again when he turns to pull his chair back.

It takes me back to my first few years in the police. How we'd piss around on shift and do things like that.

'You missed eight,' Maggie says, leaning over me to mark my card.

'Cheating!' John shouts. 'Maggie's cheating!'

'I'm helping him!'

'Fuck off!' Geoff says when Pete flicks his card away again.

'Two fat ladies. Eighty-eight!'

'Body shaming!' Pete yells.

'Fatist!' Geoff calls.

'Idiots,' the host says to the laughter going around the room. *'On its own, number 3!'*

'Line!' Maggie yells, blotting my card, then holding it up.

'That's his!' John says.

'Shut up,' Maggie says as the others in the room sip drinks and look over.

'Adjudicator, please,' the host says.

I look around to see who the adjudicator is, then blink back to Maggie looking at the card with a serious expression.

'Yeah, it's fine,' she says.

'Are you the adjudicator?' I ask with a laugh. She grins and nods.

'Maggie's the everything in this village,' John says.

'What flavour do you want?' Maggie asks.

'Flavour?'

'You've won a bag of crisps.'

'Er...' I say, momentarily stumped at this news.

'So, we got cheese and onion. Ready salted. Salt and vinegar, which you should get cos they're my favourite. And prawn cocktail.'

'Prawn cocktail, then,' I say and earn my first laughs as she swipes my arm, and a bag of prawn cocktail crisps gets thrown over.

'I'm still eating them,' she says as she opens the bag on the table. 'Gotta stay padded.'

'Not fat,' I say as the host carries on, which is way too fast for anyone to keep up, which, I work out, he does on purpose to provoke the shenanigans.

But then I figure these are hard-working people, putting in long days all year round, and I doubt very much that farmers and farm hands get four weeks paid leave every year and sick pay.

They can bloody drink, though.

The lads put pints down their necks, with forays to the bar to bring back trays holding full glasses. Which Derek tries to lift off each and every time.

They keep asking if I want a beer.

'One won't hurt, will it?' John says.

He's right.

One wouldn't hurt.

But I wouldn't stop at one.

So I stick to coke.

Maggie, however, does not and knocks the gin and tonics back, and eats my crisps and then the ones that John wins from the next line. And then comes back with more crisps that get opened up on the table for everyone to pick and munch on. And nuts. And pork scratchings.

I've never seen people eat like they do.

'HOUSE!' Gilbert yells after a while, and I can't help but smile at the look of joy on his face at winning and how he almost looks nervous when Maggie goes over to check his card.

'Yep. He's won.'

At which point, I blink from Gilbert being close to tears and rushing over to the bar to bring back his big tray of eggs.

Mind you, though. It's a bloody big tray of eggs. And they're clearly from a local farm, with feathers stuck to them.

I get another round in for my table as the lights go down a little bit and music comes through the speakers.

'...and she was like *I'll throw a pie at you!* But she loved him!'

I sit down and listen to Maggie retelling the Alice story while laughing at me and reaching over to take her drink, with her hand on my leg. But it's natural and organic, and not forced, or weird.

'You coming for a smoke?' she asks, showing me she's rolled two.

'Give it up, Mags,' John says, shaking his head as the whole table and pretty much the whole room, including John, all traipse outside for a smoke. Some with pipes. A few with cigars. A few people vaping. I gather it's a tradition from how it's done. Gilbert even comes out, holding his tray of eggs aloft like he's won a big trophy.

'But seriously, though. I thought it was legal now,' he says, as though we're midway through a conversation.

'What is?' I ask. 'Winning eggs?'

'Weed!' he says as Maggie snorts her drink.

'Winning eggs. Bloody idiot. I got G and T down me now.'

'Shouldn't be so fat, then,' John tells her.

'But is it, though?' Gilbert asks me.

'No, mate, it's not.'

'No. But it is,' Gilbert says. 'I read it on Reddit. So anyway. Did you ever shoot anyone?'

'Gil! He was a cop, not a soldier,' Maggie says as the others groan and jeer at Gilbert.

'I did actually,' I say to a stunned reaction from them all. 'I was on the tac-teams. The firearms units.'

'Oh, my god. You actually bust a cap in someone,' Gilbert says and gets walloped on his arm by Maggie.

'No. In his chest. Two rounds.'

'Fuck. So cool,' Gilbert says in awe. 'Did he die?'

'Gil!' Maggie says. 'I'm so sorry, Mike.'

'No, he survived. You can take a few rounds and live actually. It's not like the movies.'

Gilbert nods, clearly hooked. 'So, like, did you ever go undercover and, like, pretend to be a gangster or some shit like that?'

I laugh and shake my head. 'I didn't do that. I did try and apply for it. I think every cop thinks about it, but it's so hard to do.'

'Why? You just gotta be a narc!' Gilbert says, a young man full of energy.

'Why's it so hard?' John asks.

'Mindset,' I say. 'So, they have levels. A test purchaser is a low level. They go into an area and buy drugs so the police can take out a drug network, and even that is hard. The training is brutal. They teach them to be really passive and like invisible. People involved in drugs are paranoid about undercover cops, and the higher you go or deeper, or whatever, and you've got to actually believe who you're pretending to be. And that's way too complicated for me. Jesus. I struggle remembering my own name.'

'What if someone offers them drugs?' Pete asks as they laugh.

'They've got to try and avoid it, but if it's essential for

the case? They'll do it. They just need to report it as soon as they can to their handler.'

'I could do that!' Gilbert says to more laughs. 'I'm gonna be a test purchasing man.'

'You'll do well, mate,' I say, enjoying the banter and chat.

'Not for you, though?' Pete asks.

'No. I tried. I'm too chopsy,' I say, getting more laughs, 'and everyone says I look like a copper.'

'Yeah. You do,' Maggie says. 'Even now, actually.'

'Yo. But hook me up, though,' Gilbert says, nodding earnestly, as though I still have connections or contacts, and without realising just how disgraced I am.

'Too bloody cold for me,' Pete says with a shiver as they all start heading back in.

'Is it alright for you, then?' Maggie asks as we hang back to let the others go first.

'Yeah! It's really nice.'

'I thought you might be like, you know, *this is a bit shit,*' she says with a mock deep voice.

'No! It's fine. I like it.'

She nods and smiles, but I can see the questions forming in her eyes. She doesn't hide her emotions. 'I thought you and that fancy woman might be, you know...'

'Who?'

'Her,' she says. 'With the eyes and the boobs, and all that.'

'Tessa? From the café? No. I only met her twice.'

'She went back to yours, though, didn't she? Like. None of my beeswax, but Stan told everyone he saw her in the big house, and you were like, I dunno, like walking hand in hand. I mean. Nothing to do with me.'

'Yeah. No. I hardly know her. We didn't hold hands. I

think she looped her arm in mine, but I think she's just a touchy person. Tactile or whatever. She worked in fashion in the city.'

Maggie blinks at that. 'And there's me in my little diner.'

'Eh? No! Don't say it like that.'

'But she's proper hot, though. Do you like her?'

'No.'

I go to say that Tessa invited me for dinner, but I chose to go to bingo with Maggie, but it'll sound churlish or weird, so I stop myself. 'She's very attractive, but no. Not my cup of tea.'

'What's your cup of tea, then?' she asks, with that glint stealing back into her eyes. Maggie's pretty too. Brown hair, and a touch of olive to her skin. Her smile softens as she detects my scrutiny, and the moment hangs charged in the air.

At which point, my normal luck returns because her smile fades as she looks past me. Prompting me to turn and see Tessa getting out of her car.

'She's never been here before,' Maggie says.

'I was texting and calling you!' Tessa says, walking right up to me. 'And I went to the house.'

'I came here,' I say and pull my phone out to see it's on silent, with missed calls and messages.

'Obviously,' Tessa says, flicking her gaze from me to Maggie. 'So you came here instead of dinner with me?' she asks as if such a thing is unthinkable.

'Did you want me for something?' I ask politely as Tessa looks at Maggie again as though silently telling her to fuck off.

'I'll go in,' Maggie says, stubbing her smoke out while Tessa looks on in disgust.

'Yes. I did. I caught that Cooper man spying on me,'

Tessa says, making Maggie falter halfway back through the door. 'Excuse me! Private,' Tessa snaps, giving her a glare.

'I'll be right in,' I tell Maggie. She nods and goes inside.

'He was outside my place,' Tessa says before I can speak. 'I fucking saw him. I was waiting for you, obviously, like an idiot, and he was in my garden!'

'Okay.'

'Okay? It's not okay! He was wanking himself off!'

'What the fuck? Did you see that?'

'Yes!'

'Right. Okay. Yeah, that's enough for a remand,' I say and start pulling my phone out.

'What you doing?'

'Calling the police.'

She blinks once. 'I mean. I didn't actually see him wanking.'

'You said you did,' I say while holding my phone.

'I mean. It was obvious, though.'

'How? How was it obvious?'

'Cos of the tissue I found when I went outside with the bloody poker from the fire.'

'Where is it? Did you preserve it? That'll have his DNA on it.'

She grimaces. 'Shit. No. Damn. Silly Tessa! I put it on the fire.'

'Why would you do that? Have you never seen a cop movie or TV show?'

'It was disgusting and like right there, on the road.'

'Wait. What? On the road?'

'Yes!'

'You said he was in your garden.'

'Yes! On the road. In my garden.'

'The road doesn't go into your garden, Tessa. Was he inside your perimeter or on the road?'

'Like. On the road, but he was literally staring at me. And the tissue was right there!'

I exhale long and slow and slide my phone back into my pocket because finding forensic evidence on a public road or highway of that nature is circumstantial evidence at best. Any suspect would argue they dropped it while passing and thereby negate the prosecution.

Which also means there would be insufficient evidence to charge, which then means he wouldn't get remanded.

'Alright,' I say to Tessa. 'He did it at mine too. Not mine. At the house. In a secret corridor with peep holes into every room.'

'Jesus,' she says, looking horrified. 'That isn't right, Mike. He's sick and twisted. I was researching for my book, right? And I spoke to this woman who wouldn't go on the record, but she said Cooper has been a *massive* problem for the Huntingtons for a long time. Like trying to blackmail them into paying him more and poisoning their dogs and livestock and...'

'Fuck.'

'That's what I'm saying. He's dangerous! He's literally going to rape and murder someone any day now. Probably me! He's obviously got a fetish for me. Which you clearly don't share,' she says as Maggie comes back out through the door with my jacket.

'It's cold,' she says, handing it over.

'Aw, cute,' Tessa says with a sneer. 'But listen. I know we swapped pictures and all that, Mike, but this is a fucking problem.'

'We didn't swap pictures! I didn't send any,' I say as

Maggie's face grows taut, and she walks back inside. 'Fuck's sake! What did you say that for?'

'Okay, Mr Angry.'

'I'm not angry, Tessa. I didn't send you pictures.'

'Bit vocal there, Mike,' she says in a triggered voice while holding her hands up as though to plead for calm. 'Is this because you saw me with Jason?'

'Jason?'

'My gay friend! I saw you driving past.'

'I'm not cross at that. Or anything.'

'Okay. Calm down, please. You were happy enough to wank off to my pictures, though.'

'I didn't wan–! I didn't do anything to your pictures! Don't send them to me.'

'Why. Are you gay?'

'Someone doesn't find you attractive, so they must be gay?'

'You bloody do find me attractive,' she scoffs. 'Admit it. Admit you stared at those pictures.'

'I'm going inside.'

'Yeah. I'm right. And you chose that café woman over me?'

'Yep.'

'Your loss, but get your eyes checked. And what you going to do about Cooper?'

'Why have I got to do anything?'

'You're an officer! Didn't you take an oath?'

'I *was* a cop. I'm not now. Bye, Tessa.'

'No, wait!' she says as I detect her tone softening. 'Mike, please. Just hang on. Okay. I'm sorry. I misread the situation about us and was just flirting and coming on too strong. Bad Tessa! But I get like that when I really like someone. You know. When I *like, like* someone. I thought we had something,' she looks instantly sad and lost, and vulnerable, with those big, blue eyes staring up at me.

'I don't go near narcissists.'

She shrugs and pouts a little, and every receptor in my brain lights up at the signals she's giving me. Trying to look vulnerable and small to the manly protector. 'What about Cooper, though?' she asks quietly. 'I'm really scared, Mike.'

'Do you think he knows about your book?' I ask as she looks blank for a split second.

'God. Yeah. He probably does. Oh, my god. He's targeting me.'

'I forgot,' I say and reach to my back pocket for the folded paper I found in the secret corridor, then tut when I remember it's in my other jeans. 'I found a letter hidden in that corridor. It's not in English, though. I think it might be Latvian.'

'And you didn't tell me?'

'I found it when you sent those pictures.'

'So you did bloody look at them, then.'

'No! I mean. I glanced.'

'Glanced,' she says with a knowing smile. 'Should have come to dinner. You would have done more than glanced. Alright, love? Off home, are you?' she says as I turn to see Maggie in the door, with her coat on.

'Night,' she says and walks off.

'Maggie! I'll drive you!'

'Can walk.'

Maggie. I'll drive you,' Tessa mimics in a quiet voice dripping with acid. 'Jesus, Mike. Have you got a weird thing for slightly fat women? She is way beneath you.'

'Fuck you,' I snap and stride off.

'You will soon,' she calls. 'Call me tomorrow! I'll come round so we can talk about that letter!'

I get into the Landy and pull out onto the road to see Maggie walking along, and slow down next to her.

'I'm fine,' she calls in a forced cheery voice.

'Maggie, please. Let me drive you.'

'I've had too much to drink. I need to walk.'

I pull the Landy over and drop out to rush after her. Reaching her side as Tessa drives past with a toot of her horn.

'I'll be fine,' Maggie says a second or so later. 'It's not the city... I've been walking here since I was born...'

I stay at her side. 'I'm sorry about that with Tessa.'

She shrugs, and we walk on in silence for a bit. 'Up to you who you share pictures with.'

'I didn't send any.'

'Blokes don't, though, do they? They just want nudey pics so they can jerk off.'

'I didn't ask her to send any. And they weren't naked. I mean. Like. She was in the bath but... No! Hang on. You couldn't see anything.'

'Looked, though, yeah?'

'Okay. Please stop,' I say as she stops and looks at me, and I feel shitty and horrible for the pain in her eyes. 'I'm sorry. I am. But I don't know Tessa. She came back to the house once, and then she invited me to dinner the other night, but she cancelled, and that was that.'

'So you started being nice to me instead to get back at her.'

'No,' I say honestly. 'You just started force feeding me giant breakfasts and throwing tea towels in my face.'

She smiles at that, and I sense the flash of an urge inside of her wanting to banter and joke, but she swallows it down, which only makes me feel shittier.

'Then today, she sent me the pictures and invited me for dinner again.'

'To hers?'

'Yes.'

'When?'

'Tonight.'

'Tonight? Like, tonight, tonight?'

'Yes.'

'And you went to bingo instead? Are you blind?'

'No, I'm not. And no, I didn't go to bingo instead. I wanted to see you, and the bingo was just the place we went to.'

She looks at me again, like I'm the most stupidest person she ever met. 'She's so pretty. And thin. And pretty.'

'She's not. She's a narcissist.'

'What's that?'

'You never heard of narcissism?'

'I mean. Like. Yeah, it's always online and on the telly, but I don't really know what it means.'

'So. It's when someone has a really high sense of their own importance, like to the point of being obsessed with themselves, and they demand attention all the time, and they'll be lovely and amazing to get that attention, but it's not real. They don't care. They can't care. Only about themselves. And if you take the attention away, they get really shitty and lash out. Which is what she's doing now.'

'How do you know she's like that? Is that from being a copper.'

'And life. I'm just good at reading people.'

'What do you read about me?' she asks.

'That you're not a narcissist. You're kind and thoughtful, and I love it when you laugh and the way your eyes crinkle up when you smile.'

'I'm not hot like she is, though.'

'That's subjective. I think you are.'

'Yeah. I mean. Not being big-headed, but I know my face is pretty. I get attention from guys, but my arse and belly, and thighs, though...'

'Padded,' I say as she smiles and frowns up at me.

'Did you sleep with her?'

'No.'

'Did you kiss her?'

'No.'

She stays close. Looking up at me with a faint smile. 'Did you want to kiss her?'

'I think I've been very lonely for a long time, and she paid me attention, and it was nice, so maybe like for a minute, I thought–'

'Just say no.'

'No.'

The smile grows a little wider. 'Do you want to kiss me?'

I nod as the air charges, and she holds her eyes on mine, then body-bumps me away, and gives me a cross-eyed look. 'Best woo me, then,' she says with a laugh.

We walk on, with her hand finding mine. The bad air fading away.

'Do you wanna walk back to the car?' she asks.

'I don't mind walking. But I can get it if you want to drive.'

'I'm alright,' she says and holds my hand. 'So. Like. I'll say it once. Okay?'

I nod. Figuring I know what's coming.

'I don't want to get dragged into some weird thing between you and that Tessa woman.'

'Okay. There isn't, but I totally get it. Um, so, can I ask, though? You talk like you don't know her.'

'I told you. I don't know her.'

'She's been here for months.'

'She hasn't.'

'Maybe she just didn't go into the diner. Okay. So. She locked onto me cos I'm working at the house, right? And she thinks two women went missing. That's why she's up here. To research that.'

'Nobody's gone missing,' Maggie says. 'Who?'

'Vietnamese woman and a woman from Latvia.'

'Eh? No! Bugger off, have they. From where?'

'From the house.'

'When?!'

'One last year, and one the year before that.'

She pauses to frown. 'Is that why you was asking me about the August cleaning rota thingy?'

'I thought maybe those women were brought in to keep the house clean or something like that. And I found a letter upstairs written in another language.'

'What language?'

'I dunno. I haven't got internet at the house, so I can't google it. Maybe Latvian, though?'

'Where was it?'

'Behind the drawers at the end of that pervert sneaky corridor, where is says *here*.'

'That's been there for like forever. Could be anything. They get loads of guests from all over the world staying. Or one of the kiddies could have been doing like French homework or something.'

'It wasn't French. But I know what you mean. Yeah, maybe. So you never heard of an Asian or Eastern European working there?'

'We had loads of Eastern Europeans before Brexit, but

that was years ago. Every farm had them, and we had some working in the café. Really hard workers.'

'None at the house?'

'Nope. Never heard of any. And they'd come down, wouldn't they? Everyone does. Like to the shop or the café. You did it. So you working on a case with her then?'

'No,' I say quickly. 'I actually don't think she's right. I can't see it. Latvia is a modern country, and people have phones, and like you said, the village isn't far. A girl working there, feeling unsafe would report it or tell someone. I mean, the Vietnamese woman might have been trafficked. They go missing all the time. It's shocking how bad that is, but I can't see two going missing a year apart and nobody noticing it.'

'I would say something smart, but I'm really drunk,' she says, making me grin. 'Nah, though. The Huntingtons are wankers, but they don't kill women.'

'What about Cooper?'

'Oh,' she says and comes to a stop with a grimace. 'God. But no, though. Would he?'

I tell her about the problems I've been having and the tissue I found, and the inheritance issue going on.

'Mike. That's serious!' she says when I finish. 'Don't stay there.'

'I haven't got anywhere to go.'

'Come to mine! Jesus. You can't, Mike. That's not safe. What if he knifes you in your sleep or something?'

'Okay. Listen, joking aside.'

'I'm not joking! He said to John years ago. He said he'd break in and knife him.'

I take that in as we come to a stop outside her cottage. 'But obviously he didn't, though.'

'Well. No. But John backed right off.'

'But he stayed with Wendy? Even though that was Cooper's point of obsession?'

Maggie nods, then shrugs as I figure right now isn't the time to discuss the finer points. 'Stay at mine,' she urges, giving me an imploring look. 'I just met you. I don't want you getting hurt.'

That touches me again. Even more so when she reaches up to cup my cheek. I stay still. Enjoying the moment. She does too until she shivers from the cold.

'You go in,' I say.

'Coming in?' she asks nervously while trying to be light and cheery. She takes my hand to pull me through the gate to her front door.

'No. I'll walk back to the car.'

She smiles and unlocks the door, and turns to grab the front of my jacket to pull me inside. I can't help but laugh and bump into her, but I don't cross the threshold.

'Come in,' she whispers, pushing into me as I start to melt on the spot from the feel of her body and the scent of her hair and perfume. 'I want you to.'

I shake my head, enjoying the contact but refusing to go further.

'Don't you want me?' she whispers.

'Jesus. Loads. Yes.'

'Come in, then.'

'I can't.'

'Why?'

'Cos you've had a drink, Maggie, and I haven't.'

She looks up at me and smiles gently while keeping her hand on my chest. 'Only a good man would say that.'

I'm not a good man.

Not after what I did.

'You are a good man,' she says as though sensing my

disquiet. She reaches up on her tiptoes to give me a long peck on the lips. The contact minimal, but Jesus Christ, I feel incredible inside.

'I really like you,' she whispers.

'I like you.'

'Good,' she says and smiles, and steps back into her cottage.

'Café tomorrow?'

'Closed on Sundays. Text me. Or call me and don't get knifed,' she looks suddenly worried and full of angst and rushes forward to press her lips into mine, with a proper kiss this time. Lingering and growing in intensity. I grow aroused, which she detects and murmurs as she pushes into me.

But I still won't go inside.

I've made too many mistakes in my life.

I've lost too many good things.

I won't lose this.

Like I said. Women like Maggie don't come by very often.

She finally breaks the kiss and eases back into her house, with a long, frustrated groan, and slowly closes the door.

That was hard to do.

Saying no.

But it was right.

I turn to go back to the Landy.

Ready to deal with Cooper.

Except.

As ever.

My luck has other plans.

17

I drive back to the house while thinking about Maggie and become filled with a sudden surge of hope because my bleak and awful future doesn't seem quite so bleak and awful.

I temper myself not to get too excited. But I'm mad about her. The way she laughs and smiles is infectious. Her energy and aura. The thoughtfulness. That kiss.

I get images in my head of living here in Huntington. Finding work and living with Maggie. That means I need to deal with the whole Cooper thing carefully and not do anything stupid.

I know what I'll do.

I'll build a case against him, and when I know there is enough evidence to get him remanded, I'll present it to the police. Hopefully that will still gain me a bonus from Charles. He said he wanted the Cooper problem resolved.

A plan in mind and hope in my heart.

And I haven't even been here a week yet.

My phone rings in my pocket.

I smile. Figuring it'll be Maggie, with a joke about how I

need to go back to her place because of something important.

The law says you're not allowed to use phones while driving. I do it anyway and pull my phone out, with my thumb swiping to answer a fraction of a second before I see who the caller is.

Which means it's too late to stop.

'What do you want, Tessa?' I say with downward turn to my voice as she laughs down the phone at me.

Until I realise it's not laughing.

'Tessa? What's wrong?'

'He's... It's... My kitchen... I can't.'

'Tessa. Slow down. What's happened?'

'Blood everywhere. Please... He got in.'

'I'm coming to yours. Are you safe?' I ask, speeding through the village. 'Is Cooper there?'

'No... I don't– I don't know!'

'Stay on the line. Is the front door open? Go to the front door now, Tessa, and run outside. You'll see my lights.'

I look ahead to see light spilling from her cottage as she runs out. I brake hard and drop out, clutching the tyre iron I had ready in the car.

'What's happened?' I ask, seeing she's covered in blood. 'Are you hurt? Did he hurt you?'

'Not mine,' she says while panicking and gabbling words.

'Stay here,' I say and set off in full police mode. Barging in through the door, with my tyre iron gripped and ready.

'SHOW YOURSELF!' I shout in my loudest voice as the years of doing this in uniform come rushing back. I check the front room and dining room, then come to a stop in the kitchen.

The shock hitting me.

The sight of it.

A decapitated sheep's head upright on Tessa's kitchen table.

Blood everywhere. Dripping on the floor.

The dead, glassy eyes.

The wool stained red.

Words written in blood on the wall.

DIE HUMBER

Experience kicks in.

I search the house. Checking every room. No sign of him.

When I go back downstairs, Tessa is in the hallway, holding herself and looking shocked and pale.

'He's not here,' I say, pulling my phone out. 'Did you call the police yet?'

She shakes her head.

That's not unusual.

People don't trust the police so much now, and it's become instinct to call someone they do trust first.

But this has gone too far.

I make the call myself. Dialling three nines.

'Emergency services. Which service do you require?'

'Police.'

A click. The line rings again.

'Police emergency.'

'I need a response unit here, please. What's this address?' I ask, looking to Tessa.

She blinks in shock, then grabs an envelope marked for the occupier. I read the address off and give my name.

'*What do you need the police for?*' the call taker asks.

'*A local guy has broken into my friend's house and left a sheep's head.*'

'*A what?*'

'*Sheep's head. A decapitated sheep's head.*'

'*Right,*' she says slowly as my heart sinks, and in that second, I know the call taker will diminish the severity in any way she can. This was happening while I was still in the job. Call takers were being trained to deflect emergency calls to lessen the workload on response officers.

I try and get in first to stop that happening.

'*Listen. I'm ex-job. Okay? I was a detective in the Met.*'

'*And?*'

She sounds triggered already. '*Has anyone been injured? Is anyone under threat right now?*'

'*Well. No. But this guy–*'

'*Is the offender on scene?*'

'*No. I think he–*'

'*He's attacked a sheep, then, has he?*'

'*No. It's more than that. Listen. Don't take that tone with me.*'

'*I'm trying to help you. Which you should you know, being an ex-detective from the Met.*'

'*Don't say it like that.*'

'*Have you had a drink tonight, sir?*'

'*No! Listen. He–*'

'*I am listening, sir.*'

'*Which is done best by not talking,*' I snap and instantly regret it. '*Sorry. But please, this is serious. This guy is stalking people and spying on them, and masturbating and–*'

'*While he's attacking sheep?*'

'No! I don't know. But he broke in and left a sheep's head on her table.'

'Right. Did he take anything?'

My heart sinks again.

The UK doesn't have breaking and entering laws.

We have *burglary*, as defined by The Theft Act.

And the offence of burglary is only committed when someone enters a property to steal or cause GBH.

Which hasn't been done.

He's left a sheep's head.

Which means it's not even burglary.

'How did he get in?' I ask Tessa, with my hand covering the phone.

'I think. I didn't. I mean. This isn't London.'

I sag again. She didn't lock the door.

Which means he walked in.

'Were you here?' I ask in the vain hope she was while knowing she wouldn't have been.

She shakes her head.

Cooper hasn't committed *Criminal Damage*, nor has he committed the offence of *Using Violence to Secure Entry*, which requires a person to already be inside the dwelling being forced inside of.

At best it's *Trespass*, which is a civil offence, and then something like damage to livestock.

There might be some *Harassment* offences, but the one incident of him being outside on the road and then entering an insecure house to leave a sheep's head don't form enough harassment for any action to be taken.

All of which I know within a second or two.

'*I'm really worried about this guy,*' I say to the call taker, already knowing she won't despatch anyone.

She sighs. '*I'll create a report for the local countryside community officer, who will be in contact when they're next on duty.'*

'Hang on! This guy is dangerous.'

'And I've got a fatal RTI, two grade one domestics, and a pub fight, and no officers, Mr Detective from the Met. As I said. Countryside officers will be in touch.'

The line cuts off.

That's why people don't trust the police now.

I realise I didn't even tell the call taker about the message written in blood.

Which could form the offence of *Threats to Kill*. But again, it's weak.

The message written in blood is technically a statement.

Not a threat.

Defence lawyers get people off all the time because of technicalities like that.

A sense of despair hits as I realise it must be even worse for Tessa.

'This needs gripping,' I say and start for the door.

'What?! Mike! You can't just go!'

'He needs dealing with,' I say as she grabs my arm to pull me around.

'What about me? What if he comes back?'

'I'll find him first?'

'This isn't the city, Mike! He's probably watching us right now!'

Fuck.

I didn't think of that.

I get the sudden sense of being watched and close the front door. Then I go around the house and draw all the curtains. I keep hold of the tyre iron. I think of grabbing a knife, but knives have a nasty habit of getting stuck into the people holding them.

But that's what despair and fear do to people. It makes them act in desperation.

'What do we do with that?' Tessa asks as I double-check the front door is locked and bolted.

'What?'

'That!' she says.

I glance back to see her in the kitchen doorway staring in horror at the sheep's head.

'The fucking eyes,' she mutters, turning away from it as I curse at the gap in the front room curtains. I try and tug them closed, but they fold back. That's how Tessa must have seen me driving past the other night.

'We need to leave it there,' I say.

'No!' she says.

'The police need to see it.'

'Take a picture, then.'

She's right. It can't stay there. The blood will congeal within a few hours and attract scores of flies, and stink the house out.

'Bin bags?'

She looks at me. 'Er...'

'It's okay. Shock does that,' I say and open cupboard doors to find binbags and cleaning stuff under the sink. I take pictures on my phone of the head and the scene, and the words on the wall.

Then I set to it.

It's not pleasant.

But at least it's not human.

I've seen plenty of times at murder scenes and suicides.

I do the wall first. I get a bucket of soapy water and a sponge and reach up to start wiping it off, but I pause and notice the slant on the letters.

The same as on my bathroom mirror.

The same as the red chalk on the back door.

Which was before it all escalated to this dark level.

Those first few days seem almost like a game compared to now.

The wall cleans up easily.

Then I wrap the head in bin bags and take it out into the rear garden.

I go back in to see Tessa washed and changed into joggers and a baggy top.

'Why don't you make us a brew,' I suggest softly.

She nods and gets to it while I scrub the table and chairs, and floor.

When it's finished, I take the bloody water outside to pour down the drain and go back in to see her holding a steaming mug out for me.

'Thank you,' she says, with the first real show of sincerity since I met her. She looks different too. Smaller. Scared. Vulnerable.

'I can't stay in here,' she says and walks into the front room.

I follow her in. Drinking my tea. 'I think your milk is off,' I say with a wince at the taste.

'That'll be the brandy.'

What is it with women putting liquor in my drinks?

'I needed a settler,' she says, seeing my expression. 'It's only a bit. You'll be fine. Unless. I mean. Do you want a fresh one?'

'It's fine,' I say, figuring a tiny bit won't hurt.

'Gavin brought it with him the other night. He knows I love brandy.'

'Gavin?'

'My gay friend.'

'You said his name was Jason.'

She blinks. 'God. Gavin is his husband. Jason. Yes.'

'Shock,' I say again and look to the armchairs. Both with clothes folded up on the seats.

'I don't bite, Mike.'

I sit on the sofa next to her and sip the tea.

'Ten years,' she says.

'What is?'

'Gavin and Jason. They met in our office. Gav's a designer. Fashion, and Jas is this *amazing* photographer. Perfect couple. Or they were.'

'Oh.'

She nods and sips her tea.

'Gav slept with a woman,' she tells me.

'Is that bad?'

'Er, yeah!'

'No. I mean. Is it bad that he slept with a woman? God, I sound stupid. Sorry. Ignore me.'

'I asked that,' she admits.

'What did he say?'

'He said actually it made it slightly less bad. I was like *why?* And he said well, imagine Gav slept with another guy. He'd be wondering why he wasn't good enough. You know. Like what's this other guy got that I don't have.'

'Oh,' I say and drink more of my tea.

'I mean. I kinda get it,' she says to me. 'You know. So if my guy cheated with another woman, I'd be like *why her? What's she got that I don't have*. But if he was gay, and it was a man, then, you know, that's his natural sexual orientation thingy.'

I nod and drink another gulp.

'Kinda like you and Maggie,' she says as I roll my eyes.

'Really?' I ask.

'No, you, really. I mean. *Really?* Have you seen me?

Don't go! Sorry. Stay. Please,' she says, instantly softer, giving me eyes and pulling my arm to make me sit back down.

'Maggie's lovely.'

'She's fat. Sorry! Okay. Alright. Jesus. Just marry her already. God. If you've got a thing for chubsters. Oh, get off. That was funny.'

'You're clearly fine now,' I say, trying to get back up again. She laughs and pulls me back down.

'I'm joking to try and, you know, de-stress. You can't leave me here on my own.'

'Hotel, then?'

'Where?' she asks.

I think to suggest she could come back to Huntington House, but that's worse than here. At least here is somewhat defendable. Huntington House is Cooper's home territory.

'I'm sorry,' she says earnestly, putting a hand on my arm. 'I know. And you're right. I am a narcissist. I am! I admit it. Happy now? I hate not getting attention, and I *hate* losing... And that's where you say *noooo, Tess!*'

I look at her. She offers a smile, but it fades as the fear steals into her eyes. 'I am actually terrified,' she admits genuinely. 'You did this for a job. So like. I mean. In these situations. Like... What happens?'

I want to tell her they rarely get worse.

But that would be lying.

Men like Cooper do get worse. He's escalating daily. Which means his mental health and perceptions are spiralling because the voice we all have inside guiding us between right and wrong is misfiring, urging him to do things he knows he shouldn't. And with each stage and the subsequent complete lack of consequence, he gets worse.

This is how most murders happen.

Then the police or the coroners court do a serious case review and say how lessons will be learned, but they never are.

What I do know is there are two paths ahead. Two options.

The first is to try and manage the situation until Cooper gets bad enough for the police to intervene, but that carries the real risk of someone being murdered.

Namely me.

And he's showing that if he can't get to me, he'll go for Tessa.

Or maybe even Maggie next.

The next option is one I never would have thought of in realistic terms.

To negate him before he does that.

I did that once before. I stepped outside of the law and took action into my own hands, and lost everything.

I narrowly missed being prosecuted, and Scoble walked away with a payout.

Cooper, however, isn't Scoble.

For a start, I wouldn't even try and fight Cooper. The guy is twice my weight and clearly strong as anything.

That means hurting him in another way.

Or worse.

Killing him.

I felt revulsion when I first thought about it.

Now it's presenting as a credible option.

How, though?

And what about the consequences?

Could I get money from Charles Huntington and flee the country?

What about Maggie?

Would she come with me?

Jesus. This isn't a movie. What am I thinking?

'What are you thinking?' Tessa asks as I realise she's put her cup down. She shifts position to bring her head down onto my chest.

I stiffen to get up. Feeling uncomfortable at the close contact.

'I'm not coming onto you,' she says, as though I'm panicking needlessly. 'I'm just really scared.'

She sounds scared, and I detect the tremble in her body. I relax and bring my arm down over her.

I'm used to blood and death, and she might be a bitch, but anyone would feel terrified after coming home to that.

'Why me, though?' she asks and shifts position to roll over so she's facing up.

'Maggie told me he'd seen us at the house.'

'At your house? Huntington?' she asks as I nod.

'Saw us touching and told everyone we were holding hands.'

'That'll teach me to flirt with hot guys,' she murmurs in a way that makes me smile. I stretch my legs out and sigh heavily. 'You sleepy?' she asks.

'Bit,' I reply, thinking the brandy was a good settler. She takes my hands and lifts it to her forehead.

'Stroke my hair. I need attention.'

I smile again at how she says it. She gives me an imploring look. I roll my eyes but do it anyway. Her hair feels soft and fine.

'You'll fix it,' she says quietly. 'You're Mike Humber.'

'What does that mean?'

'That's why Cooper is doing all this. He knows you're not scared of him, so he's going into overdrive. I reckon he knows his days are numbered because you won't tolerate it.'

I think about the house the other night and how I set

Cooper up and caused him to have a tantrum and throw a chair through the window.

'Just don't let him murder me to death before you do,' she adds as I smile down at her. 'You will sort it, though, won't you?'

I nod as she nestles in a bit closer and closes her eyes while I smooth her hair. A while later, I think she must be asleep, but she blinks and looks up at me again.

'Did you find me attractive at all? No, seriously. I thought you really liked me.'

'I did.'

'So?'

I shrug.

'What changed?'

'You need more than me, Tessa.'

'God. Don't. Hate men telling me what I need.'

'Sorry. I meant. Whatever.'

'You got jealous because Jason came round and then sulked, and flirted with Maggie to get back at me. Now you fancy her and not me.'

I frown. Thinking that's mostly right. Except it wasn't on a conscious level.

'Okay. I'm sorry. My text was shit,' she says. 'I read it back, and I was like, *you literally dropped him like a stone.* I should have said my friend was in crisis or said come round and meet him.'

'Doesn't matter.'

She thinks for a second and looks up into my eyes. 'I am a narcissist, though.'

'I know.'

'It is a bit hot, isn't it?'

'No.'

'Admit it,' she says with a faint smile as I take in the

blueness of her eyes. She licks her lips. 'Men like you love women like me.'

'Like what?' I ask as my voice comes out deeper than intended, making me clear my throat.

Her hand finds mine smoothing her hair and gently strokes the back and then up my wrist. 'You're an alpha male. Your receptors are designed to light up around crazy, hot chicks.' I snort a laugh as she grins. 'Did you like my pictures?'

I swallow and remind myself I like Maggie. But it's warm and dark, and she's soft, and her hand feels nice. 'Did you look at them?' she asks again.

Danger close.

I tell myself to get up and go home, or sit on one of the armchairs.

Except I don't, and her hand goes up my arm.

'Did they make you think bad thoughts?'

I think about Maggie.

I think about kissing Maggie.

Which is a mistake because that only adds to the feeling inside of me. That heat and pressure.

'Did you think bad thoughts?' she whispers again as her hand goes all the way up my arm to my shoulder and along to my neck, then up to my jaw. 'Can I tell you something?'

Danger closer.

I need to get up and move away.

She hesitates as though unsure and licks her lips again. But this time slowly, and finishes off by gently biting her own bottom lip with a soft groan. 'Gets me when I think about what you did.'

I stare down at her as her fingertips trace over my lips; then, she takes her fingers in her own mouth.

I swallow again as she reaches to take my hand with her

wet fingers. She lifts it over her head, then down to kiss my fingertips. Making me stiffen and grunt.

'What you did,' she whispers, moving my hand down over her chin and neck. Inside her top. Pushing my fingers into the soft swell of her breast. She groans again, moving closer. 'When I think about it...' she murmurs. Pushing my fingers over her nipple, making it stiffen. Then drawing my hand out and down over her belly. She gasps gently. Shifting position to take my hand under the elasticated waist of her jogging bottoms. To the feel of the hair between her legs.

Danger close.

Maggie.

But I can't move.

She pivots up to lift her mouth to my neck while pushing my fingers between her legs.

Guiding me inside.

Kissing my skin. Breathing into my ear.

Her other hand starts rubbing me. She wrenches my belt open and pulls my button flies to take me in her hand while I take her in mine.

Images in my head. But they seem weird and skewed. Maggie. Her brown eyes. Her olive skin. The way she laughs. The kiss we had. Tessa's mouth finds mine. Her tongue darts between my lips. I feel weird. Hot. Turned on. Danger close. I need to go. She shifts and moves; then, her bottoms are off, and she's straddling me.

'Maggie,' I whisper and try to get up, but she's over me, pushing her breast into my mouth. Telling me to *ssshhh*. Telling me everything is okay.

She guides me inside of her with a gasp. 'Oh fuck... Oh god... I'm fucking Mike Humber... I'm fucking Mike Humber...'

I can't think straight.

Danger close.

I need to go.

Why can't I move?

'When you beat that man. So fucking hot,' she gasps into my ear and grinds into me.

That's wrong.

Scoble was evil.

I say no. I try and get her off.

She pushes harder. She grabs my jaw and kisses me hard.

I don't like it.

She's not Maggie.

She grunts and pushes hard. I ejaculate with a spasm while hating it, but I can't control what's happening. I can't get up.

She gasps and keeps going. 'I'm coming... I'm coming... Oh god, I'm coming on Mike Humber...'

She shudders, and I think about Maggie. But I can't remember what she looks like. I can't remember anything. I feel weird. I feel hot.

She slides off and slumps on the sofa next to me. Breathing hard and bathed in sweat.

'Told you you'd fuck me,' she says as my eyes close and open. 'And I told you I hate losing.'

Close and open.

Close.

Darkness.

18

Day Seven

Open.
　Awake.
　Bright light.
　The fluorescent strip in the garage dazzles my eyes. I groan and shift. My head pounds. My mouth feels bone dry.
　I scream with a sound I've never made before as I become aware of the wet pressure on my lap and first think I've pissed myself, but then look down to see another decapitated sheep's head on my legs.
　I spill from the Landrover. The head falls to the ground. I back away from it. My heart beating too wildly. My vision coming in snatches.
　Seeing the blood.
　Seeing the front of the Landrover embedded into the end wall beneath words written in dripping blood.

DIE HUMBER

How did I get here?

I don't remember leaving Tessa's house.

Oh god. I had sex with her.

I'm so thirsty.

I stagger from the garage to see the tables and chairs in the courtyard have been thrown around, and the same words are written in blood on the open back door.

Blood on the table inside. More dripping words on the walls.

I can't think straight. I can't walk properly.

I get to the sink and drink cold water until my belly feels swollen. When I stand up, I see the basement door wide open in the lobby, and my clothes filled with straw or something, forming the shape of a person now hanging from the neck.

I can't think.

Tessa.

Maggie.

What did I do?

I got drunk and fucked Tessa.

Did I?

Did I drink?

She gave me brandy.

I can't think.

I don't feel right.

'Told you you'd fuck me.'

Tessa's voice in my head.

I kissed Maggie. I like Maggie. I'm falling in love with Maggie. But I had sex with Tessa.

I get to the stairs and head up to see

DIE HUMBER

written on the hallway wall on the first floor. Then again on the second floor. On the walls in blood. On the door to my room.

On the wall inside my room.

My meagre belongings trashed across the floor.

I don't feel right.

I need to wedge the door closed.

I need to block the peephole.

Woozy.

I get to the bed.

My eyes close again.

Darkness.

◊

'Mike! Mike! MIKE!'

Maggie's voice.

Hands on my body.

'I love you,' I say, but the words slur.

'Wake up!'

Hands to my shoulders.

'Come back to bed,' I try and tell her.

'Fuck's sake! WAKE UP!'

She shouts properly. Fully. I wake up and open my eyes to see her glaring at me.

'What did you do?'

I don't know what she means.

She means Tessa.

'I...' I can't speak. My mouth is too dry again. I sit up and grimace at the congealing blood all over my top and jeans. On my arms and hands. On the walls. On her hands from touching me.

She pushes her hair back. Smearing blood across her cheeks as though in despair.

'Cooper,' I say and roll from the bed to get across into the bathroom, with a grunt at seeing more blood on the mirror. I drink from the tap. Quenching my thirst.

Then I start to cry.

It comes from nowhere.

Bubbling up inside of me.

'What did you do?' she asks again, shaking her head at me as she sees the tears falling down my cheeks. 'State of you. Come here.'

She pulls me over into the bath and unbuttons my blood-soaked shirt, and dumps it at the end of the tub. Then she starts on my jeans while I tremble and shake, and cry.

I can't think straight.

I don't know how I got home.

What's happening to me?

'It's okay. You'll be alright,' she mutters as I realise I must be saying those things.

She helps me undress down to my boxers, then grimaces as she spots the blood has soaked through my jeans onto them.

'Just take them off,' she says as the humiliation becomes complete, and I end up naked and shivering in front of her.

She turns the showerhead on and runs it till it gets hot, then starts washing the blood off me as I kneel in the bath. She scrubs my hair. My face. My body.

'Why are you here?' I ask.

'Came to murder you,' she mutters angrily. 'Fucking creep.'

I look at her.

She glares at me.

'I thought you were dead or something,' she says a second later, rubbing blood from my chest with hard, rough movements. 'Blood in the garage, then in the kitchen.'

'Sheep.'

'I know. I saw it.'

'Cooper.'

'Obviously,' she mutters and shields my eyes as she rinses the soap from my face like I'm a child. 'He did that to John way back. Kept leaving sheep heads. They're John's sheep an' all. How cheeky is that? Christ, though, Mike. He's gonna kill you. Never seen him so bad. He's obsessed.'

'Need to tell you-.'

'Shut up. Wash your bits. I'm not touching that thing. Not now or ever. You've ruined that chance.'

She hands me the shower head and stomps off while I shiver and wash. She comes back quickly, handing me a towel, then sets to work, with a bucket of soapy water and a sponge to start washing the blood from the mirror.

'Need to take a picture.'

'I've done it,' she says curtly. 'I'll send them to you. You like getting pictures.'

'Maggie.'

'Not now, Mike! Get dressed. I took that scarecrow thing down and put your clothes out for you. And drink that coffee I made.'

'We need to talk.'

'NOT NOW!'

I back off. Hearing the anger and raw pain in her voice that breaks with emotion.

I go into my room to see she's already scrubbed the blood from the walls and tidied my clothes. A steaming mug of coffee on the side. I take a gulp and get dressed.

I hear the bucket being emptied into the toilet, then refilled.

I go to help her.

'Do the hallway,' she says and walks off.

I clean the blood from the hallway walls.

When I go down, she's already cleaned the first floor and is in the kitchen.

I help right the furniture in the courtyard and almost pass out from another woozy spell.

She takes my arm and pushes me onto a chair.

'Something wrong with me.'

'Clearly,' she mutters. Folding her arms.

She knows.

'How do you know?'

She glares angrily, then pulls her phone out to show me dark video footage shot through a gap in curtains, showing a naked Tessa straddling me on the sofa.

'Cooper,' I mutter.

She nods grimly.

'I don't know what happened. He put a sheep's head in her place.'

'I know. I went there.'

'You spoke to Tessa?'

'She told me to fuck off through the door. I saw the sheep's head in the garden.'

'Maggie.'

'Don't.'

'I am so sorry.'

'DON'T! You kissed me, then went round, and fucked her?'

'No! It wasn't like that. She had that head and called me, and I went there and...'

'And what? She accidentally tripped and landed on your dick? You know what? Fuck you. I don't care. But I bloody said don't drag me into anything. I'm barely getting by, Mike! Do you know how hard it is living here? The rent on the café. The rent on my cottage. It's so...so fucking hard. And then you come along, and I think you're so nice, and you came to the bingo, and everyone loved you. Even Alice! And I would never kiss a guy on a first date. Never! What did you do? What did you fucking do?' she half yells, half cries, and slaps my shoulder. 'Am I not good enough or something?'

'No.'

'What, then?!'

'I don't know!'

'Why did you have sex with her? I asked you to come into mine! Is it cos I'm fat? Ugly? What?'

I shake my head. Not having words to give. 'She put brandy in my drink.'

'Is that your excuse?'

'I'm an alcoholic! I binge drink and do stupid things. No. No. That's wrong. I'm not blaming it like I didn't do it. I'm sorry. I am so sorry. It's just. I don't know what happened. She started flirting, and I couldn't get up and move.'

'You did get it up all right, though! Obviously from that bloody video.'

'Maggie.'

'No! Whatever. She can *fucking* have you. That's just seedy. I wouldn't do that to someone I liked. And you really need to leave.'

'You want me to leave?'

'Not me. I don't care what you do. But Stan is going to murder you, Mike. I have never seen him this bad. And what if he murders that Tessa? What if he comes for me? Look! LOOK!' she shouts, showing me her phone and pictures of her and I kissing on her doorstep last night. 'He sent them to me. He was watching us. He's bloody stalking you! He won't stop. Go back to the city.'

I snort and sag on the chair. Making her give me a look. 'What?' she asks.

'Got nowhere to go.'

'Go back to your own place.'

'I don't have a place. I was in a hostel full of migrants and refugees. And that took months to get.'

She scowls at me, but I can see the confusion in her eyes.

'I'm homeless, Maggie.'

'Jesus,' she says with a groan, pushing her hair back as I realise the blood smears are still there.

'You've got blood on your face.'

'I grew up handling dead sheep,' she says, as though that explains her lack of concern. 'Haven't you got mates? Family?'

I shake my head and reach a whole new level of humiliation.

I can't even stay at her place or with Tessa.

Not with Cooper on the rampage.

And even now. After all of this, there still isn't enough to get him remanded.

A few instances of stalking all done mostly on one night,

and again, any defence lawyer would easily argue that he was sending the sex video to Maggie to show her I'm a lowlife cheater. And that call taker last night showed how disinterested the police are.

Maggie sits down on another chair and pulls her tobacco tin from a pocket, and rolls one up. She goes to light it, then tuts, and hands it to me, and rolls another one.

We smoke in silence.

'I don't want to get murdered cos of some guy I kissed,' she eventually says.

'You know him. Do you think he would?' I ask.

She gives me a look like it's obvious he would. 'We call him psycho Stan. What does that tell you?'

'And I made a call,' she adds a moment later. 'To Bev. Head housekeeper,' she says, nodding at the house. 'They had a Latvian girl here last summer in August. It was for insurance. The house can't be empty for more than like two days or three days, or something.'

'And?'

'She went home,' Maggie says. 'Lasted less than a week.'

'The ghost?'

She stares at me. 'She woke up one night to Stan wanking in her room.'

'Fuck! Why didn't Huntington deal with it?'

'She'd gone. Literally packed and went that day. They sent her some cash apparently to say sorry and to keep her quiet. Bev reckons the same thing happened with the Vietnam woman.'

I look at her. Focussing sharply. Or at least as much as my fogged mind will allow.

'Year before. Same thing. Hired for August to house sit. When Bev and the girls came in to get it ready for the family coming back, she'd gone.'

'Gone where?'

Maggie shrugs. 'Figured she'd left. Ghost probably. Or they reckoned that at the time, but then with Stan the next year, Bev said he must have scared her off.'

'Did they call and ask her?'

'Couldn't get hold of her.'

'What if she...? I mean. What if he...?' I ask, trailing off.

She shrugs again, but I can see from her face we're thinking the same thing.

I try and clear my mind.

A missing Vietnamese woman in the UK would be very hard to trace.

'Was she agency staff?'

'Must be. Dunno. Probably hired her same way they got you.'

An advert online. That's not good. If the woman answered a random advert, and they hired her, and say, she was here illegally, there is every chance nobody knew she was staying at this house.

'Fuck,' I say into the silence. Realising this just got *very* sinister. 'She was bloody right.'

'Who? Your new woman?'

'She's not my woman.'

Maggie snorts with derision. Giving me a filthy look. 'Is that enough for the police, though?'

I flap my hands. 'If they can trace the Latvian woman and get a statement, and *if* they take into account all the pictures and the tissue I found...' I sag again. Shaking my head. 'Still really weak.'

'So what? He just gets to stalk us and take pictures, and break into houses?'

'He didn't break into Tessa's place.'

'He left that head! That's breaking and entering.'

'We don't have that in this country.'

'So he can what? Rape and kills us, then? And the police won't do anything?'

'No. I mean. Yes, obviously, if he rapes and kills someone.'

'Be a bit late when I'm already dead. And he's probably already done that Vietnam woman. What if her body is buried somewhere? Oh god. I bet he chopped her up and gave her to the pigs.'

'Are there pigs near here?' I ask with a groan.

'It's the countryside.'

Pigs will eat anything. Including human bone and teeth. That means no remains. Which means no forensics.

I rub my face. Feeling like shit.

'You need to deal with this,' she says.

'I was trying. I thought I'd get evidence together and put a case to the police.'

I also thought Maggie and I could live happily ever after.

'You're alright. You can protect yourself. He'll go for me, and although she's obviously a rancid slut, I don't want to see that Tessa getting killed cos you can't keep it in your boxers.'

I take it on the chin as my world feels like it's closing in around me and things couldn't get any worse.

At which point, a car comes down the drive and brakes hard on the gravel, followed by the sound of a door slamming and loud bangs on the front door. 'MIKE!' Tessa's voice, yelling angrily as I sink on my chair and groan, and rub my face. 'MIKE!' she yells again, the voice coming closer as she stomps over the gravel to the garage.

'Aw. You two plan a second date?' Maggie asks, with acid dripping from her tongue.

'MIKE!' Tessa yells again. Clearly furious.

'In here!' I call and listen as she walks into the garage, then shouts at the sight of the sheep's head I forgot to move.

'That fucking guy,' Tessa shouts, steaming into the courtyard with a double take at Maggie. 'You don't waste any time! He was inside me a few hours ago.'

'Jesus, Tessa,' I groan at the way she says it.

'What is this?' she demands, showing me her phone. I blink at it, and my world gets worse as I see the pictures of Maggie and I kissing on Tessa's phone. 'Was this before you fucked me? And how did that psycho get my number?'

'I don't know,' I say weakly.

'Did you give it to him?' Tessa demands, turning on Maggie.

'No!' Maggie says angrily. 'He sent me you and him on your bloody sofa.'

'You dirty fucking...' Tessa starts to say, shaking her head at me. 'You need to fix this. You said you'd fix this! I don't want to get murdered for a drunken one-night stand!'

'He was drunk, then?' Maggie asks.

'Yes! And going on about you. I only fucked him cos he's Mike Humber. I'm over it already. Trust me. Worst ten seconds I ever had. Mike! Look at me. He's going to murder someone. What if he does her?' she asks, waving a hand at Maggie. 'You're obviously in love with her!'

It's too much.

My head. My brain.

'Go back to London,' I tell her.

'I can't!' she snaps and folds her arms. 'Not now. Maybe in a few weeks.'

'You doing a book about missing women?' Maggie asks her.

'How the hell do you know? Did he tell you? Oh god.

That means everyone knows. That's why he's after me, Mike!'

'One of them was real,' Maggie says as Tessa's face grows taut. 'We think. The Latvian girl went home, but the Vietnam woman went missing.'

'Okay. Wow. This just got really sinister,' Tessa says in a voice now more terrified than angry. 'You've got to call the police, Mike. Tell them. Make them listen. You were a detective.'

'I can get them to investigate and look into it,' I say as they both look at me. 'But that will take a few weeks, and they won't arrest him until they've got something.'

'He probably chopped her up in there,' Tessa says, waving at the house.

'She was also staying here. So trace DNA evidence won't prove anything. Even blood wouldn't be enough. They'd argue she could have cut her finger and then, I don't know, ran off because of the very famous ghost, and because she's probably an illegal immigrant, they can't trace her. No body. No forensics. Maggie said there are pig farms here. Pigs eat bodies all the time.'

Tessa goes to speak, then stops, and for a weird moment, we stay in silence, somehow sharing the same peril.

'Is there anywhere you can go?' I ask Tessa. 'Take Maggie with you.'

'I'm not going with her!' Maggie says. 'What about my café?'

'There isn't anywhere,' Tessa says.

'Jason? Gavin?'

'Gav's out the country. Jas is back with his mum. I don't know anyone else.'

'Maggie? Can you go anywhere?' I ask.

'I only know people here. John and... And that's it.'

'We're fucked, then,' Tessa says, grabbing a chair and slumping down with a defeated tone. 'Some cop you are.'

'What can I do?' I ask her.

'Deal with him!'

'How?'

'You bloody know,' she hisses, leaning forward to glare at me. 'You did it before, or are we not worth it?'

'I didn't do it before.'

'You almost did! We all saw the video. The whole world saw that video.'

Scoble.

The day I caught him.

The day I saw red and beat him.

'You might not like me very much,' Tessa adds. 'And god only knows why. Most men would chop their toes off to do what you did last night, but you're clearly infatuated with her.'

'Vain,' Maggie mutters.

'Have you seen me?' Tessa asks, giving her a filthy look. 'I get it, though. You're very pretty, and you've got that earthy, *real* thing going on. God. You two are made for each other. I almost feel guilty seducing him.'

Silence again.

Awkward.

Strained.

Maggie blinks and goes to speak, but stops. I look at her. She clears her throat.

'So. Lord Charles spoke to my John. Like. Last year. Maybe the year before. And he said if John sorted Cooper, he'd gift him the farm and one hundred thousand pounds.'

Tessa's eyebrows shoot up.

Mine too.

'The farm?' I ask.

'Huntingtons own it,' Maggie says. 'Own everything here. John rents it. For a lot. Charles said he'd gift it and pay him cash.'

'To do what?' I ask.

Maggie shrugs and shoots an uncertain look to Tessa.

'Spit it out. Kill him?' Tessa asks.

Maggie nods. 'But they were in a field, and Charles told my John if he ever repeated it, he'd do him for libel and take the farm and my café, and my cottage.'

'Why didn't John do it?' Tessa asks in surprise.

'John's soft as....' Maggie says, her voice falling away as she looks at me.

'But Mike's not,' Tessa says quietly.

I think back to the comments Charles said to me the other day. That he wanted Cooper resolved, and there would be a life-changing bonus in it for me if I sorted it.

'He might gift me my café,' Maggie says, with all sorts of emotions flitting across her face.

'Aw. Well, there's your motivation, Mikey. You can do it for your new wife and run a café together.'

'I don't want him,' Maggie says.

'You two are made for each other.'

'He slept with you!'

'I gave him Viagra!'

'You did what?' I ask as Tessa pulls an innocent face, and I think back to the weird tasting tea.

'I told you I hate losing. Narcissist. Remember?'

'That's illegal,' I tell her.

'Oh, grow up. Who's gonna believe you? *Aw, the hot woman with the perfect boobs made me have sex with her.* Right. That's it, then. I'll take my cut, and then you two can stay here and run your café, and make babies. Gross.'

'Hang on. Your cut of what?' I ask.

'The fee. From Charles Huntington when he pays you.'

'What cut?' I ask again.

'Well, I can't write my bloody book after you've killed Cooper, can I?' she says, and there it is. Out in the open. The thing we were not mentioning.

Killing Cooper.

'Why would he pay you?' Maggie asks her.

'Trust me. He'll pay,' Tessa says confidently. 'I'll put Viagra in his tea like I did with Mike.'

'No. Just hang on,' I say.

'Hang on what?' Tessa asks. 'Until one of us is dead? Raped? Chopped up?'

I look to Maggie. Thinking she'll interject.

But she doesn't.

And I can see it in her eyes.

The dream of owning her café and cottage.

The way she looks at me is different too.

It has been since Tessa said she put Viagra in my tea and seduced me.

That dream comes back.

Living in Huntington with Maggie.

Could I do it?

Could I kill a man?

Yes.

I know I could.

I tried to once before, with Scoble.

And I shot a man once before.

He didn't die. But I didn't know he wouldn't die. I shot him to kill him. To negate the threat he posed. To take out the bad guy.

I never lost any sleep over it.

I didn't lose sleep about beating Scoble either.

My angst was caused by what I lost as a result of my actions.

But not the actions themselves.

The lack of vocal opposition, first from Maggie and then from me, seems to form an unspoken contract.

Like this is a done thing.

'I'll need an alibi,' I tell them.

'Say you're at mine,' Maggie says instantly.

'No. Say you were *both* at mine,' Tessa says. 'That's two people claiming they were with you.'

I nod. 'That's more believable. Need to get rid of the body. Where are those pigs?'

'Farm next to John's,' Maggie says. 'Gilbert's dad. The lad that won the eggs. His pigs are down the bottom field, out of sight of the house.'

'When?' Tessa asks, her tone now serious and low.

'Tonight,' I say as they both swallow and share looks. 'Go to Tessa's,' I tell Maggie. 'Take some wine and munchies. Mention it in the shop. *Me and Mike are going to Tessa's for dinner.*'

She nods.

'Have you got neighbours?' I ask Tessa, remembering there is a cottage next door.

'Old couple. They sleep really early.'

'The Butterworths,' Maggie says.

'Alright. I'll pick Maggie up and come to yours, Tessa. We'll go in the garden and chat, and make noise. Then Maggie and I will slip out and come back here and–'

'Why me?' Maggie asks.

'You can handle blood,' I say, nodding at her smeared face. She touches her cheeks and seems to accept it.

'Hang on. They'll hear the Landrover coming and going,' Tessa says. 'Okay. So. I'll leave my car down the lane.

You park at mine. Come in. We make noise. You two slip out and take my car, and I'll keep chatting and do different voices.'

'Okay. Go in the garden and call out to me, as though I'm in the house talking to you. They'll tell the police they heard me talking later.'

They both nod while staring straight at me.

'Alright. Okay,' Tessa says. Puffing her cheeks. 'Wow. We're really doing this, then. And we all swear never to talk about it. Right?'

'What, the fact we're conspiring to commit murder?' I ask her.

She gives me a look and flicks a middle finger.

'And then you two can live happily ever after,' Tessa says, giving a fake smile to me and Maggie. She gets to her feet. But I can see she's nervous from the tremble in her hands. She tries to hide it by being cocky. 'And honestly, forget last night,' she tells Maggie. 'It was seconds, and he kept saying your name. I mean. Why? I don't know.'

She tuts and walks off through the garage, and we listen to the crunch of gravel, then her car door slamming shut, and the engine starting, and Tessa driving away until we're sitting in silence.

The woman of my dreams looking at me with her beautiful, brown eyes.

'You'd do it?' she asks. 'You'd really kill Cooper?'

'Is that what you want?'

'God, no. But... He's sick. He'll hurt someone. And you know. We get the café and the cottage.'

She said we.

'I'm still not touching that thing,' she says, with a nod at my groin. 'I'm scrubbing it with bloody bleach before it goes in me to make a baby.'

She said baby.

'I'll make you another coffee. We need you alert,' she says, getting up to go past me. Her hand brushing my shoulder.

I watch her go. Thinking about it all.

About the dream once more hanging in the air.

A café. A cottage. A wife. A baby.

Yeah.

I'd kill for that dream.

19

'What a bitch,' Maggie says again. 'That's twisted, though. Don't you think? Like. You're so vain and full of yourself that you can't handle it when a guy likes someone else, so you literally drug him and make him have sex. Jesus.' I glance over as we drive. She tuts again. 'You're still a twat, though,' she tells me.

I nod, accepting that I am, indeed, a twat.

Woozy again.

'You okay?' she asks as I slow the car to a stop and rub my face. 'Bless. Just get through this, and we'll be okay.'

Her hand on my leg.

I open my eyes to see her looking at me in concern.

'I know you're feeling hungover, and all this is, you know, like really messed up.'

'Just a bit.'

She shrugs and offers a tight smile. 'How does it feel to be popular, though? Two women want you.'

'Do you want me, then?'

'No!' she scoffs, pulling her hand away. 'Told you. That thing is getting scrubbed before we have sex.'

I drive on.

'You think you can see yourself here, though?' she asks with a hint of nerves to her voice and manner. The way she fidgets. The way she looks at me.

'Yeah. I like it.'

'What? Coming to bingo and winning eggs?'

'I don't know what I'll do for work, though.'

She thinks for a second. 'I reckon that Tessa'll get a few quid out of Huntington. We won't even have to worry about it. I mean. If he signs the café over and my cottage, and we get cash. We could even have a holiday.'

'Benidorm?'

'I liked Benidorm! It was cheap and hot. But I don't know. We can go anywhere.'

'And you're really alright with this?' I ask as we drive through the village. 'It's a big thing, Maggie. Taking a life.'

'Grew up around it.'

'This is a person. Not a sheep.'

She falls silent. 'He ain't right, Mike. I mean. If it was anyone else, I'd be like no way. Not ever. But Stan isn't right. That Latvia girl woke up to him wanking over her.'

'Over her? You said he was in the room. I pictured him like by the door or something.'

'I bet he was standing right over her. And that's what? Like one step away from raping and murdering her? That's probably what he did to that Vietnam woman. Woke her up and killed her.' She shudders and pulls a face. 'You're a bloke. You don't know what that fear is like when you're around a strong man that's looking at you wrong. Knowing you couldn't do anything to stop him.'

She's right. Although I've dealt with a lot of victims, and I've heard it many times.

Edward Scoble's victims said the same thing.

Resolution inside of me.

Determination.

She seems to detect it.

I pull up outside her house. 'Want me to come in with you?' I ask.

'Be fine. He won't do anything in the day. Unless. I mean. Do you want to come in? I can make you a coffee.'

'I'd better get back.'

'I would offer you sex, but I did that last night, and look what happened.'

'Jesus, Maggie.'

'I'm joking. I'm just trying to. You know. Process it. Um. Question, though.'

I look at her. Sensing a sudden, strange shyness.

'Is it wrong I'm a bit horny? Is that really messed up?'

'There's a thing that happens in the body when people are near death. It gives them an urge to reproduce.'

'Really? Oh, god. I thought I was like screwed up or something. Is that for men and women?'

'I guess so.'

'Are you, then?' she asks, looking nervous.

'I feel like shit,' I say honestly.

'Well. That's twice you've blown me out,' she says and opens the door to get out.

'It's not that.'

She shoots me a smile. 'Better not be,' she says and clambers back over the seat to kiss my lips. Slow. Lingering. I do feel like shit. But I can't help my body responding to the sexual touch. She keeps kissing me, then drops a hand to my groin, and squeezes. 'Good. Just checking you do fancy me,' she whispers and pulls back. 'You coming to pick me up later, then?' she asks in a louder voice.

'Around seven?' I call through the window.

'Okay! I'm looking forward to going to Tessa's for dinner!'

I wince at the awful acting, but at least she said it. Not that I can see anyone around listening.

I drive back to Huntington House, with my mind in a tailspin.

Knowing what I have to do.

Knowing I have to take a life.

I pull into the driveway to see Lord Huntington's Range Rover outside the house.

He does the same thing as when I first arrived and stays in the car until I reach the gravel driveway.

'Mr Humber,' he says in greeting, but the cheery tone isn't there this time. He's all business as he shows me his phone screen.

I shield it from the weak autumn sun and see the footage moving past the Land Rover driven into the end wall of the garage. Me inside. Slumped over the wheel.

No sheep's head on my lap. No bloody message on the wall.

The footage shows the courtyard furniture all askew and the rear door wide open.

Cooper must have filmed me before he put the sheep's head in the vehicle with me and used the blood to write on the walls.

Huntington slides to the next clip.

Me kissing Maggie on her doorstep.

Then the next clip.

Tessa and I on her sofa having sex.

Back to Huntington House. Me passed out on my bed, covered in blood. Then he shows me pictures of the sheep's head on the floor in the garage and the blood all over the kitchen table.

'Some night you had,' he says tightly.

'Trust me. I've had worse. But what those clips don't show are the death threats written on the walls.'

He grunts and pockets the phone. 'This is becoming a significant issue, Mr Humber.'

'What happened to the Latvian woman?'

He shows surprise but recovers quickly. 'She went home.'

'Why?'

'Are you questioning me, Mr Humber?'

I don't reply.

He tuts. 'The *official* reason is the ghost phenomena.'

'And the real reason?'

'Cooper.'

'What did he do?'

'Groped her in the night.'

'That's getting worse each time it's told.' He glares at me with those piercing, cold, blue eyes. 'I heard he was masturbating.' I say.

'He was.'

I guess the groping part was played down or removed from the story. 'You pay her off?'

'I've been paying for Mr Cooper's *indiscretions* for a long time.'

'Indiscretion? You mean sexual assault. And voyeurism. And stalking. And harassment. And trespass. And mutilation of livestock. And what about the year before the Latvian woman? The Vietnamese woman. Do we add rape and murder to that list?'

His face darkens. His whole manner stiffens with discomfort.

'Did you even try and find her?'

'Of course!' he snaps.

'Did she answer an advert like me?'

He nods.

'Did she email?'

He nods again. 'Why?'

'Because emails can be traced. That would give the police a possible location as to where the email was sent from. Which could lead to her identification.'

'I didn't know that.'

'Now you do.'

'Make this go away,' he says without hesitation.

'Make what go away?'

'This. All of it.'

'Is there an inheritance issue?'

He nods again. 'Cooper's driving it.'

'So he wants the house? The lands?'

'Fix it,' he whispers.

'For?'

He looks confused.

Then he doesn't.

Understanding steals into his eyes.

'What do you want?'

'Maggie's cottage and café signed over to her.'

He balks like it's too much, then nods.

'And cash. Split two ways.'

'Two?'

'One payment to Tessa. And the other one to Maggie and I.'

'You and Maggie? Are you planning on sticking around then, Mr Humber?' he asks warily.

'Unless it's a big enough offer for me to leave and to convince Maggie to come with me.'

He stares for a long second like the greedy, entitled prick he is. Weighing up his bank balance over the worth of the mere mortals doing his dirty work.

'Or,' I say lightly or as lightly as I can, given I still feel like shit, 'you can go into any number of pubs in London or Manchester, or Birmingham, or even Glasgow, where I'm sure someone will kill Cooper for you for a fraction of that price. But then they'll get drunk. And tell their mates. And they'll keep coming back... And coming back.'

His head tilts. 'So I am paying for discretion.'

'And murder. But mainly discretion.'

He looks all manner of being bent out of shape. It's ingrained in people like this to haggle and barter, and avoid ever paying. But we both know there is too much to lose.

'Agreed,' he says curtly. 'When? Needs to be quick. I'm under pressure. Her Ladyship *dislikes* where we are residing.'

'Tonight. I need you to go to Tessa's cottage. Give her a bottle of something and stay for a quick drink. Park that big car outside.'

'Alibi,' he mutters.

'I asked you for a night off. You like me cos of what I did when I got sacked from the police, so you're bringing a bottle round. Quick chat with me and Maggie, and Tessa; then you can go. Except I won't be there.'

He nods rapidly. His blue eyes glinting with mischief and malice. His cheeks even flush a little.

'And who is going to disbelieve the esteemed Lord Huntington?' I ask.

'Quite. Understood. Er. Well. Good luck, I suppose. Do you need anything?'

I shake my head.

He falters as though unsure what to say now he's agreed for me to murder his problems away.

Then he's off in his Range Rover, and I'm left once more outside the dark and foreboding Huntington House.

20

It's a weird afternoon that follows.

When isn't it now?

The first thing I do is put a thin strand of cotton across the entrance to the tunnel behind the spiral staircase in the basement.

I can't physically stop Cooper coming into house, but if I keep checking, I'll know when he does.

Then I think about what I'm about to do, and how I will do it.

I need him in the house when the time comes.

But then he knows this house like the back of his hand and can clearly navigate it in the dark. He's also very strong, so that means not taking him on physically.

Maybe I can level the playing field.

That gives me an idea.

I'll need to show him everything is normal, and his threats haven't worked, and I'm still here.

God knows it's the last thing I want to do, but I change into my jogging gear and go outside to run up and down the drive.

Being seen.

I jog around the house on the path a few times and stop on each side to do air-squats and push-ups. I get the overwhelming sensation of being watched.

When I go inside, the cotton is still in place.

I go into the snooker room and press auto select on the jukebox. Music comes on. I go around and draw curtains, and put lights on.

Being seen.

I go into the basement. The cotton is still in place.

I get the things I need and make ready, and as the afternoon gives way to evening, I run a bath and think about murder.

I'm going to kill someone for money.

For profit.

I'm going to bypass the entire judicial system and enact justice by taking matters into my own hands.

The weird thing is, lots of ex-cops and serving cops have probably done this same thing.

We, of all people, know the limitations of the law, and that law and order is a perception rather than a reality.

People like Cooper are never dealt with fast enough. The things they do are always mitigated until it's too late, at which point the agencies all act surprised like they could never see it coming.

Which is why people like me end up doing things like this and making problems disappear, but then, to people like Charles Huntington, the law is only ever a loose set of guidelines at best. The landed gentry have been bypassing laws for centuries.

Why stop now?

I think all those things to mitigate and lessen the horror of what I am going to do.

I tell myself that Cooper is a nutjob freak, and that if I didn't do it, Huntington would find someone else. But more importantly, if I don't do it, Cooper will kill me first, or worse, he'll murder Maggie or Tessa. Or both.

Take the money.

Live a life without debt or worry.

Seek happiness with Maggie.

Start a family.

What a dream.

And that kiss at Maggie's place last night. I can't stop thinking about it.

The kiss in the car was nice. But it felt a bit colder. Like she was only seeking reassurance that I find her attractive. Whereas the kiss last night had emotional depth.

I go into my room to get changed and remember my clothes are in the dryer, and go all the way back down to the basement to get them out of the machine.

The strand of cotton is intact.

I go back upstairs, humming along to the music.

I get changed in my room and groan when I realise how creased my shirt is.

I go all the way back down to the basement and iron my clothes.

The cotton is broken.

He's in the house.

I go into the kitchen, with my clothes in my hands, and get dressed while humming to the music.

Feeling watched.

A flutter of nerves inside.

I stay calm and go into the lobby to the landline, and lift the handset, and pretend to make a call. '*Maggie! It's me. Still on for tonight? Tessa's? Okay. I'll come now and pick you up. Just for a few hours, though. I can't stay out. Alright.*

Okay. Yep. Ten minutes? Sorry? Honestly, I think just a shirt and jeans will be fine. It's only casual. Did you get the wine? Okay. Ten minutes! Bye!'

I hang up and head out the back door.

Danny Boy comes on when I reach the garage.

I figure it's just part of the auto select.

But still, though.

I drive past the house.

Feeling watched.

Being seen.

I pull up at Maggie's and gather my game face as I get out, and go to her door.

'Hey,' she says, looking nervous when she lets me in.

I go into her front room. Pictures of her and John on the walls. Pictures of other people. Her mum and dad. 'What happened to them?' I ask as she bustles around.

'Mum had cancer years ago. Dad had a heart attack.'

'I'm really sorry.'

'Thanks,' she says. 'Ready? I've got a change of clothes in here,' she shows me a small rucksack. 'Old, black clothes. Figured we'd burn them after?'

We go out to the Land Rover. I open the door for her. She smiles again, but the nerves are there.

'I went to the shop and said about the dinner,' she says. 'Wendy was working. She'll text everyone.'

'Good.'

We pull up at Tessa's. 'This must be weird for you,' I say.

'Yeah. God.'

'Not just Cooper. Coming here. All of it.'

She nods. Wide-eyed. 'You okay?' she asks.

'I had a bath and told myself why it's important.'

'Like convinced yourself? Yeah, me too.'

'I saw Charles. He came to the house.'

'What did he say?' she asks.

'He said that the Latvian woman was groped in the night. And he also said he doesn't want me around after it's done.'

'Where will you go? Back to London?'

I look at her as she frowns and looks worried.

'My life is here,' she adds. 'But. I mean. I want to be with you. So. I could try and live somewhere else.'

'We might have to. Just for a little while. Let's get through tonight first.'

◊

'There they are!' Tessa says, coming out of the front door to greet us in the garden. Big hugs. Big voices. 'Wine!' she says with a cheer, taking the bottle from Maggie like they're the best of friends.

We go inside. Music on. She opens the wine and pours it into glasses.

I get changed in the front room.

Out of my nice jeans and shirt and into my black trousers and black top.

'Not the first time you got your kit off in here,' Maggie remarks. Giving me a look as I figure it will be a while before she lets that go. 'Do I change now?' she asks.

'Not yet. Right. We ready?' I ask as powerful headlights sweep past the window, with a big Range Rover coming to a stop outside. 'He's here. Let's go out and meet him.'

It's a phony, awkward charade, but we go through the motions. Greeting Lord Huntington loudly.

He responds in kind. A bottle of something in his hands.

We go inside to the kitchen.

Weird energy in the air. Everyone nervous and excited.

'Okay. Me and Maggie will slip out. You stay for a bit,' I say to Charles. 'Say bye to me and Maggie when you leave.'

'Yes. Got that. I'll make a show of it.'

'Ready?' I ask Maggie. She looks a bit shell-shocked, but she nods.

We slip out the back door and out the side gate onto the lane, then along to Tessa's car.

'It's too close,' I say and release the handbrake to push it another few hundred yards.

We get in and set off.

Maggie exhales loudly. Fidgety.

I stay calm.

Focussed.

I feel woozy again. I slow the car.

'You okay?' she asks.

'My head. It keeps coming on.'

'Stress,' she says, rubbing my back. 'I'll look after you. I promise. What you're doing for me is... I mean. God. You're amazing.'

She makes me feel better.

I drive on.

But I don't go to Huntington House.

I go to the lane I found that first day.

I ditch the car and leave Maggie inside, and set off at a jog until I reach Cooper's cottage.

Lights on inside.

I skirt the outside. Thankful he doesn't have dogs going nuts. Nobody inside. The front door is locked.

The back door isn't.

Offenders are weird like that. They often assume nobody else could commit a crime.

His house is what I expect.

A gorgeous, old, thatched roof cottage with big fireplaces.

It also looks how I'd expect from a man like Cooper living on his own.

A fucking pigsty.

Crap everywhere. Clothes on old chairs. Unopened letters on the sides and table.

I cast my eyes around and drift slowly through the front room into the kitchen. Notes on the side. Old shopping lists in scrawly handwriting.

I find the two things I need.

The first in his wardrobe in the bedroom on a shelf.

A pair of night vision goggles. Older. Worn. He must have upgraded so he could see more when he was jerking himself off, sneaking around the corridors being a pervert.

I slip them on and can see they still work.

I dread to think what traces of fluids are on the casing and strap.

Then I find the other thing I wanted.

'Lady H won't have them in the house.'

The firearms cabinet.

Bolted to the wall in the other bedroom.

The law says they have to be kept locked and secure.

But checks aren't often, and someone like Cooper won't want to arse around to get them out.

Which means the keys will be nearby.

They are.

They're on the top.

Shotguns and rifles inside.

I take them all and wrap them in a sheet to take with me. Ammunition too.

They're heavy. It takes time and makes me sweat, but eventually, I hide the weapons and go back to the car.

If it all goes wrong, and he gets away, at least he won't be able to readily arm himself with a gun.

'I was worried! You were ages!' Maggie whispers when I get into the driver's seat and sit for a moment for the sweat on my face to dry.

'Okay. Next stage. Ready?'

She nods.

I drive out onto the road, then back to Huntington House. Onto the driveway. Then down to the gravel parking area.

'I pretended to call you and said I'd be home in a few hours, so he won't be expecting us now. But just go with my flow.'

'What flow?' she asks.

I don't reply.

I stop the car. We get out and go straight for the front door.

I hear a slight knock inside the house. Probably from Cooper panicking at me coming back too soon and trying to hide.

We go into the lobby.

'No! That's not fair,' I say with a laugh and such an instant switch to humour that it makes Maggie blink in surprise. 'I said for you to get the wine!'

'Yeah, I, er...' she says, faltering.

'Whatever!' I singsong, rolling my eyes. 'I can grab one from his Lordship's stash downstairs. You don't think he counts them, do you?'

'Eh? Oh. Er. No. No! Course not,' she says, snapping herself into the mood that's needed. 'And I'm sorry. I forgot!'

I stop and grin at her, and stay that way for a few long seconds until she looks confused.

'You didn't forget,' I say with a tone that makes her blink. 'I know what you were thinking. Eh? Suggesting we *nip back* for a bottle?'

'Yeah. That was...' she falls quiet as I close the gap and clasp my hands to her cheeks and kiss her passionately. She's stiff. Surprised. For a second, I think she'll pull away. Then she relaxes into it.

'Shall we, then?' I ask in a breathy voice. 'Upstairs?'

'Okay,' she says, the same voice. Excited. Scared. Nervous. All sorts of reactions and emotions.

We start up the stairs, hand in hand. Stopping to kiss on the first-floor landing, then on the second floor.

Hand in hand, to my room.

We go inside. I push the door closed with my foot.

She swallows nervously.

We kiss again.

We keep kissing and go onto the bed, and despite it all, I'm still a guy, and I still grow aroused.

Whether she's acting or not, I'm not sure, but she moves and makes noises, and I get that overwhelming sensation of being watched again.

But nothing else.

Come on, already.

It's starting to look fake. We're kissing too long without doing anything else.

Maggie seems to sense it.

She unfastens the buttons on her shirt and tugs her bra down to expose her breasts. I strain to listen for a foot scuffing or anything coming from the secret corridor on the other side of the wall while, knowing Cooper has been moving around this house silently for decades.

But he'll still want a better view now she's exposing herself.

Which means I have to give him that view.

So I work down her chest. Kissing her breasts and then to her stomach as she arches her back and groans with pleasure.

It works.

A sudden shout of pain from the other side of the wall, followed by a hard thud from Cooper pulling back into the other wall.

I'm off Maggie in a second. Moving for the door as she tugs her bra up and pulls her shirt closed.

Another yell of pain from the secret corridor. Footsteps, and someone heavy bouncing off the walls.

'Wait here,' I say, and I'm out the door and running along the hallway, then down the stairs. I picture Cooper doing the same on the other stairwell. Now blind, but as I said, he knows this place like the back of his hand.

Which is why I needed to level the playing field.

I get to the front door and grab the night vision goggles I left behind the front wheel of the car, and set off running along the side of the house for all I am worth, then over the lawns. Slipping on the wet grass.

My head spinning.

My heart thudding.

My lungs bursting.

I try and pull the goggles on. But Cooper's head is bigger than mine, and they slip as I run. I yank them off with a curse and run as fast as I can. Faster than I should. I start losing air and power. I feel weak and drugged.

I will myself on. Knowing what I have to do before it's too late.

I reach the mausoleum, gasping for air, and hear a great shout of pain coming closer.

Coming through the tunnel.

Footsteps. Gasps.

Cooper reaches the steps and starts up.

In pain. In fear. A dangerous man.

One side of the trapdoor is already open.

The other flies back with a crash as he surges up clutching his face.

His eyeball popped and bleeding from impaling on the needle I'd pushed through the peephole closest to the bed.

His other eye red and weeping from the chilli powder I put on the walls next to the hole. Knowing he'd cover his hands in it when he leant in close.

Knowing he'd push his hands to his eyes when the needle went into his eyeball.

Knowing the combination would blind him.

Levelling the playing field because I needed time to get ahead of him.

To the guns wrapped in the sheet I left here.

To the shotgun I just loaded and now slam closed as I tug the goggles on one handed and aim.

'Cooper,' I say as he comes to a stop, grinning in agony as he pushes his newer night-vision goggles to his good eye.

The silence of a second.

'Fuck you' he starts to snarl and come at me.

I fire the gun and shoot him.

He flies back.

I drop with a cry of pain from the muzzle flash blinding me through the night-vision goggles.

Murder.

Money.

I go down the stairs to the tunnel.

Back to Huntington House.

Back to the basement.

Forgetting I've got the goggles on and stepping out from behind the stone staircase into the bright, blinding lights of the cellar.

I wrench them off.

What did I do?

I just killed a man for money.

For my own future.

For Maggie.

'Mike,' she says, rushing my name out. I blink my eyes that still smart from the light to see her ahead of me.

Waiting.

The woman of my dreams.

I start towards her.

She pulls a face.

Worry.

Regret.

Pain.

A look of fear in her eyes.

A look of terror.

A gun.

In the back of my head.

I stop.

My eyes adjust.

Maggie looking terrified.

Tessa next to her.

Smiling.

I turn slowly.

Charles Huntington holding a shotgun.

I cock my head over to see the serial number has been filed away.

Meaning it's unregistered.

I straighten up and look into his piercing, blue eyes.

'Gun down,' he says.

I put my shotgun down.

'Don't shoot,' I say to Charles and slowly extend a hand to point at Maggie standing on the other side of me. 'You'll hit my future wife.'

His eyes show uncertainty.

Tessa too.

I glance to Maggie frowning at me as to why I just said that.

'Shoot your niece instead,' I say and look at Tessa and the same piercing, blue eyes.

The air charges.

I tap the top button on my black shirt.

'Testing. Testing. One, two...' I say and smile slowly. 'You can come and get me now, guys.'

'What the fuck,' Tessa whispers.

'What's he doing?' Maggie asks.

'He's bluffing!' Charles says.

Doubt in his eyes.

His finger on the trigger.

'I fucked him. He wasn't wearing a wire,' Tessa says.

'Wire? He ain't got a wire,' Maggie says. 'I stripped him off in the bath. He was naked! He didn't have one!'

'Technology has come a long way,' I say and look around at them all.

My head woozy.

My brain fogged.

From the coffee they laced.

The coffee they left here for me to drink.

From the drugs Tessa put in my tea at hers.

To make me slow-witted and pliable, and paranoid.

To weaken my mind.

So they could convince me to commit murder.

Murder for money.

For a cottage. A café. A wife. A baby.

I believed in that dream.

I wanted it to be true.

I really did fall for Maggie.

I still feel it now.

But then I told her and the farm lads outside the community centre the night we played bingo that to be an undercover officer means believing what you are doing with everything you have.

Until it becomes your truth.

Your reality.

I'm not a good person.

But I am good at this.

That's why they recruited me after I beat Edward Scoble.

Because everyone saw it.

And who the hell is ever going to believe a disgraced former cop who tried to murder a paedophile is an undercover officer?

These three certainly didn't.

I clear my throat and stand upright for what feels like the first time in a week. Straightening my back from pretending to be cowed and sick, and vulnerable.

The drugs in the coffee are still making me woozy.

But we get trained to deal with things like that.

And like I said. It takes a very special mindset.

'My name is Detective Mike Humber. I am arresting you all on suspicion of conspiracy to commit murder, in addition to the murder of *Linh Thi Lam,* and for perverting the course of justice by the payment made to one Alise Ivanova, who, on her return to Latvia, and after receiving that payment, contacted the Metropolitan Police, cos, you know, like I said, Latvia is a modern country... I shall now give you the caution and your rights.'

Several things then happen all in an instant.

'Shoot him!' Tessa yells. Although that's not her name. Her name is Beatrice Cooper-Huntington. Niece to Charles Huntington, whose father made a baby with Stanley Cooper's mum, which means Stanley Cooper is also her uncle.

And who said countryside people are all inbred.

'No!' Maggie shouts at the same time as Charles tenses to fire.

Although Maggie is her real name.

Maggie Cooper to be exact.

Cousin to Stanley Cooper.

That being the same Stanley Cooper, who lurches out from behind the stone stairwell, clutching one of the other shotguns.

Which is a fucking miracle, considering I shot him in the legs for groping poor Alise Ivanova while she was asleep, which was after the poor girl was offered lots of money and drugs, and booze to join in with some messed-up incest sex stuff with Charles and his niece Beatrice while Stanley watched from the walls. They liked to drug people and play mind games until they became paranoid and vulnerable.

That's what we think happened to *Linh Thi Lam*.

We traced her from the email she sent, responding to the job advert. She was never seen again after she left London.

She was an illegal immigrant.

She did some sex-work sometimes. To get by. To eat. To live.

They probably terrified her with the same gaslighting they did to me. With the bangs. The bumps. The jukebox. The chairs.

They probably drugged her.

They probably raped and murdered her.

We'll never know.

Pigs will eat anything. Including bones and teeth, and Huntington has a lot of piggeries.

But Alise, though.

She wasn't an illegal immigrant.

Alise Ivanova was a fucking legend.

Or to be more precise, a former championship long distance runner.

So she did what she was good at when she woke up to Cooper jerking off while grabbing her breasts. Which was after they'd tried gaslighting her. But see, Alise liked the supernatural, so it didn't have the same impact. She was also incredibly fit, which counteracted the drugs in the coffee.

Hence why I've been running and making myself puke.

And that was also after Charles and Beatrice made repeated visits. With booze. And drugs. And money. And tried to get her to join in with their weird shit.

And so, when Alise woke that night, she did the thing she did best.

She ran.

She ran twenty miles to the next town and phoned family to get home.

Which is when Charles Huntington pretty much made her a millionaire.

But she was still a fucking legend cos she took his money *and then* phoned the police.

Hence why I am here.

And hence why I am specifically right in this spot when Beatrice shouts *shoot him,* and Maggie shouts *no.*

And Stanley Cooper staggers on legs shot to bits so much you can see the bones.

And Charles flinches.

And I slap the barrel of his shotgun aside as he shoots, and Cooper shoots.

Which is two very loud gunshots in a confined space and two very bright muzzle flashes.

And also, two shouts of pain and shock.

One from Charles from being shot in the back at close range from a shotgun.

Which isn't a pretty sight.

And the other from Beatrice, who was also shot at close range from a shotgun by her uncle, who just tried to shoot me. Which again, isn't a pretty sight.

Maggie, however, and me, and Stanley Cooper then stand and stare, and blink in shock at Beatrice and Charles now dead on the floor.

At which point, Stanley reverses the shotgun and puts the end in his mouth.

Maggie and I both shout.

But we're drowned out by the third gunshot.

Which, again, is not a pretty sight.

But I've seen lots of death and violence now.

And as Maggie said, she's been around dead sheep all her life.

I look at her.

My ears are ringing. Hers too. Gunshots are deafening.

'He was blackmailing them,' she says, meaning Cooper.

I figured as much.

There had to be a reason for them demonising him and urging me to murder him.

All I knew was we had a missing woman, and Alise was paid off.

The rest developed when I got here.

That's what my covert police unit does. We go in and go with the flow.

Which, like I said, takes a very special mindset.

I do, however, know that the writing done with chalk and blood on the walls and with a finger on my mirror was done by Tessa.

It was the same slant and angle from the words she wrote on my cigarette papers.

And it was done from her height.

She's five three, at most.

Cooper is over six feet.

Beatrice also didn't know her own address and had to find an unopened letter marked *for the occupier* to give to me when I called the police. The Huntington Estate owns it. She doesn't live there.

I also saw the numbers used to send the footage of the kissing and sex to the phones.

Maggie recorded me and Tessa having sex and sent it to herself and Tessa, and Charles Huntington. Her number has three 4s.

Tessa recorded Maggie and I kissing and sent it to all three.

I also saw the shopping list in Cooper's cottage. The guy couldn't spell the word *apple* properly.

And how did Maggie get to this house to find me in bed covered in blood? She lives miles away. She doesn't drive. One of the other two brought her, and Maggie said she'd seen the sheep's head in Tessa's garden. I'd wrapped it in a bin liner.

I was drugged. But I still clocked all of those things.

I've no idea about the whole Jason and Gavin thing, though.

'Who was Jason and Gavin?' I ask Maggie.

She blinks at me and shakes her head, then sharpens her gaze. 'Mixed race bloke?'

'Yeah.'

'From Manchester. Gangster guy apparently. They had him ready in case you bailed.'

'Ready for Cooper? Or ready to kill me?'

She shrugs. 'Both probably. Never said. She had sex with him, though. Same spot on the sofa. She boasted about it; then, Lord Charles went off at her cos she should have been seducing you instead, but then you started fancying me, and she got all bent out of shape. That's why she did that with the Viagra.'

I grimace at the memory. 'Why did you agree, though?' I ask.

She pauses, like she's either accepting it or she's not quite grasping how serious it all is. 'Told you. He was a freak.'

'That was true then? About Cooper? And the other stuff. Your brother?'

She nods. 'Caught him jerking off in my room when I was like eleven or whatever. And I said he left sheep heads when John and Wendy got together. Girls who worked here hated him. He was always pushing himself into them and spying through those holes. Filthy creep. And I told you. I'm barely getting by. Cottage. Café. Lord Charles kept putting the rents up. He said he'd sign them over to me and give me cash.'

'When?'

'When you didn't fall for her,' she says, motioning Beatrice.

'Oh,' I say, figuring that makes sense.

'Am I in trouble?' she asks.

I look over to her beautiful, brown eyes and the laughter lines, and I see a normal woman trying to escape a bleak and hopeless future.

'Yeah,' I say quietly.

She nods, and I realise she isn't showing that much of a reaction to being in a room with three dead bodies. She's made of stern stuff. That's for sure.

'You really wearing a wire?' she asks.

'It's not a wire. It's a recording device.'

'In a button?'

'My phone,' I say and pull it out. 'I sent a code in earlier. They'll be here soon.'

She falls silent again and looks to say something, then stops, and frowns.

'What?' I ask.

'Why me?'

'You just said. They knew you were desperate.'

'Not them. You. Why not her?' she asks, flicking her hand in the general direction of Beatrice's body. 'She's stunning.'

'Just because.'

'Because what?'

'Because... Because of who you are.' She looks confused. Not getting it. 'I meant it,' I tell her. 'I fell for you.' She looks at me like I really am the most stupidest man she ever met. 'Did you?' I ask as the moment hangs in the air. The dream still there. The promise of a future.

'Oh god, no. I am like sooo gay.'

'What the fuck!' She nods. 'The kiss!' I say. Meaning her cottage. The Land Rover. Upstairs.

'I know. That first one took lots of G and Ts. So gross,'

she says, pulling a face, and thereby instantly destroys my entire fantasy and all my dreams as I look around at the bodies, then back to her. 'My brother was happy, though. He thought you made me un-gay. I told them not to mention it.' Sirens in the distance. She flinches and looks panicked. 'But like. We can still have a baby and, and... And do sex.' I sag on the spot as a chair falls over in the kitchen.

We both look up the stairs as the basement door slams shut.

And the music starts.

Oh, Danny boy, the pipes, the pipes are calling
From glen to glen, and down the mountain side.

We share a look.
    Then I hear the impact and see her reaction.
    How she jolts forward and goes rigid.
    From an invisible hand that just slapped her backside.
    I don't believe in ghosts.
    But I've no bloody idea what that was.

21

Some Months Later

I hate court.

I always have.

I'll take being undercover and getting drugged and covered in sheep's blood any day of the week over going to court and giving evidence.

I still can't believe that kiss with Maggie was fake.

I mean. I know the kiss was real.

But she was faking it.

Like all of it.

Jesus.

She convinced me so well.

She should work undercover.

That makes me frown as I look to my boss waiting next to me.

'What?' she asks.

'Have you recruited Maggie?'

'No,' she says with an eyeroll.

I look forward, then turn to look at her again. 'Would you tell me if you did?'

'No.'

I look forward again and sigh.

This is how they recruit people.

From situations like this.

I don't even know my boss's real name.

Or her rank.

And I've never met any of the people I work alongside of in my team.

That would defeat the purpose of being completely covert.

It would put us at risk if two covert officers ended up crossing paths during a job and each knew the other was secretly a copper.

Even a flicker of recognition at the level we operate at would be enough to get a bullet through the head.

Still, though.

That kiss.

Seriously. That's my number one, top best kiss ever.

The court clerk comes in.

'You ready?' my boss asks me.

I nod. She moves away out of sight of the camera that's facing me. A screen next to it. They both get switched on.

I see the judge looking at me.

The judge can also see me.

That's all that is allowed.

My real voice won't even be heard in the courtroom. It goes through a distortion machine that makes it sound different.

'Officer X, as we are to call you,' the judge says, peering over his glasses at me, 'oath or affirmation?'

'Oath is fine,' I say. The clerk hands me a thin bible, with a printed verse that I read out, promising to God that I'll tell the truth. The affirmation card in the clerk's other hand says the same thing, just without the promise to God.

I get cross-examined by Maggie's defence barrister.

Although the barrister can't see me. I can't see them either. I hear the questions, and I give my answers to the judge, and the court hears my warped voice.

Or at least, the defence barrister tries to cross examine me, but my boss signals to the clerk at what seems like every other question, who, in turn, goes out of the anteroom and into the courtroom to speak to the judge.

'Redacted,' the judge says each and every time.

My unit will not allow me to impart any information that might directly or indirectly give any methods used during the covert policing operation.

The judge has seen enough of my full evidence to be satisfied that we are allowed to redact key parts.

In turn, the defence barrister is required by law to be satisfied that the judge has examined and accepted that my evidence has met the various threshold tests and is admissible.

In the end, the defence barrister only really knows that officer X was sent to Huntington House following an investigation commenced by the Metropolitan Police as a result of Alise Ivanova reporting her experiences.

But that's it.

Nearly all of the specifics of what I did at Huntington House and everywhere else is redacted.

Getting drunk.

Having sex with Beatrice.

Kissing Maggie.

Planting a needle in the wall to blind Cooper. Using the

chilli powder, knowing he'd rub it into his eyes. Shooting him in the legs.

All of those things are redacted.

The judge knows about those things.

So does my boss.

Both went apeshit at me.

'You fucking idiot!' my boss said. Mostly because I had sex with Beatrice.

'A fine line, detective!' the judge said. 'A very fine line, indeed!' Again, mostly because I had sex with Beatrice.

In my defence, though, the video footage does show me completely out of it and trying, somewhat feebly, to push Beatrice off.

They didn't seem that bothered about Cooper blinding himself on a needle and then being shot in the legs.

But then as I said to Maggie and the farm lads - undercover officers are allowed to break the law if the greater risk justifies it.

For instance, undercover narcotics officers might be in a position where they have to take cocaine or heroin, or other class A drugs to prove they're not a copper.

In my case, I allowed myself to become drugged and went with the flow of events in order to complete my mission. Which meant I had to respond to the initial honey trap from Tessa.

And yeah. I did go too deep.

It became my reality.

That's what I mean about it requiring a certain mindset.

What I wasn't expecting was for the honey trap to switch to Maggie.

I really didn't see that coming.

Jesus. That kiss.

None of that stuff about me falling for Maggie comes out in court.

Only that I was undercover, and only that, as a result of being undercover, I was able to make recordings on my phone.

And those recordings *are* played out in court, introduced and explained by the prosecution barrister.

'The first voice you will hear in this recording is that of Lord Charles Huntington. The second is Officer X, which has been altered to disguise their real voice.'

- **RECORDING ONE.**

CHARLES HUNTINGTON AND OFFICER X.
'THIS IS A PROBLEM, MR (REDACTED)'
'I CAN LEAVE TODAY.'
'I DON'T WANT YOU TO LEAVE. I WANT TO FIX IT.'
'FIX IT? THE WINDOW? HAVE YOU GOT ANY PLY ANYWHERE?'
'NOT THE BLOODY WINDOW!'

- **RECORDING TWO.**

CHARLES HUNTINGTON AND OFFICER X.
'HE'S BEEN A PROBLEM FOR A LONG TIME.'
'COOPER? SACK HIM, THEN.'
'NOT THAT SIMPLE.'
'YOU'RE A SMART MAN, MR (REDACTED), AND CLEARLY NOT FRIGHTENED OF BEING HERE. WHICH ARE ATTRIBUTES WE NEED RIGHT NOW. ALONG WITH DISCRETION AND UNDERSTANDING.'
'KEEP THAT HOUSE IN MY FAMILY, AND I'LL CHANGE YOUR LIFE.'

. . .

- **RECORDING THREE.**

CHARLES HUNTINGTON AND OFFICER X.

'I'VE BEEN PAYING FOR MR COOPER'S INDISCRETIONS FOR A LONG TIME.'

'INDISCRETION? YOU MEAN SEXUAL ASSAULT. AND VOYEURISM. AND STALKING. AND HARASSMENT. AND TRESPASS. AND MUTILATION OF LIVESTOCK. AND WHAT ABOUT THE YEAR BEFORE THE LATVIAN WOMAN? THE VIETNAMESE WOMAN? DO WE ADD RAPE AND MURDER TO THAT LIST?'

- **RECORDING FOUR (EDITED FOR SALIENT POINTS).**

CHARLES HUNTINGTON AND OFFICER X.

'MAKE THIS GO AWAY.'

'FIX IT.'

'WHAT DO YOU WANT?'

'MAGGIE'S COTTAGE AND CAFÉ SIGNED OVER TO HER. AND CASH. SPLIT TWO WAYS.'

'TWO?'

'ONE PAYMENT TO TESSA. AND THE OTHER ONE TO MAGGIE AND I.'

- **RECORDING FIVE.**

CHARLES HUNTINGTON AND OFFICER X.

'OR YOU CAN GO INTO ANY NUMBER OF PUBS IN LONDON OR MANCHESTER, OR BIRMINGHAM, OR EVEN GLASGOW, WHERE I'M SURE SOMEONE WILL KILL COOPER FOR YOU FOR A FRACTION OF THAT PRICE. BUT THEN THEY'LL GET DRUNK. AND TELL THEIR MATES. AND THEY'LL KEEP COMING BACK... AND COMING BACK.'

'So I am paying for discretion.'

'And murder. But mainly discretion.'

🔥

When that one ends, the prosecution barrister plays the next one.

'In this recording, the first voice, the female voice, is that of Beatrice Huntington-Cooper, known to Officer X as Tessa. The second voice, as before, which again has been altered, is that of Officer X.'

- **Recording Six.**

Beatrice Huntington-Cooper and Officer X.

'You'll fix it. You're (redacted).'

'What does that mean?'

'That's why Cooper is doing all this. He knows you're not scared of him, so he's going into overdrive. I reckon he knows his days are numbered because you won't tolerate it.'

- **Recording Seven.**

Beatrice Huntington-Cooper and Officer X.

'You need to fix this. You said you'd fix this!'

'What can I do?'

'Deal with him!'

'How?'

'You bloody know.'

'And in these next recordings, you will hear the voice of the defendant, Margaret Cooper, known to Officer X as Maggie. As before, the other voice is Officer X.'

- **RECORDING EIGHT.**

MARGARET COOPER TO OFFICER X.
'HE DID THAT TO JOHN WAY BACK. KEPT LEAVING SHEEP HEADS. THEY'RE JOHN'S SHEEP AN' ALL. HOW CHEEKY IS THAT? CHRIST, THOUGH, (REDACTED). HE'S GONNA KILL YOU. NEVER SEEN HIM SO BAD. HE'S OBSESSED.'

- **RECORDING NINE.**

MARGARET COOPER TO OFFICER X.
'STAN IS GOING TO MURDER YOU, (REDACTED). I HAVE NEVER SEEN HIM THIS BAD. AND WHAT IF HE MURDERS THAT TESSA? WHAT IF HE COMES FOR ME? LOOK! LOOK! HE SENT THEM TO ME. HE WAS WATCHING US. HE'S BLOODY STALKING YOU! HE WON'T STOP. GO BACK TO THE CITY.'

- **RECORDING TEN.**

MARGARET COOPER AND OFFICER X
'AND YOU'RE REALLY ALRIGHT WITH THIS? IT'S A BIG THING, MAGGIE. TAKING A LIFE.'
'GREW UP AROUND IT.'
'THIS IS A PERSON. NOT A SHEEP.'

'HE AIN'T RIGHT, (REDACTED). I MEAN. IF IT WAS ANYONE ELSE, I'D BE LIKE NO WAY. NOT EVER. BUT STAN ISN'T RIGHT. THAT LATVIA GIRL WOKE UP TO HIM WANKING OVER HER.'

۵

'And finally, in this recording, you will first hear the voice of the defendant, Margaret Cooper, along with the voice of Beatrice Huntington-Cooper. The two are markedly different, and I see no issues with audible recognition. The defence has examined this evidence and offered no legal challenges. The male voice, as before, is the altered voice of Officer X.

- **RECORDING ELEVEN.**

BEATRICE HUNTINGTON-COOPER, MARGARET COOPER, AND OFFICER X.

'SO. LORD CHARLES SPOKE TO MY JOHN. LIKE. LAST YEAR. MAYBE THE YEAR BEFORE. AND HE SAID IF JOHN SORTED COOPER, HE'D GIFT HIM THE FARM AND ONE HUNDRED THOUSAND POUNDS.'

'TO DO WHAT?'

'SPIT IT OUT. KILL HIM?'

'BUT THEY WERE IN A FIELD AND CHARLES TOLD MY JOHN IF HE EVER REPEATED IT, HE'D DO HIM FOR LIBEL AND TAKE THE FARM AND MY CAFÉ, AND MY COTTAGE.'

- **RECORDING TWELVE.**

BEATRICE HUNTINGTON-COOPER, MARGARET COOPER, AND OFFICER X.

'I CAN'T WRITE MY BLOODY BOOK AFTER YOU'VE KILLED COOPER, CAN I?'

'Why would he pay you?'

'Trust me. He'll pay. I'll put Viagra in his tea like I did with (redacted).'

- **Recording Thirteen.**

Beatrice Huntington-Cooper, Margaret Cooper, and Officer X.

'I'll need an alibi.'

'Say you're at mine.'

'No. Say you were both at mine. That's two people claiming they were with you.'

'That's more believable. Need to get rid of the body. Where are those pigs?'

- **Recording Fourteen.**

Beatrice Huntington-Cooper, Margaret Cooper, and Officer X.

'Alright. Okay. Wow. We're really doing this, then. And we all swear never to talk about it. Right?'

'What, the fact we're conspiring to commit murder?'

◊

'And the final recording the prosecution presents to the court is immediately prior to the deaths of Lord Charles Huntington, Beatrice Huntington-Cooper, and Stanley Cooper. The first voice is that of Officer X. You will then hear Beatrice shouting *shoot him,* and Margaret Cooper shouting *no.*'

- **RECORDING FIFTEEN.**

OFFICER X. BEATRICE HUNTINGTON-COOPER. MARGARET COOPER. ALSO PRESENT BUT NOT SPEAKING ON THIS RECORDING ARE LORD CHARLES HUNTINGTON AND STANLEY COOPER.
'MY NAME IS DETECTIVE (REDACTED). I AM ARRESTING YOU ALL ON SUSPICION OF CONSPIRACY TO COMMIT MURDER, IN ADDITION TO THE MURDER OF LINH THI LAM, AND FOR PERVERTING THE COURSE OF JUSTICE BY THE PAYMENT MADE TO ONE ALISE IVANOVA, WHO, ON HER RETURN TO LATVIA, AND AFTER RECEIVING THAT PAYMENT, CONTACTED THE METROPOLITAN POLICE, COS, YOU KNOW, LIKE I SAID, LATVIA IS A MODERN COUNTRY... I SHALL NOW GIVE YOU THE CAUTION AND YOUR RIGHTS.'

'SHOOT HIM!'

'NO!'

※

Two near simultaneous gunshots. Yells of shock and pain.

Silence for a second. Then Maggie and I both shout, and the third shot rings out.

I don't flinch when I hear the gunshots.

I've heard the playback many times over.

The recording ends.

The court takes a break.

My boss goes off and comes back after a few minutes.

I look at her questioningly.

'Maggie Cooper didn't flinch when the gunshots were played back,' my boss says and drums her fingers on her knee like she's thinking.

The court resumes.

The judge announces the defence are entering a guilty plea for Margaret Cooper conspiring to commit murder.

That's it, then.

Job done.

The other three people in the case, Charles, Beatrice, and Stanley are all dead by either each other's hands or by suicide.

Which means it will be for a coroner to deal with and rule accordingly.

Which will also be done very discreetly.

For me, though.

My part is done.

I get taken to a private side room, where I need to wait for the entire landing to be cleared to allow me to slip away and disappear.

I lean against the wall and stare out the window, down to the road and the park opposite.

It doesn't take long.

Maggie comes out within ten minutes. She looks nice, in dark trousers, a dark blouse, and a dark jacket. She speaks to her legal team. They shake hands, and they go off, and I watch Maggie walk across the road into the park opposite.

To a bench, where she sits down.

I snort and shake my head.

Knowing what's happening.

Knowing a deal was made.

The CPS had to have a conviction after multiple deaths were recorded, including the probable but as yet still unproven murder of *Linh Thi Lam*.

Whereas the police, or specifically my boss, needed Maggie *not* to go to prison.

Because she'd tell people Mike Humber was the undercover cop. Mainly to the other prisoners. Who are criminals. Who would then tell their criminal mates.

So, Maggie has been released.

She'll be sentenced later. Probably within a few weeks,

and most likely she'll get something like a conditional discharge. Which is still the conviction the CPS need.

For *Conspiracy to Commit Murder*.

Which should carry a life sentence.

'Smart woman,' I murmur, wishing her the best.

I don't hold any ill will to Maggie at all.

She saw a way out of her bleak life and took it, and like she said, she wouldn't agree to murder anyone else. She knew Cooper was a wrong'un.

She looks up at the windows, and for a second, I feel watched again.

But I know the outside of these windows is reflective glass.

'Landing's clear,' the clerk says, leaning in through the door.

'Cheers,' I say and start to turn, then stop, and smile to myself, shaking my head and glancing back through the window. 'Fucking knew it.'

I head down and out the back and stay clear of the park and the bench, where Maggie Cooper is sitting.

That being the same bench I just saw my boss strolling towards.

Jesus.

I only hope Maggie knows what she's letting herself in for.

But I think she'll be alright.

As for me.

I'm back to being a disgraced former detective.

Until my boss decides otherwise.

One thing I never found out, though.

What was on that letter I found behind the chest of drawers?

22

Exhibit AI/HH/1

One handwritten letter produced by Alise Ivanova.
Translated from Latvian into English.

I'm writing this down because of what happened in the leisure room. I'm really freaked out about it. And I don't feel right. I keep feeling dizzy and weird. I can't text or email.

I arrived a few days ago. The first night I was here, the jukebox kept coming on and chairs would fall over, and doors kept slamming closed. I love ghosts, though, so I'm totally not scared. I said hello to the ghost and that I was not going to cause it harm.

I went for a long run the next day to the village and saw a cute diner place, and I met the owner called Maggie. She's so pretty. We clicked straight away. She invited me to hers for a drink one night. No way I thought I would meet another gay woman in such a small place. She's so nice, though. Really funny and sweet.

But when I got back, a big, older man was in the kitchen. He's super scary! He said he's called Stanley and he is the gamekeeper. He was staring and brushing passed me, and touching me. It was so gross!

Then that night, Lord Huntington came to the house with a really pretty woman called Tessa. I was told the family would be away for the whole of August. He said he wanted to check on me. We had beers in the leisure room and put some music on. They were really nice to me. Tessa was funny and very flirty. I'm openly gay, and I thought Tessa fancied me.

She kept dancing with me like really flirting and pushing into me, and I only had two beers, but I felt really drunk. Then Tessa kissed me, and I thought it was nice. She was touching me a lot, and I sort of went along with it because she's so pretty and nice, and I forgot Lord Huntington was there.

Then he was behind me and touching me, and he said I could have the money, and I saw cash on the bar, and he had his penis in his hand and was jerking off and kissing Tessa. Tessa said she gets turned on when Stan watches, and they both tried to get me to kiss them and take my clothes off, but I totally freaked out and ran to my room.

I shut the door, but I could hear noises in the walls. Like grunting and heavy breathing.

I felt really sick the next morning and tried to go for a run to the diner again. I told Maggie what happened. She told me to find the spot in the servants' corridor where I could get phone signal. I just found it, but I can't get signal or anything, so I wrote it all down, and I'll put this behind the big chest up here. But if they do that again, I'm literally going straight home.

Alise

ALSO BY RR HAYWOOD

Washington Post, Wall Street Journal, Audible & Amazon Allstar bestselling author, RR Haywood. One of the top ten most downloaded indie authors in the UK with over four million books sold and over 30 Kindle bestsellers.

DELIO. PHASE ONE

*WINNER OF "*BEST NEW BOOK*" DISCOVER SCI-FI 2023*

#1 Amazon & Audible bestseller

A single bed in a small room.

The centre of Piccadilly Circus.

A street in New York city outside of a 7-Eleven.

A young woman taken from her country.

A drug dealer who paid his debt.

A suicidal, washed-up cop.

The rest of the world now frozen.

Unmoving.

Unblinking.

"Brilliant."

"A gripping story. Harrowing, and often hysterical."

"This book is very different to anything else out there - and brilliantly so."

"You'll fall so hard for these characters, you'll wish the world would freeze just so you could stay with them forever."

*

FICTION LAND

Nominated for Best Audio Book at the British Book Awards 2023

Narrated by Gethin Anthony

The #1 Most Requested Audio Book in the UK 2023

Now Optioned For A TV Series

#1 Amazon bestseller

#1 Audible bestseller

"Imagine John Wick wakes up in a city full of characters from novels – that's Fiction Land."

Not many men get to start over.

John Croker did and left his old life behind – until crooks stole his delivery van. No van means no pay, which means his niece doesn't get the life-saving operation she needs, and so in desperation, John uses the skills of his former life one last time… That is until he dies and wakes up in Fiction Land. A city occupied by characters from unfinished novels.

But the world around him doesn't feel right, and when he starts asking questions, the authorities soon take extreme measures to stop him finding the truth about Fiction Land.

*

EXTRACTED SERIES

EXTRACTED

EXECUTED

EXTINCT

Blockbuster Time-Travel

#1 Amazon US

#1 Amazon UK

#1 Audible US & UK

Washington Post & Wall Street Journal Bestseller

In 2061, a young scientist invents a time machine to fix a tragedy in his past. But his good intentions turn catastrophic when an early test reveals something unexpected: the end of the world.

A desperate plan is formed. Recruit three heroes, ordinary humans capable of extraordinary things, and change the future.

Safa Patel is an elite police officer, on duty when Downing Street comes under terrorist attack. As armed men storm through the breach, she dispatches them all.

'Mad' Harry Madden is a legend of the Second World War. Not only did he complete an impossible mission—to plant charges on a heavily defended submarine base—but he also escaped with his life.

Ben Ryder is just an insurance investigator. But as a young man he witnessed a gang assaulting a woman and her child. He went to their rescue, and killed all five.

Can these three heroes, extracted from their timelines at the point of death, save the world?

*

THE CODE SERIES

The Worldship Humility

The Elfor Drop

The Elfor One

#1 Audible bestselling smash hit narrated by Colin Morgan

#1 Amazon bestselling Science-Fiction

"A rollicking, action packed space adventure..."

"Best read of the year!"

"An original and exceptionally entertaining book."

"A beautifully written and humorous adventure."

Sam, an airlock operative, is bored. Living in space should be full of adventure, except it isn't, and he fills his time hacking 3-D movie posters.

Petty thief Yasmine Dufont grew up in the lawless lower levels of the ship, surrounded by violence and squalor, and now she wants out. She wants to escape to the luxury of the Ab-Spa, where they eat real food instead of rats and synth cubes.

Meanwhile, the sleek-hulled, unmanned Gagarin has come back from the ever-continuing search for a new home. Nearly all hope is lost that a new planet will ever be found, until the Gagarin returns with a code of information that suggests a habitable planet has been found. This news should be shared with the whole fleet, but a few rogue captains want to colonise it for themselves.

When Yasmine inadvertently steals the code, she and Sam become caught up in a dangerous game of murder, corruption, political wrangling and...porridge, with sex-addicted Detective Zhang Woo hot on their heels, his own life at risk if he fails to get the code back.

*

THE UNDEAD SERIES

THE UK's #1 Horror Series

Available on Amazon & Audible

"The Best Series Ever..."

The Undead. The First Seven Days
The Undead. The Second Week.
The Undead Day Fifteen.
The Undead Day Sixteen.
The Undead Day Seventeen
The Undead Day Eighteen
The Undead Day Nineteen
The Undead Day Twenty
The Undead Day Twenty-One
The Undead Twenty-Two
The Undead Twenty-Three: The Fort
The Undead Twenty-Four: Equilibrium
The Undead Twenty-Five: The Heat
The Undead Twenty-Six: Rye
The Undead Twenty-Seven: The Garden Centre
The Undead Twenty-Eight: Return To The Fort
The Undead Twenty-Nine: Hindhead Part 1
The Undead Thirty: Hindhead Part 2
The Undead Thirty-One: Winchester
The Undead Thirty-Two: The Battle For Winchester
The Undead Thirty-Three: The One True Race

Blood on the Floor
An Undead novel

Blood at the Premiere
An Undead novel

The Camping Shop

An Undead novella

*

A Town Called Discovery

The #1 Amazon & Audible Time Travel Thriller

A man falls from the sky. He has no memory.

What lies ahead are a series of tests. Each more brutal than the last, and if he gets through them all, he might just reach A Town Called Discovery.

*

THE FOUR WORLDS OF BERTIE CAVENDISH

A rip-roaring multiverse time-travel crossover starring:

The Undead

Extracted.

A Town Called Discovery

and featuring

The Worldship Humility

*

www.rrhaywood.com

Find me on Facebook:

https://www.facebook.com/RRHaywood/

Find me on TikTok (The Writing Class for the Working Class)

https://www.tiktok.com/@rr.haywood

Find me on X:

https://twitter.com/RRHaywood

Printed in Great Britain
by Amazon